You Bring the Coffee, I'll Save the World

By Michael James Emberger

You Bring the Coffee, I'll Save the World

ISBN-13: 978-1497432680
ISBN-10: 1497432685

Contents

Prologue

Dr. Berg woke to the sounds of unfamiliar voices surrounding him. He raised his head quickly to see what was going on and felt a sharp pain as it struck a hard object.

"Ouch!" came a startled grunt from behind him.

"Quiet over there," someone barked angrily.

Berg perceived only the faintest traces of light when he turned to look in the direction of the voices. His mind was spinning from the impact and he felt that there was some sort of cloth wrapped around his head and covering his eyes. He attempted to raise his hands to investigate but couldn't move them. Confusion was suddenly replaced with dismay as he recalled the events of the night before and how he'd ended up in this predicament. Then, his attention was drawn to the sound of a vehicle driving by outside.

"Go see what that is!" the guard shouted.

"Yes, sir," replied another.

Footsteps pounded across the floor. The guard had just left the room when a deafening boom ripped through the air and shook the ground. The other men rushed out of the building and the door slammed shut behind them.

Sensing they were alone, Berg began to frantically struggle with his bonds. "Paul, we have to get out of here!"

"How?" Paul moaned. "I can't move."

"We have to try," Berg pressed, "this could be our only chance."

Chapter 1

Several days earlier...

Dr. Gary Berg breathed in the steamy aroma of the Chai tea he'd purchased near his departure gate at the airport. He closed his eyes and took a sip, relaxing as the warmth of the flavorful brew spread through his body. Despite all the planning and packing over the last several weeks, he'd still been up much later than he intended getting ready the night before. Now he wanted nothing more than to go back to bed after so little sleep and a three hour ride in the university van with ten students who had caffeinated themselves to levels beyond his comprehension.

Berg had celebrated his fortieth birthday a couple months previously and was beginning to realize that there were limits to his energy. He taught courses in Botany, Mycology and Plant Pathology at Harrisville University, where he'd recently been granted a full professorship. Regular jogging and a love of hiking kept him in excellent shape, weighing in at a muscular 160 pounds for his five feet seven inches. His typical attire in or out of the classroom was a pair of blue jeans with a green plaid shirt and dark brown loafers, which he'd left at home in favor of a trusted pair of hiking boots. Running a hand through his thinning brown hair, he inwardly groaned as he thought over the crazy schedule they'd planned for the next two weeks and hoped he would be able to catch a nap on the plane.

"Hey there!" Dr. Richard Stenvick exclaimed as he fell into the seat next to Berg, startling him from his thoughts and nearly causing him to spill his tea. "Trying to catch a few winks?" Stenvick gave Berg a heavy slap on the shoulder and took a swig from a cup of coffee that looked like it would hold half a gallon if someone bothered to measure it. "Cheer up. You're going to have a great time in Costa Rica. I've been leading this trip for twenty two years now and we always have a blast. There will be plenty of time for shuteye when we come home, but you'll see we'll be far too busy down there to even think about sleeping."

Stenvick leaned back in his seat and took another long draw on his coffee. He'd always enjoyed the drink, and it had become a rare occurrence for him to be spotted around campus without a mug in his hand. In addition to his work as the Dean of the School of Psychology, he channeled a lifelong passion for bird-watching and identification into the Ornithology course he gave each semester.

Stenvick was in his early fifties, five feet five inches tall and a slender 140 pounds of wiry muscle, honed from decades of competing in triathlons and hiking the world in search of rare avian species. A neatly trimmed full grey beard, round wire framed spectacles and a ring of short grey hair around his head gave him a mature scholarly appearance. However, that was often offset by his preferred outfit of cargo khaki pants, sandals and one of a large selection of well worn t-shirts from the many races in which he'd participated.

Berg yawned and turned to face his colleague. "How can you be so chipper? It's only five in the morning and we've been up for hours."

Stenvick just smiled, shaking his head from side to side, and then rose from his seat saying he would go check on the students.

Berg glanced up at one of the television monitors in the waiting area and caught the end of a commercial for a breakfast cereal he'd never heard of. He wondered how a box of sugar-covered flakes and marshmallows could bring such excitement and happiness as he watched the family of four with perfect smiles laughing their way through their meal.

The picture faded out and the morning news anchor came back on. "Dignitaries from around the world are beginning to arrive in Oslo, Norway for the annual Nobel Peace Prize ceremony. The recipient this year is Dr. Nathan Fiker, CEO of Hallita Corporation. He is being honored with the peace prize for his successful campaign to eliminate world hunger. We now go live to-"

Berg was distracted by the vibration of the phone in his pocket. He smiled when he saw the picture his wife had sent him of her and their son holding a handwritten sign with the words *"Have A Good Trip, We LOVE You"* boldly written in marker. After typing back a quick response, he got up to stretch and use the restroom before the airline started announcing boarding calls.

Berg returned a few minutes later to a lively conversation between Dr. Stenvick and Katrina Witmer, a senior student who'd taken several of Stenvick's Psychology classes.

"Katrina," said Stenvick, "I want you to observe what this crowd does when the gate attendant announces boarding for the preferred customers."

As if on cue, the attendant picked up the microphone and announced, "American Airways would now like to welcome all passengers in our platinum preferred priority premier program to board."

Katrina studied the crowd. "Ok, I see those three men in suits checking in. They must be frequent business travelers. There's a couple waiting a few feet from the counter, and the woman over there is gathering her bags and standing. The other passengers appear to have noticed her, and now they're all forming a disorderly queue."

"Are they all preferred customers?" Stenvick inquired.

"No," responded Katrina.

"Then why have they all rushed into the line?" asked the professor. "Coach hasn't been called yet, or first class either."

Katrina pondered for a moment. "I think what we're seeing is an expression of people's unconscious fear of isolation. They find comfort in being with the crowd, even if what the crowd is doing doesn't necessarily make sense, or move them to a position of any advantage compared to sitting in the waiting area."

"You could look at it that way," mused Stenvick, "but it's my opinion that this reflects nothing more than the primal instinct to be the first to the kill, to borrow an expression. It's basic human nature to grab what we can before, and at the expense of others, be it our seat on the plane, space for our luggage in overhead storage or just the thrill of beating someone else to our goal."

"Isn't that a bit cynical?" Katrina asked. "People may feel some of those things, but their nature is certainly better than what you're describing. Many of these people would willingly put another's needs before their own if presented with an opportunity. Our sense of compassion and need for community must outweigh our selfishness or society would crumble."

Berg interrupted them. "Rich, Katrina, they're calling our rows. It's time to go fight over the peanuts with the savages."

The three of them hoisted their bags and hurried to catch up with the rest of the students to claim their seats. Minutes later they were soaring through the clouds en route to San José via a connection in Houston.

Chapter 2

Berg awoke to the chime of the fasten seatbelt light illuminating on the overhead panel and brought his seat into the upright position as the captain announced they were on approach to land in San José. It had been an uneventful flight and he felt much better, except for the stiffness in his neck from the awkward position his head had assumed for the last few hours. He put up the tray table and turned to Stenvick. "Rich, are we arriving on time?"

"Yes," replied Stenvick. "We should be at the gate at 11:24 AM, and we'll be good to go as long as the luggage shows up. Hopefully we won't have a repeat of my trip a few years back when all our bags ended up in Paris. They didn't get to Costa Rica until after we'd already come back home! Fortunately I had all my essentials in my carry-on, but that was a rough trip for some of the students. Nothing says 'group of Gringos' like a bunch of college kids wearing matching Costa Rica tourist t-shirts from the souvenir store in the airport. At least the locals got plenty of laughs at our expense."

Berg chuckled at the thought as the plane touched down with a bump. The students chatted excitedly as they disembarked and were processed through customs.

"I'll carry this for you, Katrina," Kevin Archer said eagerly as he helped her pull a duffel bag off the luggage conveyor.

"Oh, that's ok, I'll be fine," she said as Kevin hoisted it onto his shoulder opposite his own bag.

"It's easier this way. Now they're balanced," Kevin replied with a grin.

Kevin was in his senior year as a Biochemistry major and had been good friends with Katrina ever since they were lab partners in Organic Chem.

"I thought you were being a gentleman," Katrina said mockingly, "but I guess you're just concerned about your comfort."

Kevin gave an exaggerated expression of hurt and replied in his most gallant impression of an English knight. "My lady, though thine baggage may my burden ease, tis for your sake I would carry this load that thy fair hands should labor not."

"You're such a goof," said Katrina. "Come, brave knight, my bus lies yonder."

They both laughed as they followed the rest of the group to the University of Costa Rica (UCR) bus waiting at the curb. Kevin paused at the door of the bus as Spencer Baumgaertner blocked his path.

"Give the bag to me," ordered Spencer in a thick Austrian accent. "I will put them away."

Spencer was a tall, muscular student attending the university on a full scholarship for wrestling. His English had improved considerably since coming to the United States, but was still characterized by numerous and often humorous errors that served to endear him to the other students.

"As you say, sir giant," Kevin said, handing the bags over to Spencer who effortlessly hefted them up to the roof where the driver was tying them down. When everyone was settled and the luggage was secured, Stenvick instructed the driver to proceed.

Derek Fimmell and Ben DuPont had taken the rear bench of the bus in order to have the best vantage point from which to throw airline peanuts at the other students. The pair of juniors had been best friends since childhood.

"It wasn't me!" Ben protested as Michelle De la Puenta, a highly dramatic senior from Spain whirled around in her seat and glared at him imperiously.

"Don't make me come back there," she steamed as she picked the peanut out of her hair and threw it at Ben.

"Uh oh, you've made her mad now," said Derek, lobbing a peanut towards the front of the bus.

"Don't let them get to you," Melody Foo said to Michelle. "They're just immature boys."

Melody's hand flew up to the back of her head as she felt a peanut hit her hair. She sighed and rolled her eyes at the boys, who were trying to stifle their laughter.

Stenvick stood as the bus pulled up to the university dorm. "All right folks, we'll take our bags to the rooms and meet back at the lobby in fifteen minutes to head to lunch. See the residence director for your keys and room assignments. We're all in the north wing, women on the first floor and men on the second."

"I will get the bags off of the bus," Spencer yelled as he pounded down the stairs.

"What is with him?" asked Katrina.

Kevin replied, "He's afraid he'll get weak if he doesn't work out enough on the trip. He's finished first place in the heavyweight class at the Division One National Wrestling Championship the past two years, and he's on track to set a school record if he wins three years in a row."

"Oh," said Katrina with realization, "that would explain why he kept doing push-ups and sit-ups in the aisle on the plane. Perhaps you could be a gentleman and let him get my bag for me."

"No problem," Kevin said, "I'll let him get mine too."

Berg dropped his luggage in the room he would be sharing with Stenvick and then pulled out his cell phone. He sent a message to his wife that he'd made it safely to the university, then selected P. Hargren from his contacts and dialed the number. After a few rings he heard the familiar voice of his friend.

"Hello?"

"Hi Paul, this is Gary. We've arrived at UCR."

"Oh good, how was the trip?"

"I can't complain. We all made it and so did our bags. I only have a minute before we head to lunch, but I wanted to let you know that I'm here and confirm we're still on for dinner at five."

"Yes," Hargren replied. "I'll pick you up in front of the dorm. Thanks for fitting this in, we have a lot to talk about."

"Sure," said Berg, "I'll see you at five."

Stenvick had entered the room as Berg was finishing the call. "Was that Paul Hargren?"

"Yes," Berg replied. "I was just confirming our plans for dinner."

Stenvick furrowed his brow. "He was a student of yours, right? Remind me again what he's up to down here."

Berg explained as he began unpacking his bag. "Paul was in my Botany lecture and a couple Plant Pathology courses during the first few years I taught at Harrisville. He stayed on to get his Masters and we became pretty good friends. Now he's doing doctoral research on corn here at UCR."

Stenvick let out an amused grunt. "People have been growing corn for thousands of years. What's left to figure out?"

Berg was about to reply when Stenvick glanced at his watch and cut him off. "Hold that thought, it's time to round up the kiddos for lunch."

Chapter 3

An hour later Berg, Stenvick and the students assembled in an empty classroom and formed a circle with their chairs.

"Now that we've gotten settled in, I'd like to officially welcome all of you to Costa Rica for our winter term cross-cultural," said Stenvick. "As you know, we have a lot of sites to visit and a good deal of hiking ahead of us. I always like to start off these trips with an ice-breaking introduction session and we need to go over the rules and expectations for the course. First, let's do introductions. Name, major, career goals, interests etc... I'll start and we'll go around clockwise. I'm Dr. Richard Stenvick, Dean of the School of Psychology. As all of you willingly signed up to come on this trip, I assume you didn't give much credit to the rumors about me hiking students to death. They all died from sickness, animal attacks or unfortunate accidents, not hiking.... Just kidding, but I do set a fast pace so hopefully you've all been following the preparatory exercise regime I gave you. I'm an avid bird watcher and outdoorsman. I enjoy leading this trip every year for the teaching and birding opportunities it affords, plus hiking at higher altitudes is good conditioning for running triathlons. My wife and I enjoy gourmet cooking and we're always on the lookout for interesting artwork and sculpture from Central and South America. You can take it from here, Dr. Berg."

"I'm Dr. Gary Berg. Many of you know me from the Botany and Plant Pathology courses I teach. This is my first foreign cross-cultural trip. I'm excited to show you the fascinating array of plants and trees growing in this climate that you'll never get a chance to see on our excursions back home. I also teach a course on Mycology which is a subject of great interest to me. I take every opportunity to attend forays and I travel to several conferences each year with the North American Mycological Association. We should have no trouble finding numerous species of fungi here, and if we're lucky I'll find some prime edible examples that we can prepare. I must caution you, never eat wild mushrooms unless you're absolutely sure of the identification. Even with proper training, there are many species that are too risky to eat, as subtle nuances can be missed or key features are not distinguishable on the specimen. As the saying goes, 'there are old mushroom hunters and there are bold mushroom hunters, but there are no old bold mushroom hunters.' My other hobbies include gardening and visiting sites of historical interest."

"Thanks, Gary," said Stenvick. "Kevin, you're next."

With his athletic build, short black hair and piercing dark eyes Kevin gave off an air of unsettling intensity interspersed with spontaneous grins and humor that took many people a while to get used to. His close friends appreciated his intelligent wit and brutal honesty. "My name is Kevin Archer, and I'm a senior Biochemistry major. Next year I'll be starting on my Masters in Biochemistry at the University of Wisconsin-Madison. I plan to pursue a PhD and go into research, but I'm not sure exactly what direction that will take yet. I enjoy playing racquetball in my free time, as well as occasional video gaming to relax. I also like serious discussions on science and morality."

Kevin turned to Katrina. "You're up."

Her petite frame, light blue eyes and ponytail of sandy blonde hair made Katrina appear younger than she was, but her keen intellect and maturity were quickly noticed once she was engaged in conversation. She made friends with ease due to her disarming personality and radiant smile. "I'm Katrina Witmer and I'm a fifth year senior with a double major in Developmental Psychology and Micro-Agriculture. I home schooled all the way through high school and started college a year early. After graduation I'll be working for a non-profit called Global Proactive. They work in developing countries all over the world to teach good farming practices to impoverished villagers. Their strategy is to apply the 'teach a man to fish' principle to small scale farming so that the villagers can become self-sufficient and generate income rather than rely on the government or charities. I also enjoy doing volunteer work whenever I get a chance. Ok, next?"

"Hold on," Kevin interrupted. "You left out A.T. club and your work with the kids."

Katrina blushed. "Well, my passion is helping those in need. I'm a student leader of the Appropriate Technology club, where we design products that can be easily reproduced in third world villages from inexpensive locally available materials. We work on projects such as water filtration systems and stationary bicycle powered machinery. We'll be going to Haiti this summer to install a solar powered irrigation system. I also volunteer on Saturday nights with a local church program for underprivileged children. Those kids are so adorable that I don't consider it work at all to spend time with them."

Katrina gave a self-conscious smile as she saw the looks of awe on the other faces around the circle. She whispered to Kevin, "This is why I don't tell people everything," then gently nudged Jennifer on the arm.

Jennifer was a fun-loving brunette of fairly short stature, known for being both a class clown and also one of the top students in her major. "My name is Jennifer Pilchman. This is my senior year in Pre-Med. I'm going to the University of Maryland School of Medicine and I'd like to eventually work at a children's hospital, maybe in cancer treatment or surgery. I enjoy swing dancing, camping and working as a summer counselor at a children's camp."

Spencer looked rather awkward trying to wedge his six foot four inch 280 pound bulk into the one piece desk and chair. He wiped the sweat from his brow on his sleeve and cleared his throat before speaking in his customary rushed and nervous sounding manner. "My name is Spencer Baumgaertner. I came from Austria to wrestle and crush the enemies. I am a junior student doing Plant Pathology. I hate poison ivy. I get rash from it very bad. I will use my education to find its weakness and kill it everywhere. I like watermelon. That is all."

Michelle tried to conceal a laugh by pretending to cough, but ended up letting out an embarrassingly loud snort which elicited the giggles the rest of the group had been trying to contain. She was the picture of a Spanish beauty with caramel skin, raven black hair and an aura of mystery in her cold black eyes. She carried herself like a princess and had the expensive wardrobe and attitude to match.

"I am Michelle De la Puenta," she began. "My father owns hotels in Europe and sent me to America to get an education. Thank goodness this is my last year. As soon as I graduate I'm going to start my career in movies and singing. I majored in Musical Theater to pass the time and I came on this trip because I needed the credits and it was the only cross-cultural with an opening."

An awkward silence fell over the group until Melody spoke up.

"I'm sure you'll enjoy the trip, Michelle. We're all glad to have you with us."

As the oldest daughter in a Chinese American family, Melody was used to watching over her siblings and maintaining calm and order. She was soft spoken and polite, of medium height and slender with long black hair.

"My name is Melody Foo. I'm majoring in Library Management and this is my sophomore year. I love books and reading, and I hope to run a library someday. During the summers I work in a book store back home. I enjoy crocheting, designing crochet patterns and many other arts and crafts."

"I like to crochet too," said Stephanie who was sitting next to Melody. She was small in stature with fiery red hair and a fair complexion indicative of her mother's Irish ancestry. Sparkling green eyes reflected her high spirits and mischievous personality.

"My name is Stephanie Krukowsky. I'm a junior majoring in Horticulture. My family owns a garden and landscaping business with several stores, and I'll continue working with them after college. It will really help to have training in proper plant care and disease management for our own stock and for the many customers who seek advice in those areas. I'm interested in hiking, swimming and céilidh dancing, and I love to fiddle in a little Irish band with my brother and sister."

Geraldo was sitting next to Stephanie, casually leaning back in his chair with his legs crossed at the ankles and his head resting against his interlocked fingers while he flexed his biceps in an alternating pattern. At five foot two inches and barely topping a hundred pounds he was not an imposing figure, but his brash Italian temper and outgoing personality more than compensated and served to keep him at the center of attention in most situations. He spoke while loudly smacking on a piece of gum.

"I am Geraldo Vitellaro and I'm a senior in Religious Studies. All my life I've known that I'm going to be a religious leader, but I haven't decided yet which religion I want to be, which is why I'm learning about them all. I'll try my hand at a few and see which one seems to work best for me. My hobbies are guitar, drums and extreme sports. Last summer while you useless piles were sitting on your butts, I went coast to coast on a Razor scooter to raise money for charity and used the money to buy a new truck. I was all over the news and got a bunch of sponsorships. I'm selling autographed Razor wheels for fifty dollars if anyone is interested."

"That's crazy!" said Derek.

"Not when you're awesome like me," replied Geraldo in a joking but condescending manner.

A scraggly full beard and bushy brown hair gave Derek a bit of a wild mountain man look. "My name is Derek Fimmell and I'm a junior in Medicinal Botany." Striking Ben on the knee with his palm he said, "Ben and I are going to start a business as wilderness expedition guides. We'll lead hikes, backpacking trips, canoeing, rafting, pretty much anything people are willing to pay for. I'm learning all about medicinal plants and I've been taking first aid and EMT training on the side, so I'll be able to deal with most medical emergencies when we're far from civilization. Obviously I'm really into outdoor activities, but I also play guitar and I like to write music and sing at cafés and coffee houses."

Silence filled the room once Derek finished.

"Ben," he said, "it's your turn." Getting no response, he elbowed his friend and shouted, "Ben, stop texting Sarah, you're up!"

Ben looked up startled from his phone. "Oh, sorry, I'm Ben DuPont."

Ben was tall and athletic, with dark brown hair that covered his ears and often had to be swept to the side to keep from obscuring the view through his glasses. His friends were envious of his ability to get a deep red sun burn but have a perfect bronze tan by the next day with no ill effects.

"I'm a junior Business major. Derek and I are going to go into a wilderness guide business together and I'll handle the marketing and financial aspects of our company. We've been doing crazy stuff outside for as long as I can remember. Now, instead of getting grounded for coming home late we'll get paid to do what we love. I play the electric guitar and I might open a music store someday when I'm too old to keep working as a guide."

"Thank you all for sharing," said Stenvick. "Now I would just like to go over a few things you'll need to know. First, this course does not have any tests or writing assignments. We're here to experience the natural wonders of Costa Rica. The important thing is the memories you take home with you. Keep a positive attitude, stay attentive to Dr. Berg and me, participate in our discussions and most importantly keep up with the group. Second, always be prepared. We'll be out in the wilderness where there are no convenience stores or visitor centers. Make sure you have everything you're likely to need with you, such as first aid supplies, extra clothing, food and water. Accidents and injuries happen and you never know when we might get separated, or be forced to stay on the trail longer than expected due to weather or other factors. Third, keep up with the pace and don't complain. We have a tight schedule to keep so we can't afford to slow down or take a lot of rest breaks. Your grades will be based on how well you do in those three areas over the duration of our trip. Also keep in mind, you can drink the tap water here at UCR, but whenever we're outside of San José drink only water that you brought with you in a canteen or purchased in a bottle. That's basically it. Go unpack your bags and we'll meet at the cafeteria at five for dinner."

The students filed out of the classroom and walked back to the dorm. Stephanie was a bit anxious. "I hope I can keep up on the hikes. It sounds like this is going to be really hard."

"I've heard this trip is basically nonstop hiking," said Derek, "and that Dr. Stenvick even starts jogging once in a while to make up time."

"Nonsense!" said Geraldo, "look at the guy, he's like fifty-something and half bald. I bet he'll be asking us to stop every ten minutes so he can keep up. This should be a breeze."

Ben piped up, "Part of the reason I chose this trip was the cost. It was half as much as all the others, even the ones that stayed in the U.S."

"Welcome to the Stenvick style cross-cultural," said Jennifer. "All of his trips are inexpensive because he does everything cheap. Harrisville has a reciprocal agreement with UCR for us to stay in the dorm and eat at the cafeteria at no cost. Dr. Stenvick gets the least expensive bus charters available, sometimes with companies that have been shut down shortly after for too many safety violations and unlicensed drivers. I got the scoop from Dr. Frazur. He said most of the science faculty won't accompany Dr. Stenvick on his trips anymore. They all go for the ones with hotels and air conditioning, where they don't come home with a million mosquito bites or botfly larvae growing in their skin. I'm pretty sure Dr. G only agreed to go because he didn't know any better."

"Dr. G?" Stephanie questioned.

"Oh, that's just what I call Dr. Berg," Jennifer explained. "You know, Gary, Dr. G. I'm probably his favorite student."

"Why?" Stephanie asked. "Have you had a lot of classes with him?"

"Some," said Jennifer, "but actually my Dad has been good friends with him since they were kids so we're almost like family. The only drawback is that I have to be on my best behavior in his classes. Any bad news would surely make its way to my parents."

As the group entered the lobby of the dorm, Spencer stormed over to the residence director's office and pounded on the door until it was opened. "Where is the weight room?" he demanded.

Chapter 4

Paul Hargren pulled up to the dorm at exactly five o'clock in his Isuzu Trooper.

"Hello Paul," said Berg as he climbed into the passenger seat.

"Hi Gary, it's good to see you. It's sure been a while."

Hargren put the Trooper into first gear, glanced over his shoulder and pulled away with a chirp of the tires. He was of similar height and build to Berg, with wispy light brown hair, a mustache, glasses and a jovial demeanor. "I hope you're hungry," he said. "The restaurant we're going to is one of my favorites around here."

"I'm looking forward to it," Berg replied, "but I think my body's sense of meal times is a little off from getting up so early this morning. Paul! Watch out!"

Berg gasped as a battered pickup truck with a bed full of pigs suddenly entered the lane right in front of them from a side street. Hargren cut the wheel to the left, downshifted to second and floored the accelerator. He deftly swept out around the truck and back into his own lane, narrowly missing an oncoming car by a matter of inches.

"Wow that was close," said Berg as the alarm wore off.

Hargren shrugged his shoulders. "One of the first things you learn living in this country is how to drive. Traffic is highly unpredictable here, nothing like in the states. You get used to it after a while and accident avoidance becomes second nature. You just have to keep your eyes open."

Upon arriving at the restaurant they were welcomed by the hostess and led to a table. It was a lively place, brightly lit with a Spanish stucco theme and exotic plants filling every crevice. A pair of Mariachis was playing for a young couple on the other side of the room. "Don't let those guys play for you," Hargren warned. "They're all smiles until they finish and then you have to pay them or they turn unpleasant very quickly." He translated some of the menu items for Berg and conveyed their orders to the waitress. Then, after eating some tortilla chips he took on a serious expression. "So, Gary, it's time I explain why I wanted to have this meeting. As I mentioned in my emails, I've made a troubling discovery in my research and I could really use your expert advice. I'm sorry I couldn't be more specific up until now, but this could be a very sensitive issue and you're the only person I know and trust who would understand the science."

Berg leaned forward. "I gathered you were really bothered about something. Taking this cross-cultural with Rich was about the last thing I wanted to do given his reputation, but I couldn't pass up the opportunity to come see you. I know you well enough to trust that you wouldn't ask me to come all this way with no explanation if it wasn't truly important. So, what's going on?"

Hargren looked around warily and leaned closer, keeping his voice low. "As you already know, part of my research involves tracking the yield statistics of isolated corn plantings utilizing different variations of barrier crop strategy. I selected combinations of plants with natural defense mechanisms to grow around the corn. I monitor disease, insect damage and levels of consumption by wildlife. One of the reasons I chose to come to UCR was that Costa Rica is one of the few remaining countries in the world where genetically modified corn has not been widely implemented. The varieties grown here require the use of pesticides and herbicides to produce a satisfactory yield. If I can significantly reduce or eliminate that need, we can retain non-GMO corn and other crops as viable options for agriculture. As a scientist, I'm sure you can appreciate the risks inherent in relying on just a few modified seed strains. If a problem surfaces with disease or resistant predators, the devastation could easily extend far beyond a few fields."

Berg nodded in agreement as he finished chewing. "I understand. We're taking a big risk the way things are going."

Hargren continued. "My test data was making sense for a couple years. I could see definite variation in the effectiveness of the barriers on the different fields, but this year I started to notice some odd changes in a few of the northern test sites. The first sign that something was different was when I found some stalks growing along the streams that run by the fields. Most of the test fields are located near water sources for ease of irrigation. I thought it was odd but didn't think too much of it at the time. I went to the area again about two weeks later and was surprised to see that at each site the stream banks were covered with more corn stalks and the patches had spread. Over the ensuing months, I witnessed these stalks encroach on the test fields, grow within the barrier zones and come up within the established corn."

Berg was puzzled. "Corn doesn't spread. It only grows one plant per seed where it's planted. What you're describing sounds more like Japanese knotweed."

"It gets more interesting," Hargren said, pausing as the waitress arrived and set their dishes on the table. "The existing vegetation died away everywhere this new corn came up, even the established corn stalks in the test fields. I also started seeing other changes. These particular sites had previously shown some of the higher levels of insect infestation and animal consumption. It wasn't long after the new corn started growing within the fields that I started recording drastic drop-offs in the levels of insects and eaten kernels. Soon there were no traces whatsoever of insects or animals, and in fact I started finding dead animals strewn about. I ran some tests on the carcasses and found kernels of the new corn in their digestive tracts."

"Any idea where the new corn originated from, or what strain it is?" Berg asked between bites of his fajita.

"I'm getting to that, but first you've got to try some of this rice and beans dish, the spices are incredible."

Hargren pulled a sheet of paper from a manila folder and set it on the table. It was a printout of a map with various markings and highlights. He pointed out a detail with his fork and continued. "These sites circled in red are all the test fields in the northern region. The ones highlighted in yellow are the fields with the new corn. I've highlighted the streams flowing by all the sites, and marked the direction of flow with arrows. See anything interesting?"

21

Berg studied the map for a few moments and pointed to a spot. "It looks to me like all the sites with the new corn are by streams flowing through this region here." Pointing to other details he went on. "This site is not by a stream and it's not highlighted, and these sites here and here are on streams that don't intersect with the ones by the highlighted fields. I'm guessing this strain of corn is being spread out of this region by the current."

"Exactly," said Hargren. "I've done some exploring. In each case this new corn is growing along the stream banks all the way back to this originating region, and it's more widespread the closer you get."

Berg looked closely at the map. "So what's in this area? It's just blank space."

Hargren sighed. "That, Gary, is the problem." He tucked the map back in his folder. "The region in question is an area covering many thousands of acres held by the Instituto Nacional de Investigación Agricola Sostenible, INIAS for short. The name translates as National Research Institute for Sustainable Agriculture. You might assume it's a government program but that's not the case. I've done my research. The site used to be a biological preserve jointly owned by several international universities with facilities for visiting scientists to use, but about twenty years ago it was purchased through a private sale by a company you've certainly heard a lot about. They turned it into an 'agro-tourist' attraction and research center."

Hargren paused and nervously looked around the restaurant before proceeding. "The buyer was Hallita."

Berg's eyes went wide open. "Oh. This is serious." He sat with a stunned expression as the waitress cleared their plates.

Hargren paid the bill and they walked back to his car. "If you're up for a manly mission there's another place I have in mind to go."

Berg gave him a worried look. "I hope you're not planning to storm the offices of the world's largest corporation to ask about their runaway death corn."

Hargren laughed. "No, sorry, it's just an expression my father used when my mother needed him to go to the grocery store for something. 'Want to go on a manly mission son?' he'd ask me. It meant we were stopping for ice cream on the way home without my Mom knowing."

Berg was visibly relieved. "Ok, that's fine with me. I don't have anything scheduled tonight."

A little while later they were sitting on a secluded bench with cones of delicious mango and guava ice cream. "So what's your next step?" Berg asked.

Hargren gave a thoughtful look. "That's what I'm hoping you can help with. I have a mountain of data on the test fields, and I've run several types of analysis on the corn and the animal carcasses, but I don't have the background in these areas to know what to look for in the data. I could really use your advice."

Berg considered for a minute and then his face brightened with an idea. "Paul, I have it in mind to offer an educational alternative to what Rich has planned tomorrow. I can bet you we'll have at least two inquisitive students to keep attention off of us as we take a look at this INIAS place. Then, you can give us a tour of your lab and explain your research. While the students ask you questions, I can take a closer look at what you've found."

Hargren beamed. "That's perfect. Give me a call once you've talked to the students and we'll arrange the details."

They walked back to the Trooper and Hargren opened the hood.

"Is something wrong?" Berg asked as he came around to the front of the vehicle.

"No, it's fine. I was changing the oil a few months ago and somehow I lost the fill cap. I stuffed this old rag in its place, but it gets loose sometimes and falls off so I check on it periodically."

Berg eyed the oily rag warily. "Paul, isn't that kind of dangerous? Why don't you buy a new cap?"

Hargren shrugged as he closed the hood. "I haven't gotten around to it with all the work I've been doing out in the field. Sometimes you just have to improvise to keep things going until you can fix them properly."

When he arrived back at the dorm, Berg discussed his plan for the following day with Stenvick and then gathered the group together in the lobby. "I know you're all looking forward to the beach tomorrow, but if anyone is interested I have an opportunity to take a few of you on an educational trip. We'll go tour an agricultural research station

23

owned by the Hallita Corporation, and meet with a former student of mine who's doing research on chemical-free corn cultivation."

Most of the students returned blank stares of disinterest, but just as Berg had predicted, Katrina jumped at the chance.

"Can I go?" she asked excitedly. "That would be fascinating. I would love to see what kind of research Hallita is doing here. They're the largest corporate contributor to Global Proactive, the organization I'll be working with."

"Certainly," replied Berg, fighting to keep a straight face as he asked if anyone else would like to go. He knew how much the students were looking forward to visiting the warm turquoise waters of the Pacific, and was pleased to see his suspicions confirmed when Kevin's expression betrayed the conflicting desires in his thoughts.

After a few moments, Kevin finally spoke with uncertain awkwardness as his face blushed red. "I want to go too. I, um, like, I mean, corn is my favorite."

"Ok, great," said Berg. "We'll leave right after breakfast."

Chapter 5

Kevin stirred drowsily from a dream in which he was on a sailing ship rising up and down on the waves of the ocean. It took his brain a moment to realize he was awake, but he still felt the movement of the ship. The room was dark with only faint moonlight coming through the window, but he could see the ceiling above him getting closer and then farther from him as the bed moved. As the fog of sleep cleared from his brain he lay still and listened intently. He could hear gentle snoring coming from Geraldo in the bunk below and also the sound of slow heavy breathing. Silently turning his head, he peered through the darkness across the room to the other set of bunks where Spencer was sleeping, but the bed was empty and the sheets were all made up.

"Spencer?" he whispered softly. At that instant he felt the movement of the bed cease and the heavy breathing stopped, leaving only Geraldo's rhythmic snores to fill the silence. "Spencer?" he repeated a little louder.

"Apologies," came Spencer's voice from somewhere below him in a not so quiet whisper.

Kevin felt the bed hit the floor with a thud and a moment later Spencer was standing facing him. "The weight room is not open," said Spencer with a bit of desperation in his voice. "I have to work out my arms."

"Can't you use your bed?" asked Kevin.

"No, not heavy enough."

"What's going on? What time is it?" Geraldo asked from the bunk below.

"4:30 in the morning," replied Spencer at his usual volume, all attempts at whispering forgotten. "Almost time for breakfast. Get up. Make ready. We have to go."

Half an hour later Berg took a seat across from Stenvick in the cafeteria, setting down his tray with a vegetable omelet, bowl of fruit salad and orange juice.

"Are you going to eat all that, Gary?" Stenvick chided him with a pretend look of horror.

"Probably, but I'd sure like to know where you plan on fitting that," Berg said, looking with amazement at Stenvick's collection of sausage, bacon, eggs, gallo pinto, fried plantains, two bananas, a bowl of cereal, a loaf of baguette bread and four large mugs of steaming coffee.

"Well, Gary, I have to make up all the calories I burned off on my ten mile jog this morning. I guess you didn't notice when I came back to the room and hit the shower. So, anyway, you'll be off to this research place today. I prefer not to break up the group on these trips but I guess this is the best day for it. I don't think you'd find many mushrooms on the beach, and today is really more about getting the kids into the routine. By the way, will this trip cost anything?"

Berg chuckled. "Don't worry, Paul is driving us and I'll cover any expenses out of my travel account. This won't show up on your statement."

"Good," said Stenvick. "I planned all of this down to the penny and there's no room in the budget for extras."

The professors ushered their respective groups of students outside after breakfast. Hargren was waiting in his Trooper behind a rusted green school bus with a faded *"Happy Conquistador Tours"* logo painted on the side.

"We're going in that?" Michelle said in disbelief with a disgusted look on her face. "It's ancient, there's no way that can be safe."

"Just like I said," stated Jennifer. "No expense paid when it can be spared."

"Come on kids, we need to get going," said Stenvick. As the students boarded the bus, he shook hands with Berg and told him to have a good trip.

"You too, Rich," said Berg. "We'll see you back here for dinner."

Berg, Katrina and Kevin walked over to Hargren and introductions were made. Berg joined Hargren in the front and the students climbed in the rear seat. Hargren fired up the engine and drove away as Stenvick gave a last wave before hopping on the bus.

"Where's the driver?" Melody asked no one in particular.

"I don't know. I didn't see anyone," Stephanie said as she looked around.

They jumped at the sound of the engine cranking and turned their attention to the front as the motor wheezed to life.

"No way!" Ben exclaimed. "He's driving?"

The overhead speakers crackled as Stenvick keyed the intercom mic. "Alright everyone, sit back and relax. Our next stop is Manuel Antonio National Park. Estimated travel time is two hours thirty one minutes. Enjoy the ride and remember to keep your heads and limbs inside the vehicle."

Stenvick closed the entry door, pushed the gear shift into first and eased the bus ahead. Derek leaned over to Jennifer. "Lowest priced driver, huh? Does he even have a license here?"

☐ ☐ ☐ ☐ ☐

A few miles outside of San José, Hargren had the pedal to the floor as they drove north on route thirty two. Kevin and Katrina held on to the seats in front of them for support as the Trooper swerved between the lanes, passing slower moving vehicles and darting back into the right lane in time to avoid oncoming traffic. Katrina gasped as Hargren veered to the left to pass an old Land Rover chugging its way up an incline at the start of a blind curve. She stared wide-eyed at the precipitous drop-off past the edge of the road a few feet from her window.

"If you want to get anywhere on time," Hargren was explaining, "you have to drive a bit aggressively."

The tires squealed as he cut off the Land Rover and hugged the inside of the curve, just missing a semi truck barreling down the hill in the opposing lane.

"It really helps to drive a standard," continued Hargren. "You have to anticipate your next move to know when to shift."

With expert precision he downshifted, hit the throttle to bring up the engine revs while re-engaging the clutch and put on a burst of acceleration to pass another vehicle before his window of opportunity was cutoff.

"There's too much lag in most of the automatic transmissions. By the time they respond it's too late to make a move and then you're in trouble."

Katrina closed her eyes as Hargren bore down on another vehicle and prayed that they'd make it through the next hour.

☐ ☐ ☐ ☐ ☐

Stenvick held the bus at a steady five kilometers per hour under the posted speed limit as they traveled west towards the coast along route three. Ben and Derek had rushed to claim the seats in the back but had to settle for the next row forward. They'd found that the floor under the rear benches had rusted so badly that they could feel it giving way when they stepped on it. Also, there were several holes through which they could see the road below.

"Derek, we've got to get an old bus when we start our guide business," Ben said enthusiastically. "We could charge extra to transport the groups and all their gear."

Derek agreed. "That would be sweet. We could give it a cool paint job and get our logo put on the sides. It would certainly help us look more official to have a company bus."

"We'll need to find one in better shape than this though," Ben stated, "or people will have a hard time trusting us with their lives."

"Here's another uphill," Derek said excitedly.

The boys turned to watch out the back windows as the old diesel engine strained to pull the bus up the grade and emitted an opaque cloud of black exhaust from the tailpipe. Ben laughed. "I'd sure hate to be behind us."

28

Katrina breathed a sigh of relief as Hargren turned the Trooper off the highway and took a narrow paved road. A gate with an overhanging sign marked the entrance to INIAS. It had been a harrowing journey and she felt a little queasy as her adrenaline levels slowly subsided. For the past hour and a half she'd barely spoken a word, and it took her a moment to realize that Kevin was talking to her.

"What?" she said as if coming out of a trance.

"I think you can let go of the seat now," Kevin said, pointing to her hands which were still gripping the sides of the driver's seat.

"Oh, right," she said and willed her tendons to release. Her fingers and forearms were stiff from holding the seat for such a long time. When she opened her hands, the muscles automatically clenched them back into fists.

Kevin leaned forward in his seat. "That was an awesome drive, Paul. You sure know how to handle this thing."

Hargren grinned and patted the dashboard affectionately. "This old girl has seen me through a lot of miles and never let me down. My parents bought me this car for my sixteenth birthday and I've had it ever since. I even drove it all the way down here from the states when I came to the university. Ah, here we are."

Hargren pulled into a parking lot and chose a spot in the shade. There were a good number of people walking around the grounds despite the early hour. Berg pointed down the path to the nearest building. "Let's go check out the visitor center."

Minutes later they entered a large circular atrium that was illuminated by sunlight streaming through the glass dome in the middle of the high ceiling. Various informative displays lined the perimeter of the room, and several professional looking staff in matching polo shirts manned a circular counter in the center. Hargren approached the counter and after a brief conversation returned and informed them that they were signed up for the English speaking tour at nine. In the meantime, they could look through the displays and gift shop.

As Katrina and Kevin headed off to explore, Hargren took a brochure from a display stand and motioned for Berg to follow him to a bench by the wall. "Here's a map of the property showing the tour route and walking trails. We're right here," he said pointing to the visitor center. Pulling a pen out of his pocket, he made some marks on the margins and explained. "Our test fields with the mystery corn are off the map in these approximate locations if you follow the routes these streams take." He traced the blue lines of the streams with the pen to where they met at a common juncture, and then crossed out an intersection with a small creek a little ways upstream. "This creek leads to a test field that has shown no sign of the corn, so I'm guessing the source is located between here and the junction of the other streams."

Berg pointed to a section of the tour route. "Stop number seven is about as close as the road gets to that area. Does the pamphlet list what's there?"

Hargren flipped the pamphlet over and found the section detailing the tour. He looked up with a grin. "Stop number seven is the maize research sector."

□ □ □ □ □

"Did we make it?" Michelle asked groggily as Stenvick guided the bus into the parking lot at Manuel Antonio. The ride from San José had been worse than she anticipated. It started off tolerably enough when Melody took the seat next to her and gave her some basic instruction in crocheting. Setting her mind to the task gave her something to do and she began to enjoy it as she picked up the technique, but things quickly went downhill from there. A traffic jam on an uphill section of route thirty four would have been merely annoying in most other vehicles, but as they were hardly moving, the exhaust of the bus permeated the holes in the floor and slowly filled the cabin with a pungent haze. Despite opening most of the windows, the students were feeling a bit light-headed by the time traffic cleared up and they got moving again.

Already nauseated from the exhaust, Michelle quickly developed a pounding headache from the vibration of the bus as it traveled a lengthy section of highway that was graded for resurfacing. She winced in pain as the abrupt transition back to finished paving jarred the suspension and bounced her a few inches off her seat. Then, Geraldo got the other boys in the back to join him in a percussion circle.

As time went on, their rhythms became louder and more complicated as they stomped on the floor and pounded or slapped every surface with their hands. It wasn't long until Stephanie and Jennifer joined them and Stenvick pulled out a small reed whistle he'd purchased on a trip to Guatemala. The shrill tones echoed through the bus as he played along in a high pitched tune. After several minutes of this, Michelle began sobbing and collapsed against Melody, who put an arm around her and tried to comfort her as best she could until she fell asleep to much needed relief.

When they arrived, the students gathered in a semi-circle around Stenvick who was adjusting the straps on his trail pack. "Have you all brought your hiking boots?" he asked with a wry grin, knowing full well that the entire group had come prepared with little more than sandals, beach towels and assorted light clothing over their swim suits, with the exception of Spencer who was wearing hiking boots.

"I am wearing boots," said Spencer. "My feet are tender. The sand itches them and burns."

"Ok," Stenvick continued, "good, but let me remind the rest of you that it's essential to come well prepared to all of our site visits. From the looks of it you're all expecting to just sit on the beach and swim all day, but we have a trail to do first."

Stephanie looked with dismay at her flip flops and raised her hand. "But, Dr. Stenvick, you didn't say anything about hiking today."

Stenvick beamed. "Ah, true, but I also didn't say anything about not hiking today. In fact, I didn't say anything at all about what we were doing today. Let this be a lesson to always be prepared. Don't worry, today's hike is short and easy, but I guarantee you'll all come properly prepared tomorrow."

The professor headed in the direction of the beach at a moderate pace with the students falling in line behind him. Derek was wearing an old pair of leather moccasins. They'd become his outdoor slippers after being lost in roadside vegetation and buried in a snow bank for several months as a result of a late night game of *"throw the shoes and find them."* "Ben," Derek said, "I'd say today should be nothing compared to that time we hiked Mount Monadnock barefoot."

"Huh?" Ben mumbled as he tapped on his phone.

"Monadnock, barefoot, this will be easier," Derek repeated.

31

Ben looked up for a moment. "Yeah, but I don't think I'd do that again unless all the snow was melted." He pointed ahead at Michelle who was walking in high heel sandals. "I bet the Spanish princess is going to have a rough day. I hope she has better shoes for tomorrow."

The group reached the end of the paved path and Stenvick maintained his pace as they hit the soft sand of the beach that formed a land bridge connecting the island summit of Punta Catedral to the mainland coast. Spencer and Derek kept up well enough, but the rest of the students had to remove their footwear to continue through the sand, struggling as their feet sunk in with every step. Jennifer sidled up to Geraldo and elbowed him on the arm. "Think the old man will be begging us to stop soon?"

Chapter 6

Berg, Hargren, Kevin and Katrina boarded an open safari style bus outside the visitor center for the tour. They were joined by a few vacationing families and a young couple on their honeymoon. A boisterous group of retirees with matching tee shirts advertising their membership in the San Francisco Sightseeing Seniors club climbed on at the last minute.

A young woman in her twenties stood at the front with a microphone. "Hello and welcome to the INIAS tour. My name is Megan Monet and I'll be your tour guide today," she said in a high airy voice.

With her perfectly straightened brown hair, fitted white dress shirt, black mini-skirt and towering stiletto heels, Megan looked completely out of place in the middle of the jungle. The name badge hanging around her neck read *"Megan Monet, Intern."* With her obviously American accent she explained, "I'm an intern here, not a real Costa Rican. I'm majoring in Public Relations in college. Cool, right? Yeah, so my advisor got me this internship and said I'd learn a lot about the real world, and talking to the public. It was only supposed to be, like, a year but he said I was doing such a good job that I should stay longer. Anyway, let's start this tour!"

"Is she for real?" Kevin whispered to Katrina.

"Now, before we get going I need to go over the safety procedures," Megan said as she picked up a laminated sheet and read. "Please remain seated at all times when the bus is moving. There are no windows, but please don't lean out over the side or try to touch anything while we're under way. In the event of an emergency there are exits in the front and in the back." She pointed dramatically towards the doors of the bus. "We'll make several stops where everyone may get off the bus to walk around and see things up close. Please don't go too far though. We don't want to have to go hunting for you if you get lost. Please keep any disposables with you until we return to the visitor center, where you may put them in the proper waste or recycling bin. Also, don't take anything from the grounds or walk into the planting fields. Please keep in mind that this is a scientific research area. We are here to see and observe only, so please step lightly and don't touch any of the crops unless I specifically tell you to." She turned to the driver. "Ok, let's go!"

Bracing herself with one hand on the seat next to her, Megan began her well-rehearsed monologue as the bus traveled slowly down the road. "As you all probably know, INIAS is an agricultural research facility. It's run by the Hallita Corporation. Hallita was founded in 1974 by Dr. Nathan Fiker, our CEO and chief scientist. Dr. Fiker graduated college at the top of his class in 1967, received his master's degree in 1969 and then began his doctoral research in the genetic engineering of DNA. When DDT was banned in 1972, Dr. Fiker saw an opportunity and targeted his work to engineering crops that would self-produce safe insecticide compounds. His first success was inventing a type of corn that could fight off insects without any pesticides. As the company grew, he developed herbicide resistant wheat, beetle and fungus resistant potatoes, rice capable of growing in dry fields, allergen free peanuts and numerous other crops. I'm sure many of you use products from the Hallita Home brand such as our Forgettables line of house plants modified to store water like cacti."

Most of the tourists nodded their heads in affirmation.

"The company has certainly been successful," Megan continued, "but that's not Dr. Fiker's only motivation. The tragic loss of two brothers in the Vietnam War deeply affected him. Early in his career he determined to develop crops that would revolutionize farming and put an end to world hunger, thus eliminating food shortages and famines, which are the causes of so many conflicts. In just a few days Dr. Fiker will be awarded the Nobel Peace Prize for his work and philanthropic efforts. We're all very proud of him."

One of the retirees raised her hand. "When are they going to fix the taste of the corn? It tasted so much better when I was young before they started messing around with the gnomes or whatever you call them."

Megan smiled and gave a patronizing little chuckle. "I'm sorry but you must be mistaken. Dr. Fiker invented corn in 1974, so you couldn't possibly have eaten it when you were young."

The woman looked appalled but calmed down when her husband patted her hand and whispered something in her ear. Katrina leaned over to Kevin, "I guess that wasn't part of her script."

□ □ □ □ □

Stenvick stopped suddenly and raised his hand to signal the students to halt and be silent. He cocked his head to the side and listened intently. "*Chloroceryle americana*, Green Kingfisher," he whispered.

The students could barely discern a faint rattling call off in the distance.

"They're small birds of primarily green coloring," the professor said softly. "They would be difficult to spot in this vegetation."

Stenvick continued moving, nimbly ascending the steps that composed the steep section of trail heading towards the summit. He felt satisfied that the day's lesson was sinking in each time he heard one of the students yelp as they stepped on a sharp stone or twig. He never enjoyed the pain the first day of these trips caused the kids, but experience had shown that it was a necessary step to ensure they took things seriously and gave sufficient thought to planning and packing for the remainder of their days together.

Melody fell in step next to Geraldo. "I've been meaning to ask you, how can you know you want to be a pastor but not have a religion? Don't people decide to go into ministry because they feel strongly about the faith they already have?"

Geraldo laughed. "That's probably how most of them do it, but I'm thinking more about the big picture, like which religion will offer the best career opportunities, or the best benefits and perks."

Melody was puzzled. "Isn't it important to you what the religion believes? They're all so different."

"A little bit, but if one doesn't work out I can always switch. I figure most people just want their leader to preach what they want to hear, so I'll pull a couple verses out of whatever book they use and then make up the rest. I'll need to look at things like which day of the week they have their service and how that would fit in my schedule, or if they have a dress code or dietary rules that would be too restrictive."

Melody looked incredulous. "Any place that hires you will see right through that in no time if you don't really believe anything."

"I don't think so," Geraldo retorted. "I've learned more about all the major religions than most of the people who actually follow them, and I've looked at the statistics. Most Americans don't read their scriptures and can't answer pretty basic questions about what they claim to believe. Sure, there may be a few who are skeptical, but I don't care. I'll be all set as long as I keep the majority happy with health and wealth sermons."

Melody shook her head slowly. "Good luck, I guess, but I really don't think it's going to be that easy."

□ □ □ □ □

The INIAS tour bus pulled to the side of the road at a sign post with a bold white number seven on a green background. "Ok everyone, time to get off the bus again for another walking tour," said Megan cheerily.

Most of the group was still talking excitedly about the strawberry flavored bananas they'd been allowed to try at stop three, and one of the mothers was attempting to console her little boy whose older sister had put his favorite toy car in an open pod of a flytrap soybean plant at stop six.

Megan pointed to various sections of the field of corn stalks as she explained. "We're now in the maize research sector. This region is where we test new types of maize, which is a plant that looks a lot like corn and is popular in Spanish speaking countries. The type over there grows a bunch of ears at the top like a palm tree and can be harvested every week all through the growing season. This type here grows without tassels and is really easy to shuck, but they're still working to improve its flavor. That one makes chemicals that taste bad to insects so they don't eat it, and finally that type grows with a cob so small and soft that you can eat the whole ear. Let's go see them up close."

Berg and Hargren casually dropped to the rear of the group as they followed Megan on the paved walking path. "Chemicals that taste bad to insects?" Hargren whispered.

"Sounds like a possible match to me," said Berg.

They trailed the group, pleased to see that Katrina and Kevin were peppering Megan with questions which appeared to be far beyond her memorized script, judging by her nervous laughter and flustered appearance. The trail was of roughly circular shape as it touched on the four different planting varieties.

"This is it," whispered Hargren as they came up to the third type. "The stalk segmentation has that same distinctive appearance."

"Look," said Berg. "They've been cutting these stalks growing in the grass next to the path. This must have an invasive tendency."

Hargren looked ahead to see that the rest of the group was far enough away before darting off the path to the corn patch. He swung off his backpack, unzipped it and removed a knife. "Gary, take this and cut a few sections and stuff them in here."

Berg quickly cut some stalks, folded them and put them in the bag. Hargren put the knife back in the bag and then covered the contents with a crumpled up windbreaker before zipping it shut and putting it back on his shoulders.

"Quick, we need to catch up without raising suspicion," said Berg as he cautiously jogged after the group with silent steps.

As they came up behind the other tourists, the little boy who'd finally gotten over the lost toy car turned and stuck his tongue out at them, then tugging on his mother's shirt said, "Mommy, Mommy, I think that man had to go wee-wee in the corn."

Turning beet red, the mother started to apologize but Hargren laughed and brushed it off, explaining that he'd stopped to tie his shoe.

□ □ □ □ □

Stenvick turned around at the summit and watched the students stepping gingerly up the path to join him.

"Wow," Stephanie said as she gazed out at the ocean. "The view up here is incredible, and I've never seen water that blue."

"This is so cool," Derek exclaimed. "They really know how to do oceans down here. Ben, you should send a picture of this to Sarah!"

Ben looked up to see what they were talking about. "Whoa, what an intense color, Sarah would love this. I should send her a picture."

Derek shook his head as Ben raised his phone to take a photo of the view.

Spencer was looking at something in the distance. "Dr. Stenvick, what is that?"

Stenvick looked to where Spencer was pointing, raised his binoculars, and after adjusting the focus and looking for a few moments clapped his hands together with delight. "That's a *Busarellus nigricollis*, or black-collared hawk. Good find, Spencer."

Stenvick handed off the binoculars and the students took turns looking at the majestic bird of prey. "We'll take twenty minutes to look around up here," Stenvick announced. "You can see the beaches and ocean from the overlooks. Then we'll head back down to lunch."

As the students explored, Stenvick set his pack on the ground and removed a large stainless steel thermos, a smaller thermos and a container of sugar. He opened the thermoses and poured cream from the small one into the larger, then added several tablespoons of sugar. He closed the large thermos and shook it while observing Michelle, who was sitting on a fallen log with her head in her hands. "You have a headache?" he yelled over to her.

Michelle raised her head and squinted at him with obvious irritation. "Yes," she mumbled.

"I have the fix for that," Stenvick said as he pulled two thick handmade ceramic mugs from his bag and poured steaming hot coffee into them. He walked over to Michelle, holding one out to her. "This is one of my favorite brews, Costa Rican Highland Dark. It has double the caffeine of any other bean and they don't export it out of the country. I happen to know the owner of the plantation and he had a case delivered to UCR for me."

Michelle perked up considerably and thanked him as she started sipping from the mug.

□ □ □ □ □

Stop eight was an overlook where the tour group viewed strawberries growing underwater out of reach of birds and insects, and at stop nine they all got off the bus to see grapes with one grapefruit sized fruit per bunch being developed specifically for the wine industry.

"Do you think she suspects anything?" Hargren whispered as they took their seats back on the bus, referring to Megan who was telling everyone to watch their step as they approached. "I thought she gave me a funny look as we passed by."

Berg kept an eye on the tour guide, "No, I think you're just being self-conscious and paranoid. Try to relax."

"That was our last stop on today's tour," Megan said as the bus traveled back towards the visitor center. "Thank you so much for joining us and please be sure to stop in at our gift shop."

Several minutes later the tour group had disembarked and everyone was perusing the souvenirs, stopping in the restrooms or purchasing food items from the café. Katrina was looking at a toy rack full of stuffed fruits and vegetables, her favorite being the three foot tall ear of corn with velvety kernels and tassels made of yarn.

"Katrina," said Kevin coming up behind her. "I got you an orange juice from the café."

Katrina looked at the orange in Kevin's hand with a puzzled expression. "That's an orange with a straw stuck in it."

"Exactly," said Kevin. "They're modified to grow without any internal membranes or seeds, just juice and pulp. They're excellent."

Katrina took a tentative sip on the straw. "Wow, this is really good. It tastes like fresh squeezed orange juice but better somehow."

"I read the poster," explained Kevin. "Since you don't have to actually squeeze the orange, none of the bitter taste of the rind gets into the juice. Also, the flavor has been genetically optimized based on results of consumer taste tests."

"Ah, there you two are," said Berg as he approached the students, holding a bag of freshly baked rolls made with butter-wheat. "I have some snacks for the road. We're going to visit some of the fields where Paul has been doing his research, they're not all that far from here."

Hargren grinned and took a bite of the humongous wine grape he'd purchased. "Apparently there's a winery in California that's planning to grow these. The skin is thicker to maintain the correct proportion to the flesh, but it also makes them really tough and durable. They're going to offer tours where visitors can pay to hand pick a few grapes which will be made into a bottle of wine. They get to press them and fill a dedicated fermentation tank which is labeled with their name and address. Once it's ready, the wine is put in the bottle the customer selected and shipped to their home. The label on the bottle will have a picture of them holding the grapes."

"I guess if it tastes bad everyone will know who to blame," said Kevin with a chuckle.

Chapter 7

Katrina froze when she saw Hargren's Trooper in the parking lot and remembered the drive from San José.

"Are you ok?" Kevin asked her.

Katrina shuddered. "I don't know if my nerves can take another trip like this morning."

"Don't worry," said Kevin. "I think the sites are all nearby and there's hardly any traffic in this area."

Katrina reluctantly climbed in and tried to remain calm. Hargren shut the hood after checking the oil rag and slid into the driver's seat. "Alright, make sure your seatbelts are on. Most of these roads are dirt and they can be pretty bumpy."

A few minutes later Hargren pulled off the main highway onto a dirt trail marked with a numbered UCR sign. He stopped the Trooper in front of a padlocked steel gate and got out to unlock it. As they proceeded down the rutted dirt trail, Katrina was relieved at Hargren's slow and careful pace. "Dr. Berg, and Paul, thanks for taking us to see INIAS. It was fascinating to see all the crops they're working on."

"You're welcome," replied Berg, turning in his seat to face her. "I knew you'd be interested in going given your work with agriculture. As we saw today, Hallita is clearly at the forefront of the field."

"You sure wouldn't know it by their tour guide," said Kevin. "I don't know why they would ever let her talk to visitors. She didn't know a thing about the science. I tried to ask her some questions about proteins. She told me to check at the visitor center to see if they had nutrition information, but she doubted there would be any protein since they don't make meat products."

Berg chuckled, "I doubt most visitors ask her questions like that."

"Here we are," Hargren said as they entered a large clearing with a patch of corn growing near a small stream. "As I mentioned earlier, we're dealing with an unknown variety of corn establishing itself in the patch. You can see it over there spreading from the bank of the stream."

Impersonating the tour guide Kevin said, "That looks more like Maize to me," which brought a laugh out of the others.

Hargren continued. "As I explained earlier, this corn seems to be toxic to insects and animals that eat it." The pungent odor of decaying animal carcasses reached everyone's nostrils as they walked up to the patch. "And as you can smell," Hargren pointed out, "it's having a significant effect on the animal population here."

Katrina pinched her fingers over her nose. "We're not far at all from INIAS. If this corn is invasive and demonstrating unusual properties have you considered that it may be spreading from one of their testing fields?"

"Good point," said Kevin. "Also, it's growing on the side of the patch by the stream. Maybe it's being spread through the water from elsewhere. Where does this stream come from?"

Berg and Hargren looked at each other uncomfortably for a few moments. "I should have known they'd figure this out," said Berg. "We didn't want to get you involved in this, but you two just nailed it. I know you're both too inquisitive to let this drop. Paul, do you still have that map?"

Hargren pulled out the INIAS brochure and explained the locations of his test sites in relation to the corn patch. "I don't know if you noticed, but Gary and I dropped back for a minute on the tour to collect some samples of the corn that appeared to match what we're seeing here."

"Oh," observed Katrina, "that would explain why you looked so nervous when we got back on the bus after that stop. I think the tour guide was giving you a funny look."

"See, Gary, I told you she noticed," said Hargren.

"Sorry," Berg said. "I really didn't think so."

"I saw her make that face too," Kevin said, "but I thought it was just because she was trying to think."

"Don't be so mean," Katrina scolded. "I'm sure she's doing the best she can. Not everyone can be a genius like you and ace all their tests without studying."

Kevin shrugged. "I can't argue with you on that point."

Hargren cut a few samples of the rogue corn and put them in a bag with a label showing which field number they came from. "We'll go to one of my other sites and take some samples, then I want to show you some test results back at the lab."

□ □ □ □ □

"Stephanie, this water feels magical," Jennifer said as she stepped into the warm ocean to soothe her tired feet after the hike. "You need to try this."

Stephanie joined her and agreed. "This is wonderful. Hopefully Dr. Stenvick doesn't have any other surprises in store today."

"I doubt it," Jennifer replied. "I think we've all learned the lesson he intended. Anything more would just be cruel."

They turned at the sound of Stenvick calling them from the beach. "Everyone follow me. I have a surprise for you."

The girls looked at each other with alarm and reluctantly left the water to follow the professor towards the tree line.

As they reached the end of the beach, any fears the students had were quickly forgotten when they saw the pavilion set amongst the trees. A long buffet line ran along the side of the structure and park visitors sat eating at numerous picnic tables. One of the tables had a sign marking it as reserved for Harrisville University.

"I just have a few things to say before we eat," Stenvick announced to the group. "I take advantage of the buffet here every year because the price is very reasonable. Also, I have a feeling that none of you gave any thought to bringing food with you today so you'll all appreciate having this meal. For the rest of our trip everyone will need to bring food with them for lunch. The cafeteria at the University

43

will have a table set out each morning with packaged sandwiches, fruits and other items. I'll remind you as well to drink only the bottled beverages from the cooler of water and sodas. Now let's eat!"

The buffet had a varied assortment of meats, vegetables, exotic fruits and more types of potatoes than any of the students knew existed. Spencer caused a slight commotion when he took an entire serving platter of grilled chicken, but the courteous staff quickly replaced it without complaint.

Melody and Michelle sat down across from Geraldo at the table. "Pick a religion," Geraldo said before they could start eating.

"Excuse me?" Michelle asked in an annoyed tone.

Geraldo explained. "If I'm going to be a religious leader I'll be expected to offer blessings for meals, so I need to practice. Which religion do you want me to do?"

Melody took a look at Geraldo's plate and responded with a devious grin. "Jewish."

Geraldo looked at the pile of barbecued pork in front of him. "I don't think that one would be appropriate today."

Melody glared at him. "Atheist."

"Oh forget it," Geraldo said in frustration.

Chapter 8

Hargren stopped the Trooper on a dirt trail on the way to the second site and shut off the engine. "I need to check the oil," he said, pulling the hood release and getting out.

Berg opened his door and slid off the seat. "Why now?"

Hargren opened the hood. The rag had fallen out of the fill hole and was nowhere to be seen. "I could feel something wasn't right with the engine," he said, walking around to the rear and returning with some shop towels and a fresh rag. He checked the dipstick to confirm the oil level was ok, wiped some drips from around the fill hole and stuffed the new rag in place. "I make sure to keep some of these in the car just in case."

"You could also get the new fill cap and not have to worry about it," said Berg.

"And miss out on this quality time with my vehicle? I don't think so," Hargren responded sarcastically.

A little while later they arrived at the second UCR test field. "This looks a lot like the other one," Kevin said as they got out.

"The barrier crop mix is a little different here," Hargren explained, "but the invading corn is acting in much the same manner."

The group followed him around the field to the bank of a shallow stream. Stalks of corn were growing in the mud flats and areas of stagnant or slow moving water out of the main channel. Berg approached one of the stalks near the edge. "Mind if I pull this?"

"Be my guest," Hargren replied.

Berg grasped the stalk with both hands near the base and started pulling up on it with steadily increasing force. The mud made gurgling and sucking sounds as the roots shifted around but refused to yield. He paused. "This shouldn't be so difficult. In this mud the roots should come up easily. Paul, give me a hand here."

Hargren joined him and they pulled together on the stalk. As the base started to clear the mud, there was a snapping sound as the stalk broke and they both fell backward to the ground. "Look here," Berg directed as he inspected the stalk in his hands. "This should have lots of small roots attached at the base but there's just one large one where it broke."

Hargren got to his feet and brushed off the back of his pants. "I haven't thought to look at the roots yet, let me get a shovel." He ran over to the Trooper and returned with a shovel, sample bags, branch clippers and his pair of wading boots. He carefully stepped into the soft mud and began unearthing the rest of the root system of the stalk they had pulled.

"What is it?" asked Katrina.

"It's not corn," Berg replied. "Well, it is, but not any type that occurs naturally. Genetic modification is the only explanation for this I can think of."

They all stared at the network of thick, interconnected orange roots branching out from the stalk and linking it to the others. "This is a rhizome structure," explained Berg. "It's an underground stem system that connects all these stalks. The plants store nutrients in these stems and the system will continue to spread laterally and send up new shoots. If any part of it is separated from the rest, that piece can start a new network. Paul, I mentioned yesterday that the behavior of this crop sounds like Japanese knotweed or similar invasive plants. This confirms it."

"Hand me those clippers, Kevin," Hargren asked. He proceeded to cut out a section of the rhizome that the stalk had been growing from. Kevin held a sample bag open as Hargren stuffed the mass of rhizome into it and marked it with the field number. Berg put the stalk into another bag. Hargren picked up the samples and headed for the Trooper. "Give me a hand with this stuff. We should get to my lab."

□ □ □ □ □

Once they'd finished eating lunch at the pavilion, Stenvick announced that the students would have a couple hours at the beach before they had to get back on the bus. He would be snorkeling and they were welcome to join him. After spreading out a beach towel from his pack on the sand he started laying out his gear.

"I will go see the fishies," Spencer shouted excitedly as he took off his shirt and boots and ran into the water. The students watched from the beach as he yelled, "HERE FISHIES, COME TO ME," and then plunged his head in the water to look.

Geraldo smirked. "He'll scare away every fish within a mile if he keeps that up."

"I'll help him," Derek said as he ran into the surf and started slapping the surface and shouting along with Spencer.

□ □ □ □ □

After a short drive, Hargren pulled off at a restaurant on the side of the road. "I like to stop here when I'm doing rounds of the fields. They have a great slow-cooked marinated chicken dish that I order every time."

As they entered the dimly lit interior, Hargren exchanged a friendly wave with the owner who was serving customers at the bar. They sat down at an isolated table in the corner and a waitress came over to greet them and distribute menus. Hargren relayed instructions in Spanish to bring bottled water and soft drinks for everyone.

Katrina had been deep in thought since leaving the field. "Dr. Berg, I was just wondering why you invited Kevin and I to come today. Was it really just to see INIAS and Paul's research lab, or are we here for another purpose? I'm really intrigued by this mystery corn and would like to do what I can to help you figure it out."

"Katrina, Kevin," Berg said looking at them in turn, "one of the main reasons I came on this trip was because Paul asked if I could help him with this problem. We don't know if INIAS is intentionally spreading this crop, or if they are unaware that it has escaped. Either way, the highly toxic nature is very concerning, especially considering Hallita's role in the world's food supply."

Hargren continued. "I've collected many samples and run a lot of tests, but I need Dr. Berg's expertise to make sense of what we're looking at. If I'm going to approach the researchers at INIAS, I want to know exactly what's going on with this crop."

"It was my idea to bring you along," said Berg. "I was sure you'd both decide to go and that you'd distract the tour guide with questions enough for us to be able to look around and take samples without being noticed. In that respect you both performed very well today."

"So what are we going to do now?" asked Kevin. "Can we do anything to help?"

The waitress came with the drinks and Hargren ordered four chicken dishes after quickly confirming that everyone wanted to try his recommendation. Once she'd left Berg responded. "We're going to Paul's lab for the afternoon. The plan was that he would give you a tour while I looked at the data, but I think we can all do that together now that you know what we're up to. We want to find out what's in this corn that is so toxic to the wildlife. From what we've seen, it would probably be lethal to humans. If INIAS doesn't know about this then we'll hope they can help stop the spread. However, if they are aware and this is intentional then it's a very tricky situation to get involved with. We don't want to approach them uninformed."

Kevin and Katrina agreed that they would do anything they could to help review the test data.

"I really appreciate this," Hargren said to the group. "Hopefully it's just an experiment gone awry with unintended side effects. Having all of you lending a hand will be of great help to me."

After they finished eating, Katrina had a second white-knuckle experience on the highway as they drove to Hargren's lab. They were driving through a residential area in the outskirts of San José when Hargren suddenly beeped his horn and waved excitedly at a man sitting on his front porch. They all watched as the man looked up and gave a confused wave back in their direction. Hargren laughed with amusement, "Wave at this next couple with me." He beeped the horn and they all waved. The couple looked in bewilderment at the unfamiliar vehicle but returned the greeting.

"Do you know these people?" Kevin asked.

Hargren laughed. "Of course not, that's the whole point. No one was out this morning but now I can show you one of my favorite driving games. It's called 'beep and wave.' Back in the states people generally ignore you or think something is wrong, but down here people are friendlier. I get a kick out of their reactions as they try to think how they know me and wave back even though they can't figure it out. After I pass the same person several times they actually look pleased to see me and wave back enthusiastically. It's great fun."

For much of the rest of the trip to the university, Hargren beeped at strangers on the sides of the road and the four of them waved in unison, laughing at the mix of confusion and friendly recognition as they passed by. Berg turned to face the students. "Did I mention that when I had Paul in class he was quite a troublemaker?"

"We never would have guessed," Katrina answered with a laugh.

□ □ □ □ □

"Oh lovely," Michelle remarked distastefully as she approached the bus with Melody. "I feel so safe to be riding in this heap of junk."

Stenvick was adding fluids to the engine from an assortment of bottles that Michelle guessed had something to do with the multi-colored oily puddles on the asphalt under the front of the bus. Spencer was pounding a small foot pump to add air to one of the front tires that had gone flat. "One thousand three hundred," he grunted out, apparently counting the smaller numbers in his head as he worked the pump.

"Poor guy," said Melody as she looked at the half inflated tire. "That's going to take him a while."

Stenvick turned to face them. "Don't feel sorry for him. There's an electric pump on board that we could have used to inflate that in a couple minutes, but he insisted on using the little one for the exercise."

Stenvick finished topping off the fluids and shut the hood. "How's it going, Spencer?" he asked, coming around to see the progress he'd made on the tire. The other students had all assembled and were watching Spencer work the little pump, sweating profusely and nodding his head to the rhythm as he counted.

"Two thousand eight hundred sixty five, all done," he announced, stopping suddenly and bending down to disconnect the air line. Before he could stand back up he dropped the pump to the ground and clutched his leg with both hands. "Arrggh, my leg! It hurts!" he blurted out in pain as he doubled over.

Jennifer was the first one to react. "He's got a cramp. Spencer, you have to stretch it."

"I can't!" yelled Spencer in agony.

Jennifer called Derek and Ben over. "We have to straighten the leg and pull the toes up to stretch the muscle. Spencer, try to relax, we're going to help you loosen the cramp."

Ben and Derek grabbed Spencer's arms and tried to pull him upright to straighten out, but in his pain he reacted in surprise and pushed them off, sending them both sprawling on their backs. "Don't touch me! It hurts!" he bellowed.

Derek and Ben slowly sat up, each in a bit of shock from the violence of the blow they'd been hit with. Jennifer was trying to get Spencer to calm down. "You have to let them help or it won't go away."

"Oh," he grunted through clenched teeth.

The two boys warily approached him but this time he was prepared and let them pull him to a standing position while Jennifer took hold of his boot and pulled up on the toe. After a little bit he relaxed as the cramp subsided. "Sorry I hurt you," Spencer said to Ben and Derek. "And much thanks," he said to Jennifer as he gave her a quick bone crunching hug.

□ □ □ □ □

"Here's my lab," Hargren announced as he stepped through the doorway and flipped a light switch to reveal a small room with work benches lining the walls and several types of desks in the middle. The lab was located in the basement of one of the science buildings at the university. "It's not big, but it's all mine. Restrooms are down the hall to the left. Gary, you can put the samples on the bench over there and we'll prepare them for testing. Make yourselves comfortable and I'll show you my test results."

Berg, Kevin and Katrina found seats as Hargren brought up some files on his computer and laid several printouts on the table. He dimmed the lights and the group turned their attention to the screen projection on the wall. "We're fortunate to have some good test facilities here and plenty of undergrads with part time jobs to run routine lab work for the graduate program. Let me give an overview of the data and then we can discuss specific parts in more detail."

Over the next two hours Hargren presented data and test results on the invasive corn from protein analysis, chromosomal sequence imaging, radiographic molecular structure mapping and several other procedures.

Berg thought for several moments after the presentation. "Paul, would there be students available to run the same set of analysis on the samples we collected today, particularly the rhizome cuttings?"

"Let me check," Hargren said as he pulled up an application on his computer and clicked through a few screens. "Yes, if I put in an order now results will be available tomorrow morning."

"That's great," said Berg. "Go ahead and do that. Also, do you have an account with the world DNA database? I'd like to run some of the sequences you've found through it for possible matches."

"Of course," replied Hargren. "We can submit those right now. Anything else?"

Berg looked at his watch. "We have to get back to join the group for dinner, but I'd like to meet here after breakfast tomorrow to continue."

"Can we come?" asked Katrina.

Berg considered. "Let me talk to Dr. Stenvick. I'm sure we can work it out."

Berg and the students discussed the day's events as they walked to the cafeteria and arrived at the door a few minutes before the aged bus rattled down the street with Stenvick at the wheel. The highlight of the ride home had been Michelle bouncing around the bus on a caffeine high from Stenvick's special coffee. She'd spent the better part of an hour running up and down the aisle, giggling uncontrollably and tagging the other students on the head while yelling 'you're it'.

51

Stenvick brought the bus to a stop and shut off the engine, which turned a few last times until belching a ball of black smoke out the tailpipe with a loud backfire.

"Howdy," Stenvick yelled as he bounded down the stairs. "Did you have a good trip to the farm?"

"It was fascinating, Rich," Gary responded. "How was the beach?"

Stenvick gave a triumphant grin. "Everyone will have boots tomorrow. Let's go eat, I'm famished."

Katrina and Kevin shared a look of confusion at what the professor had said as they joined the group to head into the building. Geraldo walked over to them. "You two missed today's lesson. I hope you're prepared for tomorrow."

Berg took a seat across from Stenvick in the cafeteria. "Rich, I'm going to need Katrina and Kevin for one more day. We've gotten involved in some of Paul's research and we'll be reviewing results tomorrow morning."

Stenvick scowled. "Gary, we came down here to hike and see the natural wonders, not sit in a lab. Monteverde has a lot of interesting plants and mushrooms that I'm sure you'd want to see."

"I know," Berg agreed, "but this is really important and it's a great experience for them to see some practical real world research. They're both really excited about it and want to help. Depending on how today's test results come out, we may be heading back to INIAS tomorrow to meet with their researchers. It turns out their experiments and Paul's are connected. Paul really needs my help on this and the kids will be disappointed if they can't help finish the work."

Stenvick thought for a moment as he chomped on a piece of sausage. "Well, we do have a long hike tomorrow. If you must go, I suppose I won't miss you holding us up to botanize every few minutes."

"Great, I'm glad you're ok with it," said Berg. "I won't keep making you stop to stand around and get bitten by mosquitoes. You'll have a much better hike if you can keep moving. I'm sure we'll finish up tomorrow and then we'll join you as planned the next day."

When they finished eating Stenvick addressed the group. "I want everyone to get lots of rest tonight. We'll meet back here for breakfast and the bus leaves at six. Dr. Berg, Katrina and Kevin will not be joining us, so I think I'll work in a little more hiking to make up the time we would have spent learning about plants. Everyone enjoy your evening and I'll see you tomorrow."

Chapter 9

Early the next morning, Kevin dreamt again of sailing through ocean waves but it wasn't the rocking of the boat that woke him this time. Instead, he was shocked into consciousness when Spencer flipped on the lights and started yelling at him and Geraldo like a drill sergeant.

"Get up. Five in the morning. Up and at them."

"Dude," said Geraldo angrily, "what's wrong with you? Let me sleep."

Spencer ripped the covers to the foot of the bed and yanked Geraldo's pillow from under his head. "Time to work out. Get in shape. Now you will do pushups."

Kevin was laughing in the top bunk until his sheets and pillow suddenly left too.

"You get down. Do pushups," commanded Spencer.

Twenty minutes later following an intense workout under Spencer's direction, Kevin and Geraldo collapsed on the floor of the room panting and covered in sweat. "Why on earth did we just do that?" asked Geraldo.

Kevin watched as Spencer brushed his teeth so hard that he snapped the handle of the toothbrush. "Do you want to say no to him? Come on, let's get ready for breakfast."

After everyone had eaten and packed food for the day, Stenvick surveyed the group of students waiting by the bus. Each of them had stuffed their trail pack to the brim with supplies to handle any conceivable activity they could envision the professor throwing at them.

Stenvick took a swig from a giant travel mug of coffee before speaking. "I'm glad to see you're all ready for today's adventure. We're headed to the Monteverde Cloud Forest Reserve. I know you're going to enjoy it. Let's go." When everyone had found their seats Stenvick cranked the engine and brought the old bus to life. Clouds of soot filled the air as they drove away.

Hargren had picked up the test results and was eagerly waiting when Berg and the students arrived at the lab. "Good morning," he greeted them cheerily, "I've got the results from last night. The samples we took from INIAS are a genetic match to what's growing in my fields. Have a seat and I'll show you what we've found."

They turned their attention to the screen as Hargren began his presentation. "I'll begin by showing you the genetic comparison between the samples from my fields and those from INIAS. In each of these slides the INIAS sample data is on the left and the data from my fields is on the right. In all four cases the chromosomal sequencer returned a variance of less than one tenth of a percent, which you'd expect for samples of the same DNA. For comparison, I ran the data on the standard hybrid corn that I'd planted in the test fields. There was over a forty percent variance compared to the invasive species."

"That sounds about right," said Berg. "From what we've observed of the new corn, I'd say its similarity to any common crop is little more than skin deep."

"Quite true," Hargren replied. "I have some data on that to show a bit later."

Hargren brought up another file. "Here you can see the results from the protein analyzer. The INIAS corn does indeed have much in common with my standard strain. It contains over ninety percent of the proteins found in the corn I planted. The differences are mainly additional in this case. The INIAS samples returned more distinct results by a margin of about thirty four percent, due mostly to the rhizome portion of the plant."

Kevin leaned over and whispered to Katrina. "See, more protein, there's got to be meat in those plants."

Katrina held in a laugh and pushed him away with a gentle shove.

Hargren continued. "This gets interesting when we take a look at the results from the world DNA database. There were no genetic matches better than sixty two percent among all strains of corn available for review. As you may know, the database does not contain any files on products from Hallita and most of the other GMO companies due to patent protections, so there's no way to compare this to typical agricultural corns."

"Couldn't we just get a sample from a farm and run it through the lab?" Katrina asked.

Hargren chuckled. "It's not that easy. Gary, you're the expert on this."

"Paul is right," said Berg. "About ten years ago, Hallita and a few of the other major players in the GMO industry jointly developed the chromosomal sequencing technology that we all use in the lab today. This drastically reduced the amount of time required to bring new products to market, but obviously anyone with one of the machines would be able to decode years of work in a matter of minutes. It would also be a simple matter for competitors to make a few changes and introduce essentially the same product without violating the patent. So, the GMO consortium established an independent company to manufacture the sequencers and police the users. All of the machines are connected to the company over the internet. When a sample is processed, the data is sent to a server for verification that it doesn't match any patented products. If there's no match you get the results, but if there is the machine returns a patent error. The machines don't work without the connection to the company server so there's really no way to bypass the system."

"Wow," said Katrina. "I had no idea there was so much secrecy involved."

"Oh it gets better," said Berg. "The system worked as intended for a couple years, but Hallita was the largest partner going in and it didn't take long for them to succeed in buying out and absorbing the other companies. They took over all the patent rights and assumed sole control of the sequencer business. There were several anti-monopoly lawsuits, but Congress enacted a special exemption and the cases were thrown out. By that time, Hallita's products were being planted all over the world with dramatic effect. Crop yields were up and countries previously plagued with famine had enough food due to the company's relief programs."

"I remember learning about that in high school," Kevin interjected.

"I'm sure you did," said Berg. "No doubt you also remember that the United Nations named Hallita a partner organization around that same time and granted several additional privileges and protections."

"Ok, so I guess we can't compare our samples to typical farm corn," said Katrina.

"Nope," Hargren replied, "and thanks for the explanation, Gary. Now, where was I? Oh yes, the DNA database. As I was saying, the INIAS corn doesn't match very closely to any standard strains, however the database returned a high percentage match for *Fallopia japonica*."

"Japanese Knotweed!" exclaimed Berg. "What did I tell you?"

"Is that your favorite plant or something?" Kevin asked.

Berg shook his head. "No, but it took me six years to clear an infestation of it from my garden. So, I'd say we have a special relationship. Actually, before I resorted to using herbicides I did rather enjoy the strawberry knotweed pies my wife would make with it. It tastes kind of like rhubarb."

"Anyway," Hargren continued, "that brings me to some interesting results on molecular structures. The radiographic molecule mapper showed lots of expected substances typically found in corn, as well as something you might recognize, Gary. Are you familiar with this?"

Berg thought as he studied the molecular structure on the screen. "I can't say I've seen this one before."

"Well," said Hargren, "you just told us a minute ago that you've eaten it. This is Resveratrol, a substance typically found in knotweed. It's not surprising given the genetic similarity."

Berg took another look at the screen and then frowned. "Paul, nothing you've shown us so far appears to explain why this corn is so toxic to the animals that eat it. Some people believe Resveratrol has anti-aging effects, true or not I haven't seen any findings showing it to be harmful."

Hargren brought another molecule onto the screen with a much more complicated structure. The identification field on the display showed "No matches found." "What's this?" asked Berg.

"I wish I could tell you," Hargren replied. "The system found positive identifications for all molecular structures in the samples except for this one. There's no known match in any of the public databases."

The room was silent for a few moments as everyone studied the screen, then Kevin spoke up. "It seems reasonable to conclude that whatever this is, it's likely the cause of the toxicity. Would you agree that's a fair assumption?"

"Probably," said Berg. "Our lab at Harrisville could synthesize this molecule and run toxicity trials, but that would take months and I think you're probably right. We can hold off on pursuing that route for now." Berg paused with a thoughtful expression. "I have to tell you, something is bothering me about the structure of this molecule. I can't think of what it is but I feel like I've seen it before."

While Berg sat trying to rack his brain for the missing connection, Hargren pulled a takeout menu from his desk and handed it to the students. "I know it's still a bit early to be thinking about lunch, but I just realized that today might be your only chance to experience an authentic Costa Rican pizza from Sylvia's. I can put in an online order and have it delivered here, my treat."

Katrina glanced over the menu. "How do you define authentic Costa Rican pizza? Judging by the menu this looks more like Polish food. Look at these toppings; bratwurst, pierogis, beets, wild mushrooms. They even have rye crust."

"Ok, so it's not exactly your typical Central American fare," Hargren admitted. "Mama Sylvia emigrated here from Lithuania during the Soviet years and opened her restaurant. It has become one of the most popular places for students to grab a late night meal. She's like a second mother to a lot of the kids who come to the university."

Berg interrupted. "Katrina, what did you just say about the menu?"

"Um, that I thought it looked like Polish food?"

"I mean the toppings," Berg prodded.

Katrina read off the menu again. "Bratwurst, pierogis, beets, wild mushrooms, goat cheese, cabbage, dill..."

"I wonder," Berg muttered. "Paul, I need to use your computer."

Chapter 10

Ben stepped off the bus at Monteverde and breathed in the humid air. He could barely make out the visitor center ahead as he moved through the dense fog. When he turned around, all he could see of Derek was a hazy figure approaching. "Wow," Ben said, "they're not kidding when they call this a cloud forest."

The blurry form of Derek laughed at him. "Ben, take off your glasses. They're all fogged up."

"Oh," said Ben as he removed them to see a light mist all around.

Stenvick ambled over and held up a spray bottle and cloth. "Here, this will help keep those from fogging. I learned this trick the first time I visited here."

Stenvick held out a map and addressed the group. "Alright kids, we have a lot of trails to cover today so I want to get started as soon as possible. As you can see, the environment here is very moist and wet. If you have a windbreaker I'd suggest putting it on to stay at least somewhat dry. There are restrooms here at the visitor center but none out on the trails, so make sure to use them now since we won't be back this way until the end of the day. Please remember to stay on the trails, don't disturb anything and hold on to any trash until we get to a trash can. We'll start hiking in ten minutes."

Berg was logged in remotely to a computer back at Harrisville that contained his research files. After browsing through several folders he found what he was looking for. He opened an image and displayed it on the projection screen.

"Dr. Berg," Kevin said quizzically, "that's a mushroom."

Berg chuckled. "Very good, Kevin, I'm glad to see we're giving you a proper education. This is not just any mushroom. Its scientific name is *Amanita phalloides*. Hearing those toppings jogged my memory of the research I did on this species a couple years ago. Trust me. You wouldn't want these on your pizza."

"Doesn't the *Amanita* have a red cap with little white spots?" asked Katrina.

"Yes," replied Berg, "but you're thinking of *Amanita muscaria*. That's what most people associate with the genus, probably because of its use in so many cartoons and garden ornaments. There are actually several hundred species of *Amanita*. *Amanita phalloides* is known by the common name death cap. The majority of human mushroom poisoning is due to these."

"Hmm," said Kevin. "It looks like some kind of zombie mushroom with that greenish hue."

"Well, you'd be feeling like a zombie fairly quickly if you ate one of these," Berg explained. "Even with medical treatment many cases are fatal."

Hargren looked up from crossing out the mushroom selection on the pizza menu with his pen. "So what's the connection to our corn?"

Berg pulled up a different file. "This is just a hunch but I think our mystery molecule reminded me of one that I researched in the death cap. The toxicity of these mushrooms comes from a group of poisons called amatoxins. Some of them have proven to be difficult to isolate and research is still ongoing. There doesn't seem to be much interest in many of the less prominent amatoxins such as the one on the screen here. This is Amanitin D. I discovered the molecular structure through my research. I'll publish something officially when I have a chance to write up a decent report, but all the work is finished. Let me bring up that mystery molecule again so we can compare them side by side."

Berg positioned the two images on the screen and they all studied them with interest.

"They look kind of similar, but yours is a little smaller," observed Katrina.

Berg stared at the two images for a few moments. "Yes, they're certainly not an exact match, but the similarity is striking."

Kevin stood and pointed at the screen. "Look, these bond structures are the same on both, just in different places, and there are more single bonded atoms on the periphery of the mystery version. If your Amanitin D is not in the reference database yet, maybe the radiographic mapper got it wrong and picked up some extraneous bonds."

"That's a possibility," thought Berg out loud, "but at the moment we can't be sure. That's the problem with molecule mapping. The machine works great when it can find matches to the database, but there's so much overlap and interconnection between them all that isolating unknowns correctly can be tricky. Paul, can we get another test run through to see if it comes up with the same structure?"

☐ ☐ ☐ ☐ ☐

About a mile into the jungle, Stenvick was charging ahead at a brisk pace, apparently oblivious to the complaints and sounds of labored breathing coming from behind him. The forest canopy was enveloped in dense clouds which shaded the undergrowth and produced a cool, moist environment.

"Eek!" Stephanie shrieked when several ounces of water splashed on her head from the broad leaf of an overhead tree. "Get it off of me!"

"It's just water," said Jennifer with a laugh. "It won't hurt you."

"This... is... insane," Geraldo managed to say between gasping breaths as he tried to maintain the uncomfortably fast stride.

Spencer was pounding along near him with a determined look and deep regular breathing. "Did you do the exercise?"

"No... way... I... thought... it was... a joke."

Melody snickered from behind him. "You don't take many things seriously, do you? Dr. Stenvick's instructions were very clear, and

63

we had at least two months to prepare. I bet you also didn't read his suggested books on nutrition for hikers and birds of Costa Rica."

"Yeah... right," Geraldo replied.

Melody continued, "The instructions were to walk five miles a day with a sixty pound pack and build up to a pace of twelve to fourteen minutes per mile. If you'd done that this wouldn't be so bad."

Stenvick halted suddenly and signaled for silence as several of the students piled into each other behind him. "Do you hear that?" he whispered. A bell-like bird call was faintly audible from somewhere to the left. "That's *Procnias tricarunculatus*, the Three-wattled Bellbird. They have a very loud call so this one could be quite far away. If you ever see one of the males they have these three funny looking things hanging by their beak." He pulled a guide book from his pocket and held up a picture for the students to see, then took off walking again without warning.

☐ ☐ ☐ ☐ ☐

"I don't see any difference between these," Hargren concluded as he displayed the results of the second test next to the first.

"I agree," said Berg, "it's pretty likely that this is the correct structure of whatever this molecule is. The resemblance to Amanitin D is too strong to discount it, but I'm guessing there's more to the story. I think we should go back to INIAS and see if they can shed some light on it."

"What are we going to say?" Katrina asked.

"We'll definitely have to be careful with that," said Berg. "We need to find out their side of things before giving away too much of what we've discovered. We'll keep it simple. Paul has found these crops growing in his fields and we've made the assumption that they're spreading from INIAS. If they're unaware of the situation I'm sure they'll be helpful."

"And what if they are aware of the situation?" Kevin asked. "What if they purposefully engineered this corn to be toxic and made sure it spread?"

"But why would anyone do that?" Katrina challenged him. "It must be an experiment gone awry. No one would want to release such a harmful crop into the wild, especially not a company like Hallita."

"That's what concerns me," said Berg. "I don't think the properties of this corn are any accident. When it comes to genetic engineering, Hallita is the best in the business. They certainly know what this corn is capable of so I'm hopeful they're unaware of the spread outside their field. They probably have good reasons to research a crop with properties like this one without any intention of releasing it to the outside environment."

Hargren picked up his phone when he noticed it vibrating on the desk. "The pizzas are here. I'll be back in a minute. I just have to meet the delivery guy up at the main entrance. I'll join you in the break room down the hall."

A few minutes later Hargren entered the break room with two large takeout boxes and a bag with plates, utensils and napkins. "I have drinks in the fridge over there, take anything you want." He set down the boxes and flipped open the covers to reveal two large steaming pizzas heaping with toppings.

"This is delicious," Kevin raved after taking a couple bites of kielbasa, pierogi and goat cheese on a chewy rye crust with dill alfredo sauce.

"Wait till you try this one," Katrina said before taking another mouthful of bratwurst, chopped cabbage and farmers cheese on flaky sweet egg crust with a sauce of pureed beets, butter and spices.

"Thanks, Paul, this is incredible," said Berg. "My wife is never going to believe I had Lithuanian pizza on this trip. I better get some pictures of these before they're all gone."

□ □ □ □ □

Stenvick paused in the middle of a long suspension bridge so that everyone could take in the surrounding view. Michelle and Jennifer had moved to the back of the line to avoid the bombardment of assorted trailside objects coming at them from behind. Derek and Ben professed to have nothing to do with them each time the girls turned around to try and catch them in the act.

"Finally, we're stopping," Michelle said with relief. "This damp air is ruining my hair. Jennifer, can you open the top compartment of my bag and get out my brush?"

Jennifer found the brush amidst an assortment of hair care and beauty products and handed it to her. "Why would you bring all that stuff hiking? We're just going to get all sweaty and gross and then shower when we return to the dorm."

Michelle gave her a look of disdain as she ran the brush through her hair. "My dear, appearance is everything when you're going to be a star like me. I can't afford to look dreary and disheveled like you. No one cares if a doctor looks like a drowned cat, they'll assume you've been working hard saving lives, but I need to be ready for the cameras at all times. I would be horrified if I wound up on a magazine cover not looking my best."

Ignoring the insult, Jennifer took out her hair elastic and redid her ponytail. "In that case, I better get this little guy off of you," she said, plucking a small frog from Michelle's forehead where it had been perched for the last few minutes.

Everyone turned towards Stenvick when he told them to look at a tree not too far away from the bridge. "See the large black bird with the red under its throat?" he asked in a loud whisper.

"Is that the Bare-necked Umbrellabird?" Melody asked eagerly, "I remember that one from the book you assigned. It has the funny bowl-cut hairdo."

Stenvick laughed. "Very good, you are correct. That's *Cephalopterus glabricollis*. I'm glad we ran across one, they're an endangered species so sightings are not as common as they used to be."

◻ ◻ ◻ ◻ ◻

The drive from San José to INIAS passed quickly in the light midday traffic. Berg and Hargren had discussed their plans for the visit in further detail and had called ahead to request an appointment with a researcher. When they entered the visitor center, Hargren approached the information desk and informed them of their arrival. A few minutes later they were met by a petite woman with long brown hair and glasses. "Hello, I'm Dr. Sarah Lake," she said shaking hands with each of them. "Welcome to INIAS. I've been informed that you have a concern about one of our corn test crops. Follow me and we can discuss it in our conference room."

Lake led the four of them through a secure door off the main lobby. They passed several research labs and offices as they followed her down a long hallway. The walls were lined with award certificates and plaques bearing Dr. Fiker's name. When they reached the end, their host ushered them into a room with a long meeting table and chairs. "Can I get you anything to drink? We have coffee, tea, sodas."

Hargren requested coffee; Berg and Katrina opted for tea and Kevin wanted a cola. Lake dialed an extension on the speaker phone and relayed the requests. "Please, have a seat. Your drinks will be brought in shortly. So, what is it you wanted to discuss?"

Hargren placed a map of the area and some photos on the table. He explained his research with the university, describing how he'd observed the mysterious corn taking over his test plots and the effects on the wildlife that ate it. He showed pictures of the progression and the locations of his fields compared to INIAS. Berg explained that he was visiting with some students and they'd worked with Paul to identify INIAS as the likely source of the invading corn.

Lake seemed a bit doubtful. "So you think that the corn in your fields is coming from our test facility? That's not likely. We have strict controls in place to prevent any of our crops from spreading outside of their assigned areas."

There was a knock on the door and Megan entered the room carrying their drinks on a tray. "Wow, this is so weird," she said as she set the tray on the table. "You guys look just like some people that took my tour yesterday, but they were wearing different clothing. Do you all have identical twins?"

"Thank you, Miss Monet, that will be all," Lake said in an exasperated tone.

Megan left the room and Hargren offered an explanation as he tore open a sugar packet to pour in his coffee. "Actually we did come yesterday to take the tour. We wanted to see if you had any corn here that looked like the type we've been finding. It has a distinctly different type of stalk than we're used to seeing and we did spot the same thing in your field."

Berg set a sample bag on the table with a few sections of stalk. "These are from the corn that's taking over Paul's fields. If you compare them to one of the types growing in your corn area I'm sure you'll agree they look identical."

"Mr. Berg," Lake said as if addressing a student who had done poorly on a test, "I'm sure you're aware that physical resemblance does not mean this corn is related to ours in any way."

"Can we show you the field that matches it?" Hargren pleaded. "You'll see there's no mistaking the similarity. Maybe you could even test the two types in your lab."

Lake gave a dramatic sigh and agreed to take them out to the field. She escorted them to the parking lot and after a short drive they got out of her INIAS Land Rover at stop seven, where they'd just been the day before. Berg held up the sample bag. "See, these stalks are the same."

Lake took the bag and crossed the grass to the field, where she held it up against the stalks growing there. "I'll agree they look remarkably similar," she said.

"Also," Hargren added, "your tour guide told us this corn tastes bad to insects. The corn growing in my fields is toxic to insects and animals. Is yours that way? Have you noticed dead animals around the field?"

"I can assure you we have not," said Lake. "I'm not at liberty to disclose confidential information about our research, but this corn has a modification to repel insects and nothing more. They take one bite and quickly decide to eat elsewhere. Believe me we would notice if animals started dying."

"If this is the same corn though," Berg pressed, "how would you explain its invasive tendency?"

"Well," Lake said thoughtfully, "this has some of our standard disease and pesticide resistance properties built into it. If it were to be planted in a field of normal non-GMO corn you could expect it to become dominant. It's simply a sturdier crop. I'm sure that our corn has nothing to do with what you're finding in your fields, but if you'll allow me to keep this sample I'll have our lab run some analysis just in case. If we find anything I'll alert Dr. Fiker and we'll let you know right away."

They climbed back into the Land Rover and returned to the visitor center. Before they parted at the entrance, Lake pulled out a business card and handed it to Hargren. "You should hear from us about the test results in the next week or two. We're pretty busy at the moment preparing for the media onslaught after the Nobel ceremony, but once that's settled down give me a call. We can arrange for a team to come look at your corn. We're always on the lookout for naturally occurring properties that we haven't seen before, and it sounds like the plant in your fields could be of interest to us. If not, I'm sure we can lend some assistance to eradicate it so you can get back to your research."

Hargren and Berg thanked Lake for her time and they all headed back to the Trooper in silence.

"She was definitely hiding something," Kevin surmised as they pulled out of the parking lot.

"Definitely," agreed Katrina, "and did you notice how uncomfortable she seemed trying to explain away the invasive nature?"

"I'm a bit baffled," said Berg. "I don't know why they would try to dismiss us so quickly. Their corn is spreading out of control, so unless they want some unwelcome attention I would think they'd be anxious to stop it. If they follow through on the lab test they'll see we were right and maybe then they'll take us seriously."

Lake watched the Trooper drive out of the lot towards the main entrance before heading back into the building. Dr. Nathan Fiker was waiting for her right inside the door. He was short and thin with a full head of grey hair, a neatly trimmed goatee and stylish rectangular glasses. He looked every bit the distinguished scientist with a crisp white lab coat over an expensive suit. "How did it go?" he asked.

Lake considered for a moment. "I think they know more than they let on, and they've definitely found test corn C. This could be a problem."

Fiker developed a grave expression. "Test corn C? That's the version with immediate toxicity. I'd be more concerned if they came asking about the other one... but still, I don't like this development. I'll take care of this. Thank you for bringing it to my attention."

Chapter 11

"Phew, I've never hiked that hard," Derek said as Stenvick led the students out of the forest into the clearing by the visitor center and announced they were finished. Derek peeled off his heavy pack and immediately felt a cold sensation on his back as the air hit the sweat-drenched shirt clinging to his skin.

Ben dropped his pack and lay on the ground like a stationary snow angel. "That was intense. I don't know how Stenvick does it. I could barely breathe trying to keep up with him but he was talking on and on about birds the whole time."

Stephanie stumbled up next to them. "I thought I was going to collapse those times he said we were off pace and started jogging. How many miles do you think that was?"

"I don't know," said Derek, "but I'm pretty sure we covered every trail in this place."

Stephanie groaned. "Yes, and Dr. Stenvick sure was excited about getting to do that unmarked research trail."

"Don't remind me," Ben said. "My knee still hurts from where I slipped on those lichen covered rocks. You'd think we'd slow down on trails no one uses."

Stephanie sat on the ground to stretch her legs. "On the bright side, I think we saw everything this forest had to offer. The orchids were my favorite part. We sell them at the greenhouse, but seeing so many varieties growing in their natural habitat was quite a sight."

Derek chuckled. "I can't stop laughing at how Ben was making bird whistles and Dr. Stenvick was sure he'd found a Resplendent Quetzal."

"I know," said Ben. "I must have had him going for at least twenty minutes. It's too bad he never spotted it."

"Did you practice that call before the trip?" Stephanie asked.

"Yeah, the bird book was pretty dull and I got distracted watching videos on the internet instead. I wouldn't be surprised if we run into a few more species that he can't find."

The sun was nearing the horizon as Hargren pulled into a spot at the restaurant he'd taken Berg to for their first meeting. "I don't know about all of you but I'm famished. Let's stop here for dinner before we get back to the university."

"I'm sure going to miss the meal plan we've had traveling with you," Kevin said pensively.

"Speaking of that," said Berg, "I'll charge dinner to my expense account. I've already let you pay for too much, Paul."

The restaurant was quite busy and they waited several minutes before being shown to a table. Hargren took care of translating their drink and appetizer orders for the waiter.

"What are you going to do now?" asked Katrina.

"I'm not sure," he responded. "My research is ruined and by the looks of things it won't be long until the corn from INIAS takes over my fields completely. I highly doubt they are going to admit to it being from their field."

"You should probably take Dr. Lake's offer and have their people come out," said Berg. "My guess is that they'll want to clean this up and get their corn under control. You may be surprised how far they'll go to fix this. Killer corn making the news headlines would be awfully bad publicity for Hallita. It's only a matter of time until someone inadvertently eats it."

Hargren was about to respond when the pair of Mariachis sidled up to their table and began to sing to the accompaniment of their guitars.

"Oh how nice," Katrina said as she watched them play.

Hargren looked anything but happy and began to politely say no thank you to the two men, but Berg stopped him. "Just enjoy the music, Paul, I'm paying."

The Mariachis played several traditional love songs and presented Katrina with a red rose before bowing deeply in unison once they were finished. Berg handed them several bills which must have met their expectations since they smiled and moved on to another table.

"That wasn't so bad," said Berg once they'd left.

Hargren turned his chair back to face the table and reluctantly agreed. "Hey, where are my keys?" he asked while looking side to side at the table in front of him. "They were right here a minute ago."

"Maybe they fell on the floor," said Kevin as he bent to look under the table. "No, I don't see them."

Hargren groaned and slapped his palms to his forehead. "How could I have been so stupid? Someone must have swiped them when we were watching the Mariachis. I'll be right back. Maybe I can catch them before they get away with my car."

Hargren got up from the table and walked quickly towards the front entrance. Kevin, Katrina and Berg went over to a nearby window with a view on the parking lot. "Look, there's someone in the Trooper!" said Kevin excitedly when he spotted the vehicle.

Hargren appeared running around the corner of the building and then a bright flash obscured the view, followed almost instantaneously by a deafening boom and the sounds of glass shattering.

□ □ □ □ □

Stenvick tried calling Berg's cell but there was no answer. He waited for the voicemail and left a message. "Gary, it's Rich. We're stuck in a traffic jam on the way into San José so I think we'll be late to dinner. Don't wait for us if you get there first. I don't know how long this will be but I'll let you know when I have a better idea." Glancing up at the rear view mirror, he saw that all the students were still sound asleep as they'd been for much of the ride. "*Ah, to be young,*" he

73

thought as he took a swig from his coffee thermos and drove the bus forward another ten feet before anyone could cut in front of him.

Berg slowly sat up amidst a sea of broken glass and dishes. Delayed by the shock, it took a few seconds before his senses suddenly rushed back into focus. People were screaming and shouting all around as patrons from other areas of the restaurant ran over to help and see what happened. Through the missing windows, he could see a dense cloud of black smoke rising from the roaring flames engulfing the Trooper. Gradually remembering what had happened, he stretched his arms out and turned them over, then gently felt his face and head for any signs of injury.

Berg scanned his immediate surroundings as his head cleared. One of the Mariachis was sitting on the flattened remains of his guitar with a stunned expression. There were a few people lying on the floor who appeared eerily still, and the destruction around them looked worse than the other areas of the room. Berg started to panic as he remembered Kevin and Katrina. Holding onto a nearby chair for support, he carefully got to his feet and turned to look around. He noticed a large group of people on the other side of the restaurant staring in astonishment at the view before them. Many people were sitting or lying down with assorted injuries. He jumped in alarm at a flash of light and felt his heart rate skyrocket. Realizing it was only a camera flash, he took a deep breath and calmed down a bit. He spotted Kevin, but his relief quickly turned to worry as he saw no sign of movement.

Berg stumbled over and lifted an overturned table off of Kevin's back. He was lying face down on the floor with Katrina pinned under him. "Kevin, Katrina; are you ok? Can you hear me?" Berg asked frantically.

Kevin emitted a loud groan and pushed himself to his knees.

"Are you ok? Are you hurt?" Berg peppered him.

"Whoa," Kevin said as he gathered his faculties.

Berg quickly knelt down beside him. "Katrina? Can you hear me?" He pressed a couple fingers to the side of her neck and was reassured by a strong steady pulse.

Katrina's eyes popped wide open. "What happened?" she asked in a panicked tone, looking from Kevin to Berg and back again.

"Don't move," Berg cautioned her. "You could be injured. Does anything hurt?"

Katrina looked thoughtful as she tested her arms and legs until coming to the conclusion that only her head hurt.

"You must have hit the floor pretty hard," said Berg.

Kevin had stood and was looking around the room. "Wow. That was just like in the video games. I saw the flash and turned around to dive like it was instinct. Are you ok, Katrina? Sorry if I knocked the wind out of you."

"Paul!" Berg remembered suddenly. "Kevin, stay with Katrina. I have to go see if Paul is ok." Berg dashed through the crowds of people and out the door. As he rounded the corner of the building he could feel his heart practically stop when he saw a crowd of people gathered in a circle around something on the ground. "Move!" he shouted as he pushed his way through the crowd. Finally reaching the center, he looked down and stared for a moment in confusion at an unfamiliar man being given CPR by one of the bystanders.

Berg turned and pressed back through the throng, looking wildly around the lot for any sign of Hargren. He spotted a familiar looking shoe behind a parked car and ran over. Hargren was sitting with his back against the driver's door, pressing his hand to a cut on his chin.

"Gary!" he said excitedly when he saw his friend approaching, "Is everyone ok?"

"I think so," Berg replied. "What happened to you? I thought that explosion hit you."

"It did, but I was knocked off balance and fell behind this car just in time. I think I whacked my chin pretty good."

"Are you ok to get up?" Berg asked. "We should get back to Kevin and Katrina."

Hargren pushed himself off the ground and they returned to the restaurant. Kevin and Katrina were approaching the door as they entered. "What just happened here?" asked Katrina.

75

Hargren looked around warily. "Let's go outside and get some privacy." He led them out to the parking lot and found a spot away from the growing crowds of people. "That man stole my keys when the Mariachis were playing for us. Obviously he wanted to take the car. It happens often enough around here. I was running towards it and heard him start cranking the engine and then it exploded."

"It must have been a car bomb," said Kevin. "They wire them to detonate from the ignition circuit."

"You mean someone was trying to kill us?" Katrina said in disbelief.

"But for that car thief I think they would have succeeded," said Berg.

"Who would want to...?" Hargren started to say, but then stopped as the realization hit him. "INIAS. We better get out of here before the police show up so we can think this through. Come on, follow me."

Hargren led them down the street and within a few moments they heard the whine of police sirens in the distance.

Chapter 12

Hargren hailed a taxi and gave the driver directions to his lab at the university. "We can discuss what to do next when we get there," he said to the others.

The four of them rode in silence as the taxi navigated the city streets and pulled onto the university campus. "Oh no," Hargren moaned as they turned onto the street where the lab was located. Several fire trucks and other emergency vehicles were jammed into the narrow roadway in front of the charred and steaming remains of what had been the lab building. A team of firefighters was still spraying water on the rubble.

Berg checked his phone and saw that he had a few missed calls and a voicemail from Stenvick. He listened to the message and checked the time it had been left, then tried to call him back. From what he could understand of the automated Spanish message, Stenvick appeared to be out of service. He leaned forward and got Hargren's attention. "I'm guessing this fire is no accident. That would be too much of a coincidence. If INIAS is after us, they must have found out where you work and they're probably looking into what I'm doing down here. I think Rich and the students are still stuck in traffic but I couldn't get a call through to him. We should get over to the dorm to make sure they're safe."

Hargren gave the driver new instructions and the cab sped off down the street. Minutes later they took a turn and spotted the dorm building a couple blocks away. Nothing looked out of the ordinary and Hargren instructed the driver to approach slowly and let them out in front. Berg was eyeing the building carefully as they drew nearer and furrowed his brow in concentration. "Paul, tell him to pass by and keep going."

Hargren relayed the request. As the cab rolled by, Berg saw what he was looking for. "They're here!" he said pointing to a black Mercedes SUV with dark tinted windows parked near the entrance. "See the INIAS logo on the door?"

They took the next right and Hargren pointed to a place to stop, asking the driver to wait there for them. They all got out and gathered by the corner of a building which blocked them from view of the dorm. Hargren peeked around the corner and whispered. "The Mercedes is still there but I can't see if anyone is in it."

The others joined him to look. Katrina pointed to one of the windows of the dorm. "Look, I think someone is in there with a flashlight."

After a minute they all ducked out of view as the lobby doors opened and two men dressed all in black stepped out onto the sidewalk. "Nothing interesting in there, just typical student stuff," they could hear one of the men say.

"Should we rig some charges and wait for them to get back?" the other asked.

"No, two buildings and the vehicle in one night would draw a lot of attention. We'll put in some bugs and see if they know anything. The boss said to only take them out if they're involved."

"I think we should get out of here," Berg whispered. "It sounds like Rich and the students should be ok as long as they don't know what's going on. If these guys believe we died in the explosion, we have some time to think."

Hargren agreed. "We'll take the taxi and find a hotel room a few miles from here. I don't think we want to be anywhere they could connect us with."

The four of them got back in the cab and Hargren asked the driver for a recommendation. He took them across the city to a small hotel owned by a friend. The sign indicated that there were rooms available.

Stenvick tried dialing Berg again once the traffic had cleared and he was rolling along at a steady pace. He felt a mixture of worry and annoyance when the call went to voicemail. One of the things he appreciated about his colleague was that he usually answered calls by the second ring if he wasn't in class, and even then he'd return missed calls as soon as he was free. This was unusual for sure. Stenvick was thinking about the possibility of him being in an area with no service when the beep alerted him to leave his message. "Gary, Rich again. We cleared the traffic jam. There was an accident blocking one of the lanes and everyone was slowed down getting around it. Anyway, we're moving again and I think we'll be there for dinner in about twenty minutes."

□ □ □ □ □

Berg sat on the end of the bed in the hotel room looking at the missed call and voicemail notifications on his phone.

"Did someone call?" asked Hargren.

"It was Rich again," Berg answered. "I don't know what to do. What do I tell him? I can't ignore him for much longer but I also don't want to put him and the rest of the students in danger. Let me see what the message says." He listened for a few moments then put the phone away. "They'll be at dinner soon. Obviously we won't be there to meet them so I need an excuse."

"Why don't we just call the police?" asked Katrina.

Hargren shook his head. "I don't think that's a good idea. What evidence do we have? We can't give them any proof that INIAS is behind this or that their guys blew up my car and the lab. All my work is gone. They'd just think I'm a lunatic or some sort of radical activist making up stories. Plus, I have a number of outstanding speeding tickets so I wouldn't say I'm on the best terms with the cops around here."

Berg chimed in. "Even if we could get new samples from your fields, that wouldn't prove much since your records of the progress are gone. I wouldn't be surprised if INIAS has already sent out people to remove any traces of their corn from your fields."

"We can't hide forever," said Kevin. "They'll find out soon enough that none of us were in the Trooper and then what? If INIAS was willing to kill us over some corn I doubt they'll just let this go."

"Kevin is right," agreed Hargren. "It's only a matter of time before they find us, and we can't go public without proof of what we know. Gary, you think up a reason that Rich will believe to explain why we can't make it back tonight. Kevin, Katrina, see if there's any news coverage of the bombing or the fire. I'm going to make a phone call to someone who may be able to help us out of this."

☐ ☐ ☐ ☐ ☐

Kyle Shepard parked the black INIAS Mercedes several blocks from the UCR cafeteria. Isaiah Drummer sat in the passenger seat and checked the signals from the bugs they'd installed in the dorm room and the GPS tracker in the rear bumper of the bus. The two men were in their early thirties, both dishonorably discharged from an American Special Forces unit, and now working as hit-men for hire. Kyle had a solid muscular build with intense black eyes and a cautious demeanor, while Isaiah was taller and lean with a mop of curly hair and a constant grin underneath his 1970's rock-star style sunglasses.

"Are the bugs checking out?" Kyle asked.

"Yes," said Isaiah, "all of them are transmitting and we have a lock on the bus."

"Good, it won't be hard to track them and find out what they know. Plus, I even got photos of their itinerary from the dorm room. This is so much easier than trying to figure out the enemy back when we were in the service."

"That's for sure," Isaiah agreed, "and now we don't have any rules of engagement to worry about."

Kyle's phone rang. "I better get this, it's Curt."

Isaiah continued running checks on the bugs from his laptop while Kyle took the call. Kyle listened for a few minutes and was obviously agitated by what he was hearing.

"What's wrong?" asked Isaiah as he put down the phone.

80

Kyle scowled. "Curt said the police found one body in the Trooper and it appears to be a known carjacker. That means our targets are on the run and probably know we're after them. Curt's not happy about all the attention we've caused with the explosion and the fire, something about overkill."

"Whatever," interjected Isaiah.

"Anyway," Kyle continued, "the boss figures those nosy scientists will probably hide out for a while, and he said we should send a message by making sure the other professor and his group of students have an unfortunate accident."

Isaiah grinned. "That's what I was waiting to hear."

Chapter 13

"I don't know, Dr. Stenvick," Jennifer replied doubtfully as they sat at the cafeteria table. "I really do believe that it's possible to treat all patients equally if you separate your feelings about them from your professional ethics as a physician. If you approach each case viewing the patient as simply a human being with a problem to be solved, I don't see why feelings or bias should influence decisions."

Stenvick paused as he finished a mouthful of beans. "In a perfect world yes, perhaps, but studies have clearly shown that doctors don't put their best efforts into helping patients when they have a prejudice based on appearance or knowledge of the individual. Conversely, they'll go to the greatest lengths of imagination to treat patients they're attracted to or feel similar to in some way. I wish it were as you say, but even the best among us are influenced by our subconscious biases."

"We'll see," replied Jennifer, "I plan to prove you wrong on that."

"Excuse me," Stenvick said as he pulled his phone from his pocket. "Dr. Berg is calling, I better get this." Stenvick answered the call and put the phone to his ear with anticipation. "Hello?"

"Hi Rich, it's Gary. Sorry I didn't get your calls earlier but we were out of coverage for a while."

"That happens," agreed Stenvick. "There's good service around the larger cities but the more remote areas are quite spotty. You missed a good hike today. I hope you're calling to tell me you'll be here soon. We just sat down to eat a few minutes ago. Oh, and I almost forgot. One of the science buildings burned down this evening. Watch out for all the emergency vehicles on your way in."

There was a slight pause before Berg spoke. "Actually, we're not going to make it there tonight. We were on our way back but we ran into a flooded section of road. It would have taken over an hour to go back around it and find another route. Paul decided he'd try to make it through but the water was too deep and flooded the engine. Fortunately a park service truck came by after not too long and threw us a tow rope. Once they pulled us back to dry ground, the driver informed us that a levy had broken in the park."

Stenvick groaned. "Something similar happened to me a number of years ago. Our bus was swept away but we were fortunate that another college group was going through and we hitched a ride with them."

"Well," Berg went on, "we were thinking of wading through and getting a ride from someone on the other side, but the park ranger said not to go in the water since the levy break had released alligators from the park. He was kind enough to let us stay at his home for the night and we'll arrange transport back down there tomorrow morning. We should see you by the time you return from tomorrow's trip."

Stenvick sighed. "Ok, glad to hear you're alright. Tell Paul I hope his car isn't ruined and to take the long way if this ever happens again."

☐ ☐ ☐ ☐ ☐

Berg ended the call and turned to face the expectant looks from the others. "I think he bought it. He said to go the long way around next time, Paul."

A sad expression passed over Hargren's face. "I guess it hasn't quite hit me yet, but my Trooper is gone. There won't be a next time."

"Don't feel sad," Katrina said while gently putting a hand on his shoulder. "We can all be thankful that we weren't in the car when that bomb went off. We can all remember your Trooper for saving our lives by catching the eye of that car thief."

84

Hargren pulled himself together. "So, I called Bill McConnell, a friend of mine who lives over in the port of Limón. I didn't want to tell him much on the phone but I promised I'd explain when we get there. He said he would do what he can to help. Trust me, if there's anyone who can assist us now it's him. You'll understand when you meet him but I'm not at liberty to say much more. We'll figure out a way to get there tomorrow morning. Kevin, Katrina, anything on the news?"

Kevin responded. "We don't understand the Spanish but they did have some live footage on one of the news channels showing reporters at the restaurant and the lab. We're pretty sure they didn't have any real answers yet about what happened and we didn't hear any of our names or mention of INIAS."

"Also," said Katrina, "there's a special on in a few minutes about the upcoming Nobel Prize event. They have satellite here so we can watch it on the American news stations. The preview said there will be a debate about Dr. Fiker getting the prize. Maybe we can learn something."

When the time came, they all focused their attention on the television as the program began. The host of the show explained that his two guests were there to discuss the worthiness of Dr. Fiker for the Nobel. "It's a bad idea," one of them began. "What do we know about this man? He was a war protester back in college and was associated with some highly questionable groups and individuals. Ever since he made it big with Hallita he's stayed out of the spotlight, but what's his agenda? Why does his company pursue so many patent lawsuits against small farmers and do so much political lobbying if he's truly a humanitarian?"

"You can't judge him by his actions in college," the other guest rebutted. "That was decades ago, people change. Look at all the humanitarian relief efforts he's spearheaded. World hunger is almost nonexistent thanks to him, and of course Hallita has to protect its technology. They have every right to if they're going to make any profit on their work."

"Look at the politics though," the first guest continued. "Every vote goes their way thanks to all their campaign donations and lobbying. There's no oversight or regulation any more. Who's making sure their crops are safe? Even the FDA is no longer given access to their science for review. They just have to accept testing by the company. I think it's dangerous. Hallita products feed the world, but for the common good we need to be moving to make the technology open to scientific review, not putting Fiker on a pedestal."

"Oh please," said the host. "We're here to discuss the merits of Dr. Fiker for the Peace Prize, not to argue about the safety of GMO crops. That issue has been settled for years now and only a few fanatics still rage about their 'dangers'. Don't tell me you're one of them?"

The debate continued for a while longer with the obvious consensus between the host and the guest in support of Fiker that he was deserving of the prize.

Hargren turned off the television. "I don't know what to make of that, but I do agree that the lack of public oversight is a concern. We don't know what's going on with the mystery corn crop, but it makes you consider that we really don't know what's in most of the crops being grown."

"I agree," said Berg. "Our recent experience has certainly given me a lot to think about. But, it's been a long day. We should get some rest so we can get up early to go meet your friend tomorrow."

After they'd turned out the lights, Berg lay wide awake in the darkness and thought of his family. Before the explosion at the restaurant turned their world upside down he had been emailing regularly with his wife about how the trip was going and what she was up to at home. He read over the last two messages from her on his phone and smiled at the pictures she had included, and then responded that all was well and he was having a good time. He couldn't think of any way to explain what was going on and didn't want her to worry about him. He turned off the phone and prayed that he'd get to hold his family in his arms again soon, and then drifted off to sleep.

☐ ☐ ☐ ☐ ☐

Kyle and Isaiah sat in the Mercedes at the crack of dawn listening to the audio feed from the bugs they'd planted in the dorm rooms while nursing large energy drinks and sharing a dozen donuts. They were startled and Isaiah dropped a donut on his lap when

Spencer's voice suddenly broke the silence. "Up and at them! Time to push up!"

The assassins listened in amusement as Spencer focused all of his workout commands on Geraldo since Kevin was not in the room. As the minutes went by, they heard the sounds of people getting ready for the day as the occupants of each room woke to their various alarms.

Kyle had been listening to Stenvick. "The professor just said he's heading over to breakfast. We'll pick up their conversation again when they board the bus. Let's drive a few miles out ahead of them until we confirm they're sticking to the schedule."

"Sounds like a plan," agreed Isaiah. "I'm looking forward to their accident."

"You enjoy this too much," said Kyle. "Pull up the map so we can go over the plan again."

Half an hour later they were parked off the side of the highway when the microphone in the bus crackled to life. "All aboard," they heard Stenvick saying to the students, followed by the sounds of people shuffling and jostling to get up the stairs and down the aisle. They heard the door close and Stenvick speaking over the intercom. "Our drive isn't so long today. We're going to visit the Irazú volcano. There's an excellent hike from the valley up to the crater that I know you'll all enjoy."

Coughing and sputtering noises sounded from the engine and then they could hear the bus accelerating. Isaiah pulled a small transmitter out of his bag and flipped the safety cover off of a red switch.

"What is that?" Kyle demanded.

"An accident," Isaiah responded as if it were obvious.

"What do you mean an accident?"

"I put a *few* remote explosives under the bus," said Isaiah. "I just have to flip this switch and they go kaboom."

"That's not the plan," Kyle responded angrily. "Curt said this has to be clean and look like an accident. Blowing them up would make it obvious that someone is out to get them and the cops would start investigating... wait a minute. What do you mean by 'a few'?"

Isaiah replied sheepishly. "A hundred pounds of C4, maybe a little more."

Kyle shook his head. "We're going to have to get it back before someone finds it, and put that transmitter away."

"Fine," said Isaiah reluctantly as he shoved the transmitter back into his bag.

□ □ □ □ □

Katrina woke from a fitful sleep and took a few moments to remember why she was in a strange hotel room. Berg, Hargren and Kevin had bedded down with extra blankets on the floor and given her the room's sole bed. She was about to fall back asleep when Berg's alarm broke the silence with a loud ring. "Everybody up," he said after dismissing the alarm.

"What, no pushups?" Kevin asked groggily.

"Umm, no," replied Berg quizzically. "We need to be on our way. We can take turns with the shower and then head to the lobby. I think they have a breakfast buffet."

A little while later, they sat around a small table hungrily devouring an assortment of breakfast foods. "I'm starving," mumbled Kevin through a mouthful of pastry. "I just realized we never got to eat dinner yesterday."

"Don't speak with food in your mouth," Katrina scolded. "Dr. Berg," she asked, "how are we going to get to Limón?"

"I've been thinking about that," he replied. "Paul thinks we should find a vehicle and drive ourselves there."

"Too much risk to take a taxi," said Hargren. "I think we should avoid being seen as much as possible."

Kevin's gaze was fixed on the front window of the hotel. "That old VW Bus across the street has a for sale sign on it. Do we have any cash?"

Hargren looked in his wallet but only had a few bills. Berg rifled through his thoughtfully. "Paul, ask the woman at the desk if she can cash travelers checks. Rich gave me some to hold on to. And, Kevin, can you see how much they're asking for the Bus?"

"Traveler's checks?" Hargren repeated. "No one uses those anymore. You need to get with the times."

Berg threw his hands up, "I know, you don't have to convince me. Rich insists on using them. Old habits die hard, you know."

Hargren sighed and headed for the desk. He returned after a brief conversation and reported that Paula, the owner of the hotel, was reluctant but willing to cash the checks. Kevin came back with the price on the window sign.

"We don't have enough money," Katrina said with dismay upon hearing the figures.

Hargren sighed. "We won't be able to get the necessary paperwork and title transfer either, but I think I can swing it. I'll be right back."

Hargren sauntered over to the gas station and found the owner as Berg and the students watched from the lobby. After a lively conversation he returned with a wide grin. "The owner says it runs and drives. It's been sitting around for a few years and he hardly uses it any more. It's not even registered. As you probably saw, I drove it around the lot to make sure it works. We haggled on the price and I got him to take half off if we pay cash now."

"Seems a bit risky," said Berg, "but it appears to be our best option at the moment. Let's do it."

They cashed the checks at the desk and Hargren went to complete the purchase. Berg climbed in the passenger seat and Kevin cleared some empty boxes off the rear bench.

"Limón here we come," Hargren said as he turned out of the hotel lot and headed for the highway.

◻ ◻ ◻ ◻ ◻

Kyle and Isaiah watched the blinking dot showing the location of the bus as it moved along on their laptop display. They had an excellent view of the winding mountain road that Stenvick was slowly navigating from their vantage point on a ridgeline high above. "I'll count down from three and you hit the detonator at zero," Kyle instructed.

"Got it," said Isaiah as he flipped open the safety.

"Only the one for the charges we just set, not the one for the bus," Kyle reminded him.

"I know," Isaiah said with a roll of his eyes.

89

"Ok, get ready. Three, two, one."

Isaiah hit the switch and they heard several muffled explosions from the steep hillside below.

Michelle was sitting with her head pressed against the window watching the mountainous scenery pass by. Her attention was drawn to sudden movement on the cliff face up ahead. She watched in disbelief as an entire section of the cliff broke free and began sliding and tumbling towards the road just ahead of them. "Stop the bus!" She yelled in a panicked tone.

Stenvick didn't see anything wrong but he instinctively jammed his foot on the brake, startled by the urgency of Michelle's command. The students were thrown against the seats in front of them as the tires locked up and skidded on the broken asphalt. A wall of soil enveloped the front half of the bus, stopping its forward progress and pushing it over on its side and towards the edge of the roadway. Glass shattered and steel screamed against the pavement until the vehicle came to rest in a cloud of dust.

Amidst much yelling and coughing, Ben found that he was pressed against the side wall by Derek, Jennifer and Stephanie, who all fell in a pile on top of him as the vehicle tipped. He let out a gasp when he turned his head and looked down. His shoulder rested on a cracked pane of window glass, through which he could see a drop-off directly below extending several hundred feet to the bottom of the valley.

Chapter 14

"So let me get this straight, Katrina," Kevin said loudly to be heard over the engine of the Bus that Hargren was driving east on route thirty two. "You have a job lined up after graduation with Global Proactive. They're funded in large part by Hallita, and Hallita just tried to blow you up. Don't you think that's going to be a bit awkward?"

"It has crossed my mind," she responded, "but I'm more concerned with our present situation and how we'll get out of this mess alive."

"Well," said Kevin, "at least we're heading away from San José, INIAS and any place they're likely to look for us."

A sudden bang sounded through the VW, startling the four passengers. They could feel the left side of the vehicle drop and Hargren had to react quickly to maintain control. He let off the gas and let the Bus coast. "The rear tire blew out," he said after checking the mirrors.

Berg pointed ahead. "Look, there's a pull-off up there."

"Got it," said Hargren as he put on the turn signal and carefully piloted the unwieldy vehicle towards the exit ramp, trailing a shower of sparks from the bare metal wheel. He passed a few other cars and parked in an isolated spot near some picnic tables.

"Do you think we were followed?" Kevin asked.

"I was just wondering the same thing," Berg said as he looked warily at the entrance ramp coming in from the highway.

"We can't keep driving on this tire," said Hargren. "We're sitting ducks here until we get it fixed."

Berg was still watching the road. "If that blowout was no accident, I'd think whoever was following us would be here by now. It could have just been a bad tire, or maybe we hit something."

"I guess I should have checked the tires a little better," Hargren said as he turned off the engine. "The owner did say it was sitting for a number of years."

"No point dwelling on what we can't change," Berg said as he slid from his seat and got out.

Upon inspection they found that the tire had been severely dry-rotted and cracked. "I hope the spare is in better shape," Kevin said as he went to check.

"That won't do us much good unless there are some tools to change the wheel," Hargren replied.

"Can't we call triple A?" Katrina asked him. "That's what I've always done for car trouble."

Hargren shook his head. "I wish it were that easy, but they don't operate here. I really don't think it's safe for us to call anyone at the moment. The people from INIAS are likely still after us and we have no idea what their capabilities are. If they're monitoring our phones they'll know where we are pretty quickly if we make a call."

"I agree," said Berg. "We can't take any chances right now. If we want to get to Limón we're going to have to fix it ourselves."

For the next few minutes they checked every conceivable storage spot in the vehicle and came up with only the lifting jack and a bag containing a random assortment of tools. "Alright," summarized Berg, "we have no tire iron or suitable tool to get the wheel off. The spare tire and wheel are ok but there's no air pressure in the tire. We're going to need to improvise."

Hargren laughed. "Gary, I've seen you do some amazing things, but I don't see what you could have in mind to fix this."

"Give me a minute to think," replied Berg.

"Is everyone ok?" Stenvick yelled as he climbed over his seat and felt his way through the dusty haze. The front half of the bus was buried under the landslide and dirt had spilled in through a number of shattered windows which made his progress difficult. The rear half had broken through the guardrail and was angled out over the edge of the cliff. "Don't move," Stenvick said, stopping in his tracks as he comprehended the precarious nature of their resting place. "I think the only thing keeping us from falling into the ravine is the weight of the dirt on the front."

Stenvick directed the students to move as far forward as possible in hopes of shifting weight away from the rear. Aside from some bumps and bruises, everyone was uninjured and accounted for. "We have to find a way out of here and back to the road," he said. "The front door is buried so that's not an option."

"I checked the back door but it's welded shut," said Geraldo.

"Yes, I think the rental company mentioned something about that," Stenvick replied thoughtfully. "I suppose that leaves us the windows on the top side."

"They only open halfway," said Stephanie. "We've had them open every day and there's no way we'd be able to fit through."

"I know!" Derek said suddenly. "Ben and I were going to sit in the back row the first time we rode the bus, but the floor is rusted there and we could feel it giving way. I think we could break through it."

"Everyone, stay here, I'm going to go take a look," Stenvick instructed before cautiously walking to the rear. Being careful not to step through the missing side windows, he inspected the floor and pushed on the seats. The metal floor was rusted and no longer attached around the sides and back. He confirmed that it bent like a hinge a few feet in from the rear wall where it was connected over a frame member. Pushing with all his might he could get a few inches of deflection, but the metal quickly sprang back when he let off.

"Dr. Stenvick, I can do that, you come back here," Spencer shouted.

"Be my guest," Stenvick offered as he rejoined the group in the front.

Spencer shuffled down the side wall and took the same position the professor had been in a minute earlier. "Hmm," he muttered as he gave the seats a push, "this is no good." Grabbing onto the two seatbacks, he carefully walked his feet up the roof until he got them into the raised channel that ran the length of the bus. He then adjusted his position to achieve a squatting stance between the seats and roof.

"Be careful, Spencer," Jennifer yelled, concerned by the sight of him suspended horizontally across the bus over the broken window.

"I will," Spencer grunted. Growling through clenched teeth, he pushed on the seats as if he were going for a record lift in the weight room. The metal floor snapped and groaned as it slowly gave way. After the end had bent out by about a foot it seemed that something was holding up further progress. Sweat glistened on Spencer's brow. He took a few moments to recover and then let out a fearsome roar as he pushed with all he had. It looked futile for several seconds, but then there was a loud crack and the floor gave out.

Now extended with his arms halfway out past his head, Spencer slowly walked his feet back down the roof until he was standing on the side of the bus again. He took a position against the back wall and pushed the section of floor further until the two seats were rotated out through the bottom of the bus. "We can… go out… here," he said between gasping breaths. "Just a… short jump."

"Great job, Spencer," said Stenvick. "Come back here a minute and let me take a look."

They switched places again and Stenvick evaluated the scene before him. Directly below was a precipitous drop to the steep cliff side, but there was level ground about five feet from where he stood.

Chapter 15

"I think we can do this," Stenvick said to the students. "We'll go one at a time. I want as little weight in the back as possible so we'll throw all the packs to the road first. Ben and Derek, I'm going to test the jump. I'd like you to gather the packs and throw them to me. Then everyone will follow." He measured out the steps from the edge of the window to the open floor of the bus several times before attempting the jump, then stood in position ready to go. "Wish me luck," he said, then took two strides and leapt over the chasm, landing easily on the edge of the roadway.

"Made it," the students could hear him yell. "Throw me the bags."

Derek made several trips back and forth collecting the scattered packs and handing them to Ben, who heaved them over to Stenvick. Once they were all off Ben stepped back and made the jump. "That was easy," he yelled.

"I'm next," Derek said eagerly as he took his position and completed the crossing.

No sooner had Derek's foot left the bus than Geraldo darted to the back. "That's nothing," he said scornfully upon seeing the gap before him. "I thought this was going to be scary." Seconds later he'd joined the others.

"I guess chivalry is dead," Melody surmised as she looked at the other girls and Spencer.

"I will stay," said Spencer. "You all go. I am heavy. I will keep weight in the front."

"I'm glad to see at least one of them has some manners," said Stephanie. "Spencer, give my thanks to your mother for raising a gentleman. Melody, would you like to go first?"

"Ok," Melody agreed, then slowly walked down the wall to the back. She shut her eyes for a few moments to calm her nerves and then nimbly leapt to the road. "Next," she shouted for the others to hear.

"Go for it, Michelle," said Stephanie as she gave her a nudge.

Michelle clutched each seat as she walked, trying not to look down at the view through the windows. She reached the opening and froze. "I can't do this," she said with apprehension.

"Sure you can," Stenvick encouraged. "Don't look down and don't think about it. The gap is only five feet across. I know you can make it." Seeing that she was still hesitant he continued. "Remember the coffee addict's mantra?"

Michelle thought for a moment. "Caffeine lets me do stupid things faster?"

"Exactly," said Stenvick.

Michelle smiled at the thought and agreed to give it a try. She easily cleared the gap and laughed with relief as Melody gave her a quick hug and congratulated her.

Spencer, Jennifer and Stephanie remained in the front of the stricken vehicle. "You go," Stephanie said to Jennifer.

"You don't have to convince me," Jennifer said as she started for the back. Without a moment's hesitation she jumped across.

"Come on, Stephanie," Melody yelled towards the bus.

Stephanie and Spencer exchanged a parting look. "Good luck," she said, "and thanks for giving us a way out of here."

Spencer gave her a gentle hug. "You go now. I will see you soon." Then, he moved as far forward as possible to maximize the weight balance on the front.

Stephanie began to creep forward cautiously. She froze in panic when the vehicle groaned and shifted several inches.

"Go quick," Spencer yelled from behind her.

With determination she pressed on and reached the back.

"You can do it," Jennifer urged.

Stephanie's brow furrowed in concentration. She'd never been so scared in her entire life, but when she looked back and saw Spencer bravely waiting for her she knew she'd have to force her fears aside. She took two running steps and pushed off. The bus shifted another few inches under her weight, which threw her off balance as she started the jump. She flew across the void and nearly fell over as she hit the landing, but was caught by the other students. "Phew, that was close," she said as the adrenaline rushed through her body and caused her to shiver.

Spencer sat crouched next to the driver's seat. He could hear the students cheering as Stephanie made the crossing safely. The weight shift from her push off the back seemed to have tipped the balance of the vehicle. He heard the creaks and groans of metal as the bus shuddered and slowly ground against the asphalt. On the roadway, the rest of the group fell silent as they saw what was happening and began to step back to a safer distance from the edge of the cliff. Stephanie yelled out, "Spencer, get out of there!"

The bus slipped further off the road with a loud grating screech. The rear was beginning to drop lower than the road surface and twist outward over the cliff edge, which would make the jump much more difficult. When Spencer appeared at the opening in the bottom his lower half was out of view. Stenvick shouted for him to make the jump quickly. Spencer took a couple steps back to prepare for the run, but before he started to move the bus began tipping and the group watched in horror as it slid off the edge of the cliff and fell, along with the dirt and rocks that had been holding it in place.

Stenvick and the students rushed to the edge of the cliff and watched as the bus tumbled end over end for several hundred feet until coming to rest in a cloud of dust at the bottom of the ravine. "Spencer!" Melody cried out.

Everyone jumped when a reply of "what?" came from somewhere below and to their right.

"Spencer?" Melody repeated.

"I am down here," he shouted. "Give me some minutes."

"There he is," Derek yelled, lying on his stomach over the edge of the cliff and pointing somewhere below.

A minute later Spencer appeared at the edge of the roadway where the mangled guardrail was bent down over the side. Ben and Derek ran over and helped pull him up the last few feet to the road. He was covered in dust but appeared unharmed. "What happened?" asked Stenvick.

"I was doing the jump but the bus fell," Spencer explained. "I saw the guardrail hanging down. I did not think. I jumped. I caught the guardrail with both hands and hit the cliff. I hold on tight. Then I climb up."

"That was amazing," Geraldo said looking at him in awe. "I guess I'm not the only one who woke up being awesome this morning."

Everyone laughed and hugged Spencer, relieved to have him safely back with them.

□ □ □ □ □

Kyle and Isaiah watched with disappointment as the group of students stood safely on the road below. "The timing was perfect," said Isaiah. "They should have been swept right off the cliff."

"They must have seen it coming," responded Kyle. "It looked like they were braking a bit before they hit."

Isaiah had a sudden look of panic. "How are we going to get the explosives back now? There's no way to get down that ravine."

Kyle pondered for several seconds. "The bus just tumbled a few hundred feet. It's not easy to get to but someone will soon enough. What always happens in the movies when cars fall like that?"

"They explode!" Isaiah said gleefully, "but that bus is a diesel, an explosion would be highly unlikely."

"Unlikely," Kyle conceded, "but remotely possible perhaps? It would be pretty hard to gather evidence after it's all burned, and the eyewitness accounts of the explosion from a bunch of foreign students who almost fell to their deaths would probably be exaggerated, don't you think?"

Isaiah thought. "No, I don't think it would happen. It might catch on fire from leaking fuel, but I don't think it would explode."

Kyle let out a frustrated groan. "You're not getting the point. Blow up the bus with your detonator and all the evidence will be burned

98

to a crisp. Unless they bring in experts, the local police will just assume it caught on fire and move on."

"Oh," said Isaiah, finally grasping Kyle's intent. "Why didn't you just say so?"

Using the few tools available, Berg had taken apart a section of the dashboard in the VW to access the windshield wiper system. He removed the wiper arms and clamped them tightly around one of the lug nuts using duct tape to make a two sided wrench. The improvised tool had a solid grasp on the nut but was too short for any of them to be able to apply enough torque to turn it. "Paul, can you lift the rear with the jack so I can see underneath?" Berg asked.

Stenvick and the students were startled when a massive explosion rocked the valley and sent a ball of fire up high enough for them to see from the roadway. "Wow," Ben said in awe as the rumbling echoes from the blast reverberated off the surrounding hills.

"That was just like the movies," Geraldo said after a moment.

Meanwhile, Stenvick had climbed up to the top of the landslide. "Hey kids," he yelled down, "climb up over this and we'll walk the rest of the way to the trailhead."

"We're still hiking?" Melody asked in amazement.

"That's Dr. Stenvick for you," said Jennifer. "A little bump in the road won't alter his plans."

The last of the students made it over the hill of dirt and joined the group as Stenvick was conversing in Spanish with a driver who'd been traveling in the other direction. "It's only about six to seven miles to the trail," he informed them. "We can be there in less than two hours. If we hurry I don't think we'll have to adjust our route up the volcano. Let's get going."

The students obediently fell in line behind him, though they were still a bit dazed by the events of the preceding minutes.

□ □ □ □ □

"Hand me the socket set," Berg instructed from under the Bus. "I want to get this bumper off." The rear bumper was a simple set of two metal pipes that had been welded to some brackets and bolted in place of the original.

"Here you go," said Kevin as he handed Berg the sockets.

Berg found the correct size and started working on the bolts holding the bumper in place. After a couple minutes he'd removed most of them. "There's still one on each side that I can't get," he explained. "They must be an older set, they're completely stripped and I can't get a hold on them. The good news is that these brackets are rusted through pretty badly. I think we can break the bumper off."

"Why do you want to do that?" Katrina asked as Berg slid out from under the vehicle.

"Well, it's a bit large but we can slip the pipe over the end of my wiper arm tool and use it for leverage to turn the wheel nuts. Paul, take the jack out and put it under the bumper. If we lift on the bumper the weight of the van should break the bracket."

Hargren lowered the jack and moved it to a spot under the bumper. He turned the crank and raised it, but the bracket held as the rear of the vehicle lifted off the ground.

"Hmm," said Berg. "Everybody get in the van." Following his direction, they lined up in the back and jumped up and down in unison. After a few tries the bracket snapped and they fell in a heap as the vehicle hit the pavement. "Let's do the other side," instructed Berg. Hargren set the jack under the other side of the bumper and they repeated the process. Berg picked up the mangled steel and carried it to the wheel. He slipped the pipe over the end of his wrench and gently applied pressure. "It's working!" he said with satisfaction as the first nut broke free. The process was slow and awkward and they had to be careful not to break the improvised tool, but eventually they succeeded in removing the wheel.

Kyle had been listening to Stenvick with a laser microphone. He put it away as the group of students marched off around a bend in the road. "This is incredible. They're still going to go through with the hike up the volcano."

"I guess that means we're on to plan B," said Isaiah, "we better hurry."

The two assassins packed up their gear and hustled back to the Mercedes. They'd parked at the base of a dirt trail that led to the top of the mountain and hiked the rest of the way to the ridge. The access road joined the main highway about a mile past the landslide so they had to be quick to get there before the students.

Kyle pulled onto the main road and breathed a sigh of relief after a few minutes when it was clear that they'd made it down before the students walked far enough to spot them. When they reached the volcano he parked in a location far from the trailhead and well out of sight. "Let's see that trail map," he asked.

Isaiah pulled the map from his bag and unfolded it across his lap. "We could set some charges here and..."

"No explosives," Kyle said cutting him off. "We have to do this cleanly." He pointed to a spot on the trail partway up the mountain. "I think this will suit our purposes well."

Isaiah read the warning note on the map and grinned. "I don't know what you have in mind, but I like it."

Chapter 16

Kevin finished removing the spare tire from the front of the Bus as Hargren jacked up the rear again so they could replace the wheel. "We can get the new tire on," said Hargren, "but we can't drive on it without air pressure."

Berg rummaged in the tool bag and removed a set of hex wrenches and a hacksaw blade. "I think these will do the trick," he said with a knowing smile.

"Who am I to doubt MacGyver Gary?" Hargren said.

"Who?" Katrina and Kevin asked in unison.

Hargren explained. "MacGyver was a television show that was on many years ago. The main character could get out of any predicament with his pocket knife and random objects available in his surroundings. This situation reminded me of the show."

"I appreciate the compliment," Berg said with a laugh. Kneeling down by the spare tire, he held several hex wrenches next to the air valve and selected one. He handed the wrench and hacksaw blade to Katrina. "You and Kevin figure out how to cut the smaller portion of the L off of this so we have just the long portion with two flat ends." Next, he took a pair of pliers and went to the front of the vehicle, removed a wiper fluid line and two hose clamps and brought them back. "I sure hope we don't need to use the wipers for the rest of the day."

Katrina handed over the sawed-off hex wrench. "Perfect," said Berg as he inspected the work. He held up the shaft of the wrench and the length of wiper hose next to each other to compare and pinched a spot on the hose with his fingers. Using a razor blade from the tool bag he cut the hose to length. "Alright, I'll need a bit of help for the next part. Kevin, pick up the spare and bring it over here by the front tire. Paul, take these pliers and hose clamps."

Berg pushed the end of the wiper hose over the valve on the spare tire and instructed Hargren to slide a hose clamp into place to hold it. He inserted the hex wrench into the hose and then had Kevin hold the spare near the front tire with the valves facing each other. He pushed the hose onto the other valve and Hargren slid the second hose clamp into place. He lined up the hex wrench by feel inside the length of hose so that the ends fit into the valve stem on each tire. "Ok, Kevin, push the spare gently so the wrench depresses the valves."

Kevin applied pressure to the tire as Berg held the hose section until they heard the air begin to flow. The spare creaked as the bead pressed into the rim of the wheel and then started to inflate. "Stop," Berg instructed. "We'll have to take a little at a time from the other tires to fill this enough to drive."

They disassembled the custom air transfer tool and repeated the process on the other two tires. "I think it will do," Berg said when they'd finished and installed the spare. "All the tires are a little low but they have enough pressure to drive. You'll just have to take it slow and easy, Paul. Let's get all the tools cleaned up and be on our way."

☐ ☐ ☐ ☐ ☐

Stenvick fell in step beside Spencer as the group power-walked along the roadway. "Spencer, I was very impressed with how you handled the situation in the bus back there. You acted very bravely. Thanks for your help getting us out."

"It is no problem," Spencer replied. "These things happen."

Stenvick chuckled. "You're right about that. I've run into a lot of mishaps over the years running these trips, but certainly never anything that bad. It's not the first time I've lost a bus though. I think it was on the third year I led this trip that we had another incident."

"What happened?" asked Spencer.

"We were at a river crossing and I put the bus on a car ferry which was a sort of barge that got pulled across the river by a cable. I was concerned about putting so much weight on the rickety looking ferry, but the operator said it would be fine. We waited on the dock with our gear just to be safe. To make a long story short, the current was moving faster than usual and the cable broke with the ferry midway. It floated downstream, hit a rock and capsized. It was a twenty mile walk back to the last town we passed where we could get transportation. It's funny, I was at the same site again last year and that bus is still on its side in the river."

"Dr. Stenvick," Jennifer called from behind, "how are we going to get back to the university?"

"Excellent question," Stenvick replied. "I'll talk to one of the staff at the park office when we get to the trailhead. I'm sure they'll be able to arrange something for us while we're hiking."

"Do landslides like that happen a lot around here?" Jennifer asked.

"Not too frequently, but they're unpredictable. I've had to take detours on a few occasions to go around them. You just never know, I guess today was not our lucky day."

□ □ □ □ □

Isaiah and Kyle stopped when they arrived at the fork in the trail. The path to the right was marked with a metal signpost warning of danger ahead. "Let's confirm that the bridge is still there," Kyle said as he started down the trail.

A few minutes later they came to the edge of a steep ravine with a fraying rope footbridge suspended across. Several of the wooden planks were missing and a danger sign hung across the entrance. "Are we going to blow it up with them on it?" Isaiah asked hopefully.

"No," responded Kyle, "I have a much simpler plan. First we have to get rid of these danger signs. Go across and remove the one on the far side so they won't see it while they're on the bridge."

"Why me?" asked Isaiah indignantly, "that bridge might not hold."

105

"You're lighter and I'm in charge. Do it."

"Fine," Isaiah mumbled as he took a few tentative steps onto the planks before walking across and removing the sign, which he dropped to the side of the trail. When he returned, Kyle had removed the other sign and stashed it in his bag.

"Once we're done I'll put this back in place," Kyle said. "Now we have to switch the sign at the fork in the trail."

They walked back to the warning sign. After several minutes of rocking it side to side, pulling on it, hitting it and yelling at it the pole finally loosened enough for them to free it. Kyle picked up a nearby rock and handed the sign to Isaiah. "Here, hold this in place and I'll pound it into the ground on the other trail."

When they were satisfied with the placement of the sign they did their best to fill in and smooth the spot where they'd removed it from. "This looks good," Kyle said when they were finished. "Now we'll go hide off the trail by the bridge and wait for the group to pass by."

Hargren pulled off the highway and stopped at a gas station. He went into the store and paid cash for a foot pump and several emergency tools while Berg topped off the tires outside from the free air hose. "I hope we won't need any of this for the rest of the trip," Hargren said when he got back to the Bus, "but I'll feel a lot better being prepared just in case."

"We still need to take it nice and slow," Berg cautioned. "These tires are holding air but they're well worn and the rubber is pretty old. I'll be amazed if we make it without another blowout, and I don't have any ideas for improvising a new tire."

As Stenvick had promised, the walk to the trailhead hadn't set them back too far off schedule. He calculated that deducting most of the planned time for lunch and sightseeing at the crater would allow them to do the hike as planned. "The park officer will arrange a bus to return us to San José," he announced as he joined the students in the parking lot. "There's no time to waste, so let's go." Without pause he took off for the trail and started the climb.

"Ugh, I can't believe we're doing this," Michelle complained to Melody and Jennifer. "I'm tired enough after walking here from the landslide. Now we don't even have much of a break to look forward to at the top."

"I think I'm still shaking from seeing our bus go off the road," said Melody. "I don't mind the extra walking. It's helping me to avoid thinking too much about how we could all be at the bottom of that cliff right now."

"That's a sobering thought," said Jennifer. "Hey Michelle, weren't you the one that screamed at Dr. Stenvick to stop?"

Michelle nodded her head. "Yes, I was just watching the scenery and suddenly I saw the landslide coming."

"I'm glad you did," said Jennifer, "otherwise I don't want to think about what would have happened to us."

Ben and Derek walked at the back of the group as usual as Stenvick led them through the dense forest. "Check this out," whispered Ben. He cupped his hands to his face and let out another imitation bird call that he'd practiced before the trip.

On cue, Stenvick stopped in his tracks and cocked his head to listen. After a few seconds Ben projected the call again, this time ahead and to the left. Stenvick turned with a puzzled expression on his face. "I have an idea what that bird sounds like but it can't be. Its habitat is generally the Pacific Northwest, certainly not farther south than California."

The call sounded out again and Stenvick turned towards where he thought it was coming from. "I hate to admit it but I'm honestly baffled by this one."

"Dr. Stenvick," Derek piped up from the back of the line, "maybe someone brought the bird you're thinking of and released it here."

Ben had to turn away to hide his laughter as Stenvick pondered the thought. "That's possible, Derek," Stenvick replied, "but unlikely given the laws about transporting wildlife. I'm more inclined to think that we may have come upon a new species. If we're lucky we'll get a glimpse of it to confirm."

After a few moments he let out a sigh. "Well, I haven't heard it again. Perhaps it flew off."

Ben regained his composure as they began hiking again, and let out a much quieter call that sounded like it was farther away.

"Maybe another time," Stenvick said dejectedly from the front of the line.

⬜ ⬜ ⬜ ⬜ ⬜

Kyle and Isaiah crouched in hiding when they heard the group approaching. Isaiah had mounted a small wireless camera in the parking lot, so they'd been alerted when the students passed by and were also confident that no other visitors would be coming near them any time soon.

"That's funny," they could hear the professor saying as he stopped at the bridge a few feet from their hiding place. "I don't remember there being a bridge on this trail. It looks like there are some missing boards so be careful where you step."

"Are you sure it's safe?" asked one of the girls.

"It must be," responded the professor. "This park gets a lot of visitors. If it wasn't safe there would be a warning sign like they had on the other trail until it could be repaired."

The girl still looked doubtful. "I'm just feeling really nervous about heights after the bus accident. Looking at that ravine is making me feel sick."

A large muscular boy spoke in a choppy accent. "I will do it first. Make sure it is safe. Wait for me." He calmly strolled out onto the bridge and walked to the other side, then returned and pronounced it to be fine other than the missing planks.

"See, there's nothing to worry about," said the professor. "Let's go."

The two assassins let out the breath they'd been holding as they watched the professor lead the way onto the bridge with the students following behind in single file.

The bridge was approximately two hundred feet across and spanned a deep ravine with whitewater rapids running through the bottom. The professor paused at the midpoint to take in the view before proceeding towards the other side. When the whole group was facing away, Kyle signaled to Isaiah and the two men silently moved out of their hiding place and took positions at the end of the bridge. They each pulled out a serrated combat knife and quickly went to work on the ropes. With expert strokes they frayed and snapped the strands so that the ropes would not appear to have been cut, and then darted back into hiding when the remaining fibers began snapping on their own from the stress.

□ □ □ □ □

Stenvick was about forty feet from the other side when he froze in alarm upon feeling a distinct twang hit his hands, which were holding on to the side ropes for balance. Quick to react as always, he grabbed onto the ropes tightly and shouted. "Everyone hold on! We're going down!" He looked back over his shoulder and saw the students taking hold of the ropes. Then, as he expected, the far end of the bridge disconnected from the bank and began to fall. It felt like time slowed as he watched the end of the bridge plummet into the ravine and the rest follow in a downward swing.

"Hold on!" he heard himself shouting, followed by the screams of the students as the planks dropped out from under their feet. With all of them clinging on for dear life, the bridge completed its swing and crashed into the side of the ravine. Stenvick shouted out instructions for everyone to climb up the planks as he began the ascent. He reached the top and pulled himself to safety by the end posts, then turned to wait for the others.

The bridge hung at a near vertical angle due to the steepness of the side of the ravine. It took a few moments for the shock to wear off before any of the students started to move. One after another they slowly pulled themselves up the planks to where Stenvick waited to help them over the top. Jennifer looked down at the distant end of the bridge swinging in the mist. *"It's like ropes course at camp, you can do this,*" she thought to herself. She looked up to see Geraldo disappear over the edge of the ravine and Stenvick beckoning her to climb.

"Stephanie is behind me," she said shakily as Stenvick helped her over the edge of the cliff. Then, everyone was startled by the sharp crack of a board snapping, followed by a loud scream. Stenvick rushed to the edge and leaned over, spotting Stephanie hanging on to the end of a board that had broken. She was turned around with her back to the bridge and no easy way to get a handhold. Stenvick dropped his pack and pulled out a coil of climbing rope with a grapple hook which he looped around a nearby tree. He threw the coil out over the edge of the ravine and with one hand running over the rope as it unwound he took several running steps and leapt off, performing a twist in mid air.

Ignoring the burn of the rope against his palms, he clamped on to stop his fall and swung in to plant his feet on the bridge a few feet above Stephanie. "Help!" she screamed as her hands slid down the board another few inches.

Stenvick rappelled down and grabbed her in a one-armed bear hug seconds before her fingers slipped from the end of the plank. "Stephanie, grab onto the rope," he commanded. Shaking from fear she willed her hands to let go of Stenvick and take hold of it. "Now," he instructed, "grab the bridge with one hand and turn around to face it. Don't worry, I've got you." Stephanie closed her eyes to calm her nerves before letting go of the rope with one hand and twisting around to grab the next wooden plank. Stenvick helped her to gain footholds and finally take her other hand from the rope and start climbing. They ascended slowly together, keeping the safety rope between them. Multiple hands assisted them at the top and pulled them both to safety.

Everyone sat in a daze for a while until Stenvick finally broke the silence. "I'm truly surprised that there was no warning sign on that bridge. I'm going to have some words with the park office when we get back there. This is simply unacceptable."

"Hey look," said Ben as he picked up a metal sign and some rope from the side of the trail. "Maybe this was supposed to be on the bridge."

"Danger,   keep   off   bridge," Stenvick   translated. "Incompetence!" he bellowed. "What's that doing on the ground? In all my years I've never witnessed such disregard for safety in the public parks. This is intolerable."

"What a useless bridge," Geraldo muttered as he sat pouting by the side of the trail, "we could have died."

"I don't think we would have made it if we weren't so close to the end," Jennifer observed in a morbid tone. "We hit the side of the canyon pretty hard. It would have been much worse if we were farther back."

Michelle sat crying nearby. "This has been the worst day ever, I hate Costa Rica."

"Come on," Derek said as he sat down next to her. "We've just had some bad luck. You can't blame the whole country for a couple mishaps. You'll see, things will get better and we'll all be able to look back and laugh about this someday."

Michelle gave him an icy look. "Laugh about it? What about this is funny to you? We nearly died, twice! I just want to go home and forget this trip ever happened."

Stenvick had moved away from the group to cool off. He sat against a tree and pulled out one of his thermoses. The warmth of the coffee gradually calmed his nerves as he gulped it down. Once his anger had ebbed sufficiently, he stood and hoisted the pack on his shoulders, and then returned to the students. "Well, I'll talk to the park about this, but now we have to press on to the crater. We can't afford to lose more time. We'll have to come down a different trail. Come on, everyone get up. Let's get moving."

☐ ☐ ☐ ☐ ☐

"Unbelievable," Kyle said as he watched the last of the students disappear into the woods on the other side of the ravine. "I thought that would do them in for sure."

"We could have blown it up," Isaiah pointed out.

"No explosives," said Kyle as he put the warning sign back on the end of the bridge. "We need to go switch the sign at the fork in the trail, and then we can get up to the crater and think while we keep an eye on them. According to the map they're going the long way so we should beat them up there."

"What's plan C?" asked Isaiah.

Kyle frowned. "I'll need to think about that."

Chapter 17

The rest of the drive to Limón had gone pretty smoothly with no further problems from the old Volkswagen. Once they were off the highway Hargren drove through a commercial district near the harbor. He slowed as they came upon a large property surrounded by a high wall and stopped at the gate, rolling his window down to speak with the security guard. The guard had a brief discussion on his radio and then told them they were cleared to enter. Heavy metal doors retracted into the walls and a two foot high barricade and spike strip folded flush to the ground. Hargren drove into the compound and passed several warehouses and workshops before parking near what appeared to be an office.

The place was busy with numerous workers milling about and forklifts buzzing in all directions carrying pallets of machinery, gas cylinders and other industrial products. A man tending a gas grill waved as they got out of the Bus. "Hi Paul, you're just in time for lunch," he said as Hargren approached.

Hargren smiled and shook his hand. "Bill, it's good to see you. Thanks for making time for us. Everyone, this is Bill McConnell. Bill, these are my friends Dr. Gary Berg, Kevin Archer and Katrina Witmer."

McConnell was middle-aged with a lumberjack's build and short black hair. He wore blue jeans and a black dress shirt, complemented by dark sunglasses and a .45 pistol in a side holster. His eyes fell on the

Bus for a few moments. "Paul, what is this thing? Where's your Trooper?"

"We have a lot to explain," Hargren said.

McConnell cut him off as he went back to the grill and shut off the burners. "That will have to wait. The food is done. You can fill me in after lunch." He picked up a large platter heaped with chicken drumsticks, strip steaks and baked potatoes and led them into his office.

"The chicken has my special rub on it," McConnell said as they devoured the mouthwatering tender meats, "and I marinated the steak in one of my favorite mixtures. It's a good thing you showed up when you did. I was starting to worry you'd be late and the food would get cold."

Berg reached for another drumstick. "Bill, this is incredible."

The others nodded their heads and mumbled agreement.

McConnell grinned. "I'm glad you like it. I've always enjoyed working with food. Actually, I've even considered starting a restaurant someday."

When everyone had satisfied their appetites, McConnell called in an assistant and asked them to bring coffee and take the leftover food out for the guys in the shop to finish off. "So now," he said turning to Hargren, "what brings you out here to see me? I gather it's something very important since you didn't want to talk on the phone."

"That would be an understatement," Hargren replied. "Where do I even begin?"

Over the next hour Hargren and Berg detailed the events that had transpired, starting several months previously with Hargren's work and then getting into the details of their adventure over the last few days. McConnell yawned and listened politely as they explained the details of their research and visit to INIAS, but sat forward with genuine interest as soon as the car bombing came up. "I saw that on the news," he exclaimed, then listened with undivided attention to the rest of the story up to the drive that morning.

McConnell leaned back in his seat once Hargren finished the story. "I see why you came to me, and why there was such a need for secrecy. That was good thinking, Paul. You had no way of knowing this, but that explosion and the fire at the lab caught my attention. My sources tell me that both were professional jobs. I'm assuming you haven't told your colleagues here anything about me?"

Hargren shook his head. "No, just that you were a friend that could help us get through this. I'll vouch for them, they'll keep anything you tell them a secret."

"Is that true?" McConnell asked, staring down Berg, Katrina and Kevin in turn.

They all nodded in affirmation.

"Ok, now that we're clear on that I'll explain why Paul brought you here. As you may know, UCR has a satellite campus in Limón. When Paul first started his research he had reason to visit the campus with some regularity. My company is in the import/export business and we have a number of contracts with UCR for lab equipment, gas cylinders and the like. Paul and I met when we delivered some refrigeration equipment that he needed for his work. I'll let him fill you in on the details later if he chooses, but suffice it to say that events occurred where I had to step in to resolve a problem and brought him into my confidence."

"You see," McConnell continued, "the work I do here is not quite what it appears to be. While we do a good amount of legitimate commercial shipping as a cover, the main reason I'm here is to handle sensitive shipments in and out of the country for the CIA. I used to work out in the field but there was an incident overseas and circumstances required that I take a lower profile. The official story is that I retired from the service, but in reality I'm still quite involved. I have contacts and resources at my disposal to get information and take care of situations as necessary. I'd say you've certainly gotten yourselves into a situation, and I'll do what I can do to help you."

"We need some proof to show that INIAS was responsible for the corn that invaded my fields," said Hargren, "and I'm guessing they have more to hide than we know based on their attempts to silence us. You could help us sneak into their facility and find out what they're up to that's worth killing over."

"Now is probably our best chance," said Berg. "They're busy arranging for Dr. Fiker's trip to the Nobel ceremony, and showing up in their back yard is probably the last thing they'd expect us to do right now."

McConnell nodded his head in agreement. "You're probably right. If their focus is on finding you, chances are they'll be checking the airport, embassy and other likely places you might go to for help. Most people would be trying to get as far away as possible."

"That wouldn't help us," said Katrina. "Hallita can reach anywhere on the globe. They'd find us eventually for sure."

Kevin agreed. "And who can we go to for help with no evidence? We'll be laughed at, especially once Dr. Fiker gets the prize. No one would take us seriously."

"Alright," said McConnell decisively. "If we're going to find what you're looking for we have to get moving. I need to gather some intelligence on the site and some supplies, and then we'll go in tonight after sundown. Let me send off a few messages and we'll head over to my house." He activated a secure line on his phone and sent an encrypted message before returning it to his pocket. "There, the boys at headquarters will work on that for a couple hours and we can review the data at my home office. Now I'll just have my secretary clear my schedule for an 'urgent sales call' and we'll be on our way."

McConnell ushered them out of the office and locked the door behind him. "I'm sorry about your Trooper, Paul," he said while looking with disdain at the battered old VW. "I'll tell you what. I'll give my mechanic a call and have him pick up this Bus and look it over. I can't imagine it's safe to drive in the condition it's in. He'll have it back by the time we return."

"Thanks," said Hargren with a sad expression at the thought of his beloved Trooper. "I'd appreciate that."

McConnell pulled out his phone and dialed a number. After a brief discussion he explained that Ralph would be over to get it shortly. "He said he could squeeze it into his schedule. Just leave the key over the visor for him."

McConnell led them around the corner of the building to a gleaming white Mercedes sedan. "Hop in," he said as he unlocked the doors with his remote.

"Nice car," Kevin commented as he slid into the spacious interior that accommodated the five of them with ease.

McConnell grinned. "This was a thank you gift from some German colleagues for some work I did a few years ago. Imported tax and duty free of course." The silky motor purred to life and within minutes they were through the gate and driving out of the city.

"What are you doing?" Kyle demanded as he put down his night vision binoculars to see Isaiah lying on the ground with a silenced sniper rifle to his shoulder and his eye to the scope. They were situated on an observation platform along the rim of the volcano crater a few hundred yards from where the group of students had stopped for lunch. Dense fog blanketed the top of the mountain, reducing visibility to less than twenty feet.

"This is the new laser infrared scope I was telling you about," said Isaiah. "I can see them all clearly and the digital processor identifies each target and marks it with the range. I bet I can take them all out in less than ten seconds."

"Put that away," Kyle ordered. "I keep telling you, it has to look like an accident. What is so hard to understand about that? Groups of civilians don't just accidentally blow up or accidentally end up shot with high velocity rounds while hiking at tourist destinations. We have to be more creative than that."

"But this would be so easy," Isaiah argued. "No one will be able to trace it back to us. Just a few shots and this job will be finished."

Kyle groaned in exasperation. "No, no, no. We'll never get paid if you do it that way. If you want more jobs you have to follow instructions."

Stenvick sat on a park bench and sipped from his coffee thermos as he watched the dense mist swirl around him. He'd given the students fifteen minutes to eat their lunches before they would have to head back down the mountain. He thought about the events of the day as he retrieved a chicken burrito from his bag and removed the wrapper. What were the odds of having two near-miss accidents within such a short time? He'd experienced plenty of dangerous situations in his travels, but never such close calls as what had happened that day. Maybe he was getting too old for this. Maybe he was missing obvious warning signs that he should have noticed.

He wondered how Gary and the other students were doing. They hadn't been in touch since the night before and the thought of calling them had slipped his mind. They'd probably arranged a ride back to the city and he'd see them at the end of the day. Checking his phone, he saw that there was no service so trying to call now would be pointless. He imagined how they would react when he told them about the dangers they'd missed. This trip had certainly worked out differently than he'd planned, but no one had been harmed and he'd paid for the accidental damage and loss insurance on the bus. The students seemed a little shaken but they'd bounce back soon.

The students sat in a close circle eating their lunches in silence as their minds struggled to come to terms with the near fatal accident at the bridge. Spencer was staring blankly into the mist and was halfway through eating the paper bag he'd brought his lunch in before he realized he'd finished his sandwich. He spit the wadded paper out of his mouth.

Derek broke the silence. "Hey guys, I was just thinking that this is only the beginning of this trip, but I feel like it's been so much longer. It seems like breakfast this morning was a week ago." He paused to wipe away the tears that were building up in his eyes before continuing. "I know we've only been together a short time, but I'm really glad you're all ok. I think I'm going to miss you all a lot when this trip is over."

"You are making me sad," said Spencer as he wiped a tear from his eye.

Geraldo leaned over to pat him on the back. "Cheer up big guy. No one's going anywhere yet, and we all still have at least the next semester together."

"Assuming we make it out of Costa Rica alive," said Ben pessimistically.

"We will," Derek said with certainty. "Dr. Stenvick may be a bit crazy, but look how he handled those situations. Did you see the way he jumped off the edge of the ravine to help Stephanie? He didn't hesitate for a second. That's the kind of guy you can trust with your life.

118

Hopefully we won't have any more incidents for the rest of this trip, but let's all watch out for each other."

Heads nodded in agreement around the circle and Spencer proclaimed it to be group hug time which lifted everyone's moods considerably.

Jennifer and Melody were trying to comfort Stephanie, as she was shaking uncontrollably from the after-effects of the fear and adrenaline brought on by her near fall. Jennifer pulled a small blanket from her pack and wrapped it around Stephanie's shoulders. "Just try to relax, you're safe now. Your body doesn't know what to do with all the chemicals swirling around. Your mind needs to regain control and calm things down."

"I know," Stephanie said through chattering teeth. "I feel like I'm freezing."

Michelle's face brightened as an idea hit her. She got up, walked over to Dr. Stenvick and asked if he had any coffee to share with Stephanie.

"Sure," he said as he opened his pack. "Nothing calms frazzled nerves like a mug of hot coffee." After removing his climbing rope, jacket, first aid kit, gallon jug of water and spare boots, Stenvick unfolded a heavy thermal blanket to reveal at least six large thermoses nestled in the middle of his bag. He pulled one of them out and set it on the bench, then rummaged around further until he found the cream and sugar containers and one of his thick ceramic mugs.

"How do you carry all of this stuff?" asked Michelle incredulously.

Stenvick grinned as he prepared the mug of coffee and handed it to her. "I only pack what I can't do without. Sure it's heavy but I find it comforting to know that I have everything I need right here in my bag. Plus it's great conditioning for my races."

Michelle thanked him for the coffee and returned to the group. "Drink this," she said handing the mug to Stephanie. "I had a headache the other day and it picked me right up."

Stephanie took the mug and sipped at the steaming coffee. "Thanks. This is wonderful."

"No problem," replied Michelle with a smile. "I hope it helps."

A couple minutes later Stenvick appeared out of the fog and announced that lunch time was over. Then as quickly as he had come, he spun on his heel and headed away. The students scrambled to their feet and hoisted their packs in order to catch up before he vanished out of sight.

□ □ □ □ □

"Looks like they're leaving already," Kyle announced as he watched through his binoculars.

"Are we going to ambush them on the way down?" asked Isaiah.

"No," Kyle replied. "I haven't had time to come up with a good enough plan. We already tried the bridge and I don't think there are any natural features of the remaining trails that we can use to our advantage. Let's get back to the car. We'll think of a new plan for tomorrow. According to the itinerary they'll be doing the canoe trip."

Chapter 18

McConnell drove through an upscale residential neighborhood and pressed a button above his rear view mirror as he approached a property surrounded by a gated fence. His passengers noticed the security cameras mounted around the perimeter as he slowed and drove through the gate that had just opened at his signal. He pulled into a large circular courtyard in front of the house and parked the Mercedes. The brick driveway encircled a bubbling fountain that shot a stream of water ten feet in the air.

"Come on in," he said as he unlocked the front door of the mission style house and led them inside. "There's a restroom down the hall to the right. I've got cold drinks in the fridge or if you'd like coffee or tea feel free to use the espresso maker or the hot water tap by the sink."

"This is a nice place," Berg said as he surveyed the modern kitchen. "What kind of stove is that?"

McConnell's face lit with excitement as he turned to Berg to explain one of his prize possessions.

Stretching along an entire wall of the kitchen was a bank of polished stainless steel commercial gas ranges of various designs. "I had this setup custom made," McConnell began. "I'm passionate about cooking and I'm also highly impatient. When I was outfitting this kitchen I didn't find any commercial ranges or stoves on the market that would meet my requirements. I called up a friend who works for a stove manufacturer and he agreed to work with me on a special order. As you look from left to right I have two six-burner ranges with ovens, a four foot griddle, a four foot grill, and a high capacity double oven."

Hargren chuckled as he watched McConnell give his practiced sales pitch to Katrina, Kevin and Berg who were all enthralled by the equipment. He'd seen it before several times and was always amazed at how his friend never tired of telling the story over and over.

McConnell continued. "My biggest complaint with standard products is that they simply don't have enough burner power. It takes too long to bring pots and pans to temperature and the ovens just don't heat up quickly enough. We addressed all of those concerns and more with this equipment. You see, the typical gas burners used in most commercial ranges put out about twenty or thirty thousand BTU's each. I drew up the design for these burners and the engineers perfected it. Each one has four concentric flame rings with independent controls for each and a total output of a hundred thousand BTU's."

"Wow," exclaimed Katrina.

"That's not all," said McConnell. "That gives me plenty of heat from the bottom that can be fine-tuned to the pan, but check this out." He reached to the back of the range and swung out a pivoted arm with a round bulbous head on it. "This is what we call a shower head burner. There's one for each spot on the range. It puts out thirty thousand BTU's of flame from above the pan in several patterns, so you can cook the food from the top and cut down the time considerably. Watch this." He turned one of the numerous knobs on the front of the range and flames shot out of the burner, then settled to a reasonable level as he adjusted the control. "This is the standard setting which has an evenly dispersed circle of flame jets. I can turn this dial on the top of the burner and switch the pattern." He turned the dial and showed them the six different flame settings that the burner could produce.

Kevin laughed. "That's just like those multi-pattern massaging shower heads."

"Exactly," McConnell agreed. "That was my inspiration. I'll admit it's a bit unnecessary, but it sure does make cooking fun."

Over the next several minutes the group was amazed as their host explained and demonstrated the other features of the equipment, finally ending with the twelve hundred degree double oven and custom built range hood that exhausted the whole setup. Berg was obviously impressed. "This is some amazing cooking technology. I assume it must work very well, but I'm curious why I haven't seen anything similar elsewhere."

McConnell grinned. "I doubt you will anytime soon. I was able to pull some strings to get this made, but even so I had to do the final assembly and hookup on my own. No restaurant back in the states would be able to get the permits and insurance required to install something like this, at least not at a reasonable cost."

Hargren interrupted the conversation to remind them that they needed to get started on their plan for breaking into INIAS that night.

"You're right," said McConnell. "Sorry, I got distracted there for a few minutes. Let's go down to the basement and we'll get to work."

The group followed him down a flight of stairs to an ordinary looking basement with a concrete floor and cinderblock walls. "There's nothing down here," said Kevin as he looked around at the standard utility equipment, laundry machines and ping pong table.

McConnell raised an eyebrow and winked, then walked over to the clothes washer and pressed a number of buttons simultaneously and hit start. A section of the wall swung open in front of them revealing a secret passage.

"Welcome to my home office," he said as he led them down a long hallway and into a large room approximately thirty feet square that was packed with storage cabinets, gun racks, computers and file drawers. "We're actually under the garage right now. The official plans show only a slab foundation. I had this dug and built in secret with the top finished off to look like a simple poured concrete pad, which is what the contractor built the garage on. This room doesn't officially exist, just like much of the work I do here."

"Impressive," Hargren said as he surveyed the high tech equipment.

McConnell turned to them as he typed a password into the computer. "I do need to ask that you please don't touch any of the weaponry, both for your safety and so that I don't have to clean off the finger oils."

Kevin pulled his hand away in disappointment from a compact machine gun that he was about to pick up. "What do you do with all these guns?" he asked.

McConnell smirked. "It's probably best that you don't concern yourself with that." He turned back to the computer and opened up an email. "Oh good, we've got some intelligence on the INIAS compound. Headquarters sent satellite images, building plans and details on the security system."

McConnell scanned over the files, and then hit print before getting up from the desk and pulling some duffel bags out of a cabinet. He scurried around for several minutes packing the bags with an assortment of equipment, then inspected several guns and put them in protective cases once he was satisfied they were in good order. "I trust I can count on your help to carry all this stuff," he said once everything was ready.

"Sure," everyone replied in unison.

McConnell distributed the bags, shut down the computer and then led them back out to the basement. At the press of a few buttons on the clothes dryer, the lights switched off in the office and the secret door swung shut and clicked into place. Katrina watched as the seam vanished in front of her eyes where the door had just closed. "You can't see any sign of it. This wall is perfect. How is that possible?"

McConnell ran a finger over the line where the door seam would be. "The materials research lab at the CIA came up with this. It's pretty neat and I only have a basic understanding of what it does. The edges of the door and frame are lined with two parts of a special material. In its normal state like you see right now the two halves mesh with a crystalline matrix that makes a connection as hard as rock, so it looks just like the cinder block. When you add energy in a certain way the substances repel each other and each have a rubbery texture. I doubt you'll be seeing it at the local hardware store anytime soon. Now, please forget you saw any of this and let's get these bags upstairs."

□ □ □ □ □

Stephanie was on a caffeine high and rapidly talking Michelle's ear off as they followed Stenvick down the mountain. "You know what, Michelle? I almost didn't come on this trip. I was all set to go to Ireland and see where my ancestors lived. I was looking forward to that quite a bit but unfortunately it didn't work out because the professor who was leading the trip had to cancel due to personal problems or something, he didn't really explain. This was the only trip that still had an opening so I signed up for it. I barely had time to read through all the books that Dr. Stenvick assigned but fortunately I've been able to keep up ok with the hiking even though I didn't get to do the exercise plan that he gave us. All the dancing I do must keep me in good enough shape. I still want to get to Ireland someday. I want to walk along the cliffs by the sea and visit the pubs and see all the people and go to some real dances and tour the castles and run in the fields with the sheep and-"

Michelle patiently listened as Stephanie went on and on about the Ireland trip, the greenhouse run by her family and many other topics. She was amazed at the difference Stenvick's coffee made and wouldn't believe that it could be possible if she hadn't experienced the same effect just days earlier when they were hiking at the beach. She made a mental note to ask him about it at some point. Maybe the reason his favorite coffee was not exported out of the country was due to more than just the unusually high caffeine content.

□ □ □ □ □

McConnell led his guests out of the house and across the courtyard to the garage. The door opened after he punched in a combination on the keypad. He opened the rear gate of an old Land Rover and put all the duffel bags and gun cases in the back. Kevin looked at the old vehicle with disappointment. "Wow, I would have expected you'd have something newer than this given the Mercedes and all the other high tech stuff around here."

McConnell laughed. "Sorry, Kevin, but this is our ride for tonight. Paul, I'm sure you understand why I'd use a car like this, why don't you explain it to him."

"Certainly," agreed Hargren. "Perhaps you haven't noticed, Kevin, but Costa Rica has a lot of old Land Rovers and Land Cruisers still

125

on the road. If you want to blend in and avoid attracting attention while being able to travel nearly anywhere out in the rural areas, this is about the best vehicle you could choose. Am I right, Bill?"

"Yes," said McConnell, "but that's not quite the whole story. Everything you said is true and that's why I chose this vehicle for jobs like this, but this Rover is not what it appears to be. It may look like an old Series III model from the 1970's, but I had Ralph do some modifications."

Berg looked at the vehicle with curiosity. "Please do explain."

"My pleasure," said McConnell. "The old Rovers are fine vehicles, but in my line of work I can't trust my life to decades-old parts and technology. At the same time, I can't drive around in a new vehicle when I don't want to be noticed. I worked with Ralph and we came up with a plan. We picked up this old Rover from a used car lot and took it back to his shop. We lifted off the body and threw away everything else. Ralph ordered in a new galvanized steel frame from a newer model and we adjusted it to fit. All the suspension, brakes, lines and hoses are new. Everything is stainless steel or corrosion resistant material of the highest quality."

"It sure doesn't look like it," said Kevin as he knelt down to look at the underside.

"That's by design," explained McConnell. "The frame was strategically touched up with paints and various coating materials to look old and rusted. If you touch it you'll find that what looks like rust feels like spongy rubber. The metal underneath is perfectly sound. We also redid all the wiring and replaced the gauges and controls with upgraded replacements that look like the originals. The body is reinforced with bullet proof glass all around and lightweight ceramic composite armor hidden inside the doors and wall sections. It's good enough to protect from most small arms fire."

McConnell turned their attention to the front of the vehicle as he lifted the hood to reveal a spotless engine compartment with a large motor wedged in. "Obviously I needed more power than we'd ever get from the original engine. Ralph ordered a high performance turbo diesel V8 and a heavy duty transmission. I thought he was crazy when it arrived since it didn't look like it would ever fit, but that man is a genius when it comes to custom work. Check this out."

McConnell undid four clasps near the firewall and then tilted the entire front end of the body forward on a hinge concealed by the bumper. "Ralph reworked the front of the vehicle to fit around the engine. He had to alter the dimensions of the hood and fenders a little but you'd never notice unless you measured. With this nifty hinged front, we have lots of room to access the engine for repairs and maintenance." He pointed to the top of the motor. "See this air intake? Ralph said we'd need more fresh air for the engine and it would need a hood scoop. Once again I underestimated him. I said a hood scoop would be too noticeable and unusual but he proved me wrong."

McConnell lowered the front of the Rover back in place. "This looks like a spare tire mounted on the hood, just like a lot of these vehicles have, but it's been modified. If you look closely you can see that there's a mesh screen in the shape of the tread pattern. It's almost unnoticeable. The hood scoop is hidden behind the screen, and the steel wheel is hollowed out to fit it. I can't use the spare tire, but it's unlikely I'd ever need to as the tires on this vehicle are military grade and I keep two extras in the back just in case."

After ushering everyone back outside McConnell closed the garage door. "My plan is that we'll arrive at the INIAS compound after dark for our best chance of sneaking in without anyone around to see us. We still have a little while before we'll need to leave, so I'll take the opportunity to prepare a nice dinner. In the meantime make yourselves at home."

"Bill, I was wondering," Berg inquired, "is there any way we can know if it's safe to use our phones? We haven't answered any calls or contacted anyone since we left San José this morning, just in case our communications are being monitored. If I don't respond to my wife pretty soon she's going to start worrying."

"It's quite possible they've tapped your lines," said McConnell. "There are ways we could check, but it would be much easier to just have our tech guys handle this. Give me your numbers and I'll send them over to headquarters. They'll have you setup with secure lines in just a few minutes and you can use your phones with no worries."

Berg and Hargren wrote their phone numbers on a slip of paper and gave it to McConnell.

Ten minutes later a reply email arrived informing McConnell that the numbers had been secured. "Every time you use your phones the transmission will be encrypted," he explained. "It doesn't matter if the other party is on a secure line or not, you'll both be protected. The same goes for data usage such as texts, emails and internet browsing. Anyone that tries to monitor or intercept the transmission in any way will be unable to. I'll give you a contact number to call in case you run into any problems. Also, you'll no longer receive phone bills. The CIA will take care of that. Our pockets are deep when it comes to protecting sources and informants, and at my level I don't need approval to add you to the program."

Berg and Hargren thanked him and proceeded to catch up on the voicemails and messages that they'd ignored throughout the day, careful however not to give anyone information on their whereabouts or activities. Berg figured that Stenvick must have forgotten about him or was out of service on his hike since he hadn't tried calling all day. After a brief discussion, everyone agreed that it would be best if Stenvick and the other students remained unaware of what was going on.

Chapter 19

Doctor Fiker and Dr. Lake sat in the conference room at the INIAS office across from Benjamin Curt, their director of security and operations for the facility.

"I've been in touch with our two, um, 'contractors' concerning the school group," Curt explained. Curt was an imposing figure, a little over six feet tall and built like a bear. He wore his usual grey work pants, boots and tee shirt. He kept his sandy brown hair in a kind of bowl cut that came close to covering his eyes, which peered vigilantly through his rectangular framed glasses. On his belt were a radio, various tools and his trusted .40 caliber handgun. "They've made two attempts so far but both were unsuccessful. They'll be trying again tomorrow. Also, they've seen no sign of Dr. Berg or Mr. Hargren. Neither of them returned to the university after the incident at the restaurant."

"Those hit men were supposed to take care of this," Fiker complained angrily. "Their handiwork is all over the news but the scientists have dropped out of sight and we have no idea where they are. You promised they'd get this job done."

"They will," countered Curt. "Kyle and Isaiah are the best in the business. They'll come through for us, you'll see. Also, I stressed the need to avoid any more public spectacles."

"I'm concerned about the scientists," said Lake. "Chances are they realized we were responsible for the attempt on their lives at the restaurant. It's imperative that we find them soon and finish the job."

"My men put a trace on their phones this morning," said Curt. "We'll be able to pinpoint the location when they make a call."

"Sarah, how much do you think Dr. Berg and Hargren know?" asked Fiker.

"That's what concerns me," Lake responded. "I could sense they were holding back information when I met with them. They seemed to be judging what to say by my reactions and kept to generalities. It was obvious they didn't believe what I told them but they played along."

Fiker stroked his goatee thoughtfully. "What do we know about this Dr. Berg?"

Lake gave an awkward little cough. "I've been doing my homework on him. His teaching career seems normal enough, but what caught my interest was his research. He seems to have a particular passion for mycology."

Fiker's face darkened. "Go on."

"Berg is involved with a number of mycological clubs and keeps an active schedule of identification forays. He also attends several regional conferences of NAMA, which is the North American Mycological Association." Lake opened a manila folder on the table in front of her and slid a printout to Fiker. "I searched through the conference archives on the NAMA website and found this presentation given by Dr. Berg a couple years ago."

Fiker read the highlighted title of the talk. *"Amatoxins - Unlocking the Secret of Amanitin D."* He banged his fist on the table. "How did we miss this? It can't be a coincidence that he's here snooping around and asking questions. You were supposed to be monitoring anyone doing research on D."

Lake shrank in her chair at Fiker's outburst. She responded meekly as he glared at her, red faced and fuming. "Only a handful of scientists in the world have done any serious study on it so far. Until now we've been successful in keeping the research at a standstill by arranging unfortunate accidents for those whose work appeared promising. Dr. Berg never published anything. We monitor all the journals and routinely search the internet but this never came up. The file that contained that conference schedule was not linked to the website in a way that our searches would have found the reference. I apologize for the oversight but it appears Berg's work slipped under our radar."

Fiker glowered. "So, he may very well have the key to Amanitin D and I wouldn't doubt he's analyzed that test crop that got away from us. I knew we should have been doing a better job monitoring for any crops spreading outside our borders. Now he's on the loose and who knows who he's talking to. Our plan depends on keeping this molecule a secret and his timing could not be worse."

"What could he do?" asked Lake. "You'll be giving your Nobel speech in two days, and then it will be too late regardless of what he may know. Besides, it's unlikely he'll discover anything of consequence. His little group was only interested in test corn C."

"A lot can happen in two days," growled Fiker. "If he goes public or talks to the right people it could be a problem for us. What if they start an investigation? That could delay the ceremony. We can't initiate our plan if I don't get to speak live on the world stage."

"We'll find him," said Curt. "He can't hide for long."

"That's true," said Fiker. "Your men burned the lab so any data they had there is gone. Sarah, have your teams finished cleaning up our escaped test crop?"

"Yes," replied Lake. "As soon as they left after our meeting I had the lab produce enough of our experimental genetic targeted herbicide to cover a twenty mile radius surrounding us. I'm pleased to report that it worked just as well as in the lab trials. Within an hour the corn was blackened and beginning to decompose into dust. By now there should be no trace that the plants were ever there."

"Good," said Fiker. "That should leave them with nothing but their word for what they observed, which won't be enough to convince many people. Actually, that may work to our benefit. For them to go public they'll need proof of what they found and the only place they can get that now is here. It's possible they'll try to come back so we should keep an eye out. Now, I have to go pack for my trip so you'll have to excuse me." He rose from his seat and walked to the door, then turned around before he'd opened it all the way. "And Ben, tell those two

131

goons to hurry up with the school group." Fiker pushed through the double door and quickly strode down the hall. He barely returned a distracted grunt acknowledging the cheery greeting from Miss Monet who was just exiting a nearby restroom.

Berg, Hargren, Kevin and Katrina remained in their seats not wanting to move after finishing the scrumptious meal that McConnell had prepared. He'd marinated ten pounds of chopped pork in a spicy sauce which he stir-fried with broccoli and scallions in a large wok over medium heat until the meat was cooked through. To finish it off he added peanut oil and sesame seeds and turned the burner to high. The wok started to glow red as he expertly tossed the sizzling meat to create a crispy seared texture on the surface. It was then glazed with a special sauce and served over jasmine rice.

"That was the best Chinese food I've ever had," said Katrina.

"I agree," Kevin concurred.

"I'm glad you enjoyed it," said McConnell with satisfaction. "You two can thank me by helping to clean up the dishes before we head out. We have plenty of food left over, so you can pack it and we'll take it with us. There should be a cooler in the pantry and ice packs in the freezer. We should be ready to leave here in thirty minutes."

Stenvick was still leading the students down the mountain when the sun dipped below the horizon and the sky grew dark. He pulled a head lamp from one of the pockets on his bag and switched it on to light the path ahead. Finally they reached the end of the trail where it intersected with a paved road that extended several hundred yards up the mountain from the parking lot. A bright flashlight illuminated them from somewhere on the road and swept over the group.

After a few moments the light was lowered to aim at the ground and a park ranger approached them. Stenvick had a brief conversation with him in Spanish and then explained to the students.

"He says that the park closed fifteen minutes ago and he's making the rounds to check for anyone still coming down off the trails before he locks up for the night. He wants us to climb in the back of his truck and he'll give us a lift to the parking lot."

The students scrambled into the truck and Stenvick joined the ranger in the cab. A few minutes later he parked in front of the office and let them out. A small taxi bus was sitting by the office and the driver was conversing with one of the other rangers.

"Here's our ride," said Stenvick. "If we don't run into any problems we'll make it back for a late dinner."

The students took their seats as Stenvick paid the fare and soon they were on their way out of the park.

□ □ □ □ □

McConnell turned the Land Rover off the highway and studied the GPS unit mounted on the dashboard. "I'm taking us in the long way from the back of the property. We have a number of miles to cover on jungle roads and stealth will be essential to getting in unnoticed." He switched off the headlights, leaving them sitting in near darkness.

"How are we going to see where we're going?" asked Kevin.

"With these," McConnell said dramatically as he flipped a couple switches on the dash.

"Nothing happened," said Katrina uncertainly.

"Sure it did," said McConnell. "We just need a little help to see." He flipped another switch and a greenish image appeared on the windshield. The trail ahead was clearly visible as if lit by powerful floodlights.

Kevin looked around at the other windows through which he could see only darkness. "Is that night vision?"

"Yes," said McConnell. "The light bar on the roof and the headlights are equipped with infrared flood bulbs. The wavelength is not visible to our eyes but the heads-up display on the windshield shows the image from hidden night vision cameras. The system is highly advanced and auto-adjusting. We could drive on the highway with oncoming headlights and it would still show a good picture. Now we can drive in through the woods without our lights giving us away."

The Rover bumped and jostled along the dirt roads for several miles with little conversation among the occupants. After a while McConnell pulled off the path and drove down a river bank, stopping at the edge of the slowly moving water. He pressed a button by the rear view mirror and they could hear an electric whining and rhythmic clicking noise coming from something on the roof. The image on the windshield began to show computer generated grid lines representing the river bottom, complete with rocks and other objects. Depth measurements were displayed periodically with numbers in red representing sections too deep for the vehicle to enter. "Don't ask me how it works," warned McConnell, "but somehow the boys in advanced research came up with a way to combine radar and sonar in one neat little package. It can scan the water from the air, and the air from the water."

McConnell shifted into low range and slowly idled into the water. All eyes were riveted to the display as he followed a safe course through the river. At times the water rose within inches of the top of the hood, but after a few minutes they chugged up the opposite bank and he switched off the scanner. "We were lucky," McConnell said. "If that had been any deeper I would've had to get out the special snorkel." He drove up the bank and into the jungle as far as he could go before the path ahead was blocked by trees and undergrowth.

"This is as far as we can drive," McConnell explained as he shut down the vision systems and turned off the motor. "We'll have to walk the rest of the way in. There should be a perimeter fence a couple hundred feet from the river." After making sure the interior lights were turned off he instructed them all to be silent and carefully eased his door open. When they were out of the vehicle he distributed the gear, donned a pair of night vision goggles and cautiously crept into the jungle. It wasn't long until they came upon the fence. "This is most likely electric," he whispered. "I need to check before we touch it."

McConnell took a device from his bag and carefully touched a probe to the chain link fence. The display showed the voltage and confirmed the presence of a pulsed monitoring signal that would trip an alarm if a section lost power.

"Let me guess," whispered Hargren, "you have a little device that lets us just walk right through this?"

"Not quite," McConnell replied with a chuckle. "It takes a little more effort than that." He pulled what looked like a coiled rope with clothespins attached every inch or so from his bag, as well as a small metal box with wire leads.

Starting at the bottom of the fence he attached the insulated clamps one after another to the chain links. He worked his way up about five feet, then across and back down to the bottom to complete a square. One lead from the black box was plugged into a terminal in the end of the rope that he'd started with. The other lead had a metal post that he attached the rope to with the next free clamp following the one that finished off the square on the fence. He flipped a switch on the box and then set it on the ground.

"The rope is an insulated cable," McConnell explained. "The clamps are all wired into it. Once the box is connected and I flip the switch it makes a complete circuit. The circuitry in the box causes the section of fence surrounded by the cable to lose power without affecting the continuity of the fence as a whole. " He tested several points on the fence again with the probe and confirmed that no charge was present.

Rummaging in his bag again, McConnell produced a pair of wire cutters and proceeded to snip the chain links up one side and across the top within the protective square. Then he bent the section of fence so they could pass through. When they were all safely on the other side he pulled the fence back into place and adjusted it so the cut was not too noticeable. "If they have patrols scouting the fence this should avoid detection unless they look very closely, which I doubt anyone will. They'll have no reason for concern since the electricity is not disturbed."

Quietly walking through the woods single file, the group followed McConnell for a few hundred yards until he motioned for them to stop. They crouched behind some plants and took turns looking through the night vision goggles at the compound ahead.

"These buildings are not on the map of the property," whispered McConnell, "but they did show up on the satellite images. The visitor center is several miles away. Chances are if there's anything these people want to keep hidden from the public it will be here."

Chapter 20

Derek collapsed into his seat in the UCR cafeteria and slowly pushed his food around with his fork.

"Are you ok?" asked Melody. "Your eyes are all red like you've been crying."

"No," replied Derek, "I mean yes, I'm fine. I just feel really exhausted. My eyes are itchy and watering and my whole body is aching. I feel like I already went to sleep but my brain didn't realize it and now I'm stuck like this."

"I know the feeling," Melody said sympathetically. "Try to eat your dinner and then go to bed. I'm sure we'll all feel better in the morning."

Stenvick called for everyone's attention from the next table. "Kids, this has been a long and eventful day. I would never have expected we'd face so many challenges, but I was impressed with your endurance and how well each of you handled everything. I've made arrangements to rent a fifteen passenger van from the university. It may not be as spacious and comfortable as the bus we had before but I'm sure we'll manage. We have to leave early again tomorrow, so don't stay up too late tonight. Enjoy the rest of your dinner and we'll meet back here again at five."

"Dr. Stenvick," Jennifer called, "when will Dr. G be coming back with Katrina and Kevin?"

"I'm not sure," Stenvick replied with a wearied tone. "I expected they'd be here by now. They had some car trouble yesterday and were going to arrange a ride back today. I suppose they're still on their way here but I'll try to call again soon. Paul is with them and he knows the area so I'm sure they'll be fine. Maybe they had to go back to his place. Regardless, they've been on their own schedule since we got here, so if we don't see them at the van tomorrow morning we'll just have to go on without them again."

□ □ □ □ □

McConnell pulled a thermal spotting scope out of his bag and scanned the buildings from his hiding place in the woods. "There's one person inside the closest structure," he whispered. "Oh, and before I forget, make sure you've turned off your cell phones."

"Yep," said Hargren, pulling his phone from his pocket to confirm that it was turned off.

"Let me check," whispered Berg. Just as he was about to switch on the screen it lit up with the display notifying of an incoming call from Rich Stenvick and the shrill ringer piercing the darkness.

"Turn it off!" McConnell whispered anxiously.

Berg fumbled in panic until his finger found the right button and he silenced the call.

"Did they hear that?" asked Kevin nervously.

McConnell brought up the scope again. "Whoever is in there is moving toward the door. Quick, everyone duck down and be quiet." He trained the night vision goggles on the door and watched a woman emerge holding a phone to her ear. She appeared to be talking to someone, but after a moment she put the phone in her pocket and went back inside.

Still watching through the scope, McConnell explained what he'd just seen. "I don't know if she heard us or if it was just a coincidence. We better stay where we are for now."

Katrina cocked her head and signaled for everyone to be quiet. "Do you hear that?"

Within a few seconds the sounds of a motor approaching grew louder. Headlights appeared on the road coming from the visitor center and moments later an old Land Cruiser emerged from the jungle and pulled into the clearing.

Two men got out of the vehicle and approached the building, stopping outside the door and not appearing to be in much of a hurry. Strains of conversation were barely audible to the group watching from the jungle. McConnell silently unlatched one of his gun cases and lifted out a short rifle and a metal gas cylinder which he screwed onto the side of the stock.

"Are you going to shoot them?" Katrina whispered incredulously.

"No," McConnell reassured her as he inserted a narrow black cylinder with a sharp point into the chamber and slid the bolt forward with a gentle click. Taking aim through the scope on the rifle he waited until the men entered the building and then pulled the trigger just as the heavy metal door was about to shut. A puffing sound came from the rifle when he fired. The clink of the projectile hitting the metal siding was masked by the sound of the door latching closed.

"It's a silenced air rifle," McConnell explained as he pulled a radio from his bag and plugged in several sets of ear buds, distributing them so everyone could listen. "It fires a wireless transmitter. As long as it's stuck to a thin metal surface like that wall it will pick up and amplify the faint vibrations generated by sound waves in the air. We should be able to hear any conversation inside."

They all huddled around and listened intently through the ear buds as McConnell adjusted the settings on the receiver until the conversation came through clearly.

"Yes, my private jet is all set to go," one of the men was saying. "The helicopter will be here at about eleven and I should be at the airport in San José ready to board by midnight."

"That must be Dr. Fiker," whispered Berg.

"All the staff has left," said the other man. "Those involved with the program at this location have headed to San José to get the facility there up and running. The rest believe they have off for the next week as we celebrate your award. The trucks will arrive tomorrow morning and I'll get everything important packed up with my security team, then we'll join Dr. Lake in San José."

"Good work Mr. Curt," said Fiker. "Sarah, is everything ready for them to load up tomorrow?"

"Yes," she confirmed. "Ben, I've marked all these file boxes for you to take. Don't worry about the lab equipment, but make sure to bring the computers. Right before you leave pull the pin on this spray cylinder and set it inside the door. It will fog everything with herbicide which will destroy the test specimens. Just make sure you don't come back in after you've activated it."

"That's Dr. Lake," Hargren whispered.

"Got it," replied Curt. "Are you ready to head back to the office with us?"

"Yes," said Lake. "I'm finished here. We can go."

The door opened and the three of them stepped out. Curt shut off the lights and locked up, then joined the two scientists in the Land Cruiser. The engine roared to life and the headlights flicked on. Gravel sprayed from the rear tires as Curt made a tight turn and sped off back into the jungle.

No one spoke for several minutes until the sounds of the engine had faded off in the distance. "I think we're clear," said McConnell. "From what we just heard it seems they're evacuating this place."

"They're going to a facility in San José," said Hargren.

"I wonder what they're planning to do there," mused Kevin, "the timing seems odd since Dr. Fiker is leaving for Norway tonight. Maybe the plan they mentioned is related to his award."

Berg stood, "there's only one way to find out. We need to get into that lab."

McConnell stealthily crept out of the jungle and slipped across the clearing to the lab. It took him only a minute to pick the lock on the door and gain entry. He quickly shone his flashlight around to check for an alarm panel but finding none he leaned out the door and motioned for the others to join him. None of them were aware of the silent alarm indicating their entry on a display panel in the security office at the visitor center.

McConnell passed out tactical flashlights that projected red light beams. The color made it possible for them to investigate the interior of the lab while not ruining their night vision. "Keep the beams pointed down," he instructed. "There aren't many windows but if anyone

140

happens to pass by outside we want as little light visible as possible. I'm going to do a sweep through the building and make sure it's secure while you check out the lab."

As McConnell headed out of the room the rest of the group took stock of their surroundings. The lab had numerous rows of greenhouse tables with various types of plants and mushrooms in different stages of growth. Powerful lights were strung over each table but were apparently kept off at night. Computers and scientific equipment lined the perimeter as well as several desks and file cabinets.

Hargren pointed out a stack of cardboard boxes. "These must be the files that Dr. Lake wanted moved tomorrow. We should probably start here. Kevin and Katrina, see if you can access those computers."

Berg and Hargren pulled the lids off the boxes. They were full of notebooks and folders with tabs organizing each box by month and year. "Some of these date back as far as the mid 70's," Berg said excitedly.

"I've got more recent ones over here," said Hargren. "This box is dated this year."

Berg pulled out a few notebooks from the first box and quickly scanned through the pages. "I think these are Dr. Fiker's notes from grad school. He must have kept records of his whole career."

"The computer is password protected," Kevin said with disappointment.

"Don't worry about it," said Berg. "You two come help us dig through these records. We need to see if there's anything in them that would explain what's going on here."

Kevin and Katrina started in on the boxes between Hargren and Berg. Katrina pulled out a notebook from December 1981. "Hey, this notebook is an end of year summary. Check if the other boxes have anything similar."

"Yes," confirmed Berg as he rifled through the end of his box. "These summaries should help quicken our review considerably. Let's take them all out and have a look."

McConnell came back from his walkthrough and announced that the building was empty. "There's a small kitchen, a soda vending machine and a restroom. The rest is just storage. They have a bunch of potting soil, planting trays and lab supplies."

"Do you have anything to hack the password on the computer?" asked Kevin.

McConnell took a quick look at the screen. "Sure, I can break that, but I'll have to run back to the Rover for the equipment."

"Look here!" said Katrina, startling everyone. She read aloud from the notebook. "1995: March: Successfully isolated Amanitin D from *Amanita phalloides*. November: Amanitin D molecular structure identified. December: Amanitin D fatal in high concentration lab rat study."

"I knew it," said Berg gleefully. "They have been working with that molecule. Let's see what follows."

Everyone huddled in and watched over Katrina's shoulders as she flipped through the short summary pages of the following years. They gasped with astonishment as she read through the terse descriptions of the monthly events.

"1996: February: Initial lab trial of Amanitin D in modified wheat, seeds failed to sprout. July: Second lab trial of Amanitin D in modified wheat, plants died after one week. November: Third lab trial of Amanitin D in modified wheat, seeds failed to sprout." Katrina continued reading through the next several years of lab and field trials which showed gradual progress in getting the modified wheat to grow successfully. "Hand me the next one," she asked Hargren.

"1999: May: Genetic modification for protection of wheat from toxin successful. June: Field trial of Amanitin D in modified wheat, plants grew to harvest. August: Initial human field trial failed, population zero within one week."

The next books showed more field trials in remote areas of the world with disastrous results. "Here's 2005," said Hargren as he handed Katrina the notebook.

She opened it and started to read. "2005: March: Modified Amanitin D long term lab tests successful, rat life expectancy one year. July: Human lab trials commenced."

2006 and 2007 detailed numerous experiments with disappointing results, followed by apparent reworking of the toxin over the next several years.

Katrina continued reading. "2012: June: Human lab group A expired, three month duration. October: Human lab group B expired, four month duration. 2013: May: Alternate formula introduced. December: Promising results thus far."

The tension in the room was palpable as Katrina read through more books until finally coming to a statement that took everyone's breath away. "Trials concluded. Worldwide seed distribution initialized." Katrina dropped the book in horror. "What does this mean?"

"I'm not sure," said Berg, "but it looks like they introduced the toxin into the world's food supply."

"We have to tell someone about this," said Hargren.

McConnell stood up. "I'll make a call and we'll have backup here in no time." He pulled out his phone but stopped before making the call. "Maybe I need to step outside, I'm not getting a signal in here." He went out the door but was back in less than a minute. "I have no signal at all. Gary, you got a call earlier. Check if you have service."

Berg checked his phone but had the same results, as did Hargren. McConnell thought for a moment. "Perhaps this is just a bad spot, or maybe the tower is down. The Rover has an integral satellite phone. I can call from there and pick up my computer hacking gear. I'd prefer we don't stay here longer than necessary. Katrina and Kevin, can you help me carry back some of the equipment?"

Berg and Hargren went back to searching through the files as McConnell and the students gathered the non-essential gear and left the lab. They trekked through the jungle in silence until returning to the fence. "Hold on while I bend this out of the way again," said McConnell. He pulled out the testing probe to confirm that the isolated section was still safe. "Hmm," he said with worry as he touched the probe to the chain links in several spots. "There's voltage in this section. The device must have burned out." He peered closer and trained his flashlight along the line of the metal rope. "It looks like some of the links that I cut fused back together when the voltage arced across. Unfortunately I don't have a backup plan to get through this. We'll need to find another way to contact my people."

"What should we do with this stuff?" Kevin asked, looking at the heavy bag at his feet.

"Bring it back with us," replied McConnell. "We may need to move on to another building to find a phone so there's no telling what equipment will prove to be useful."

They reluctantly hoisted the bags and headed back into the jungle the way they'd just come. As the clearing came into view McConnell froze and ordered the students to drop to the ground. "There's a vehicle coming," he said as lights danced over the trees. Seconds later the Land Cruiser skidded to a halt in a cloud of dust.

"Incredible," Berg said as he put down the last of the summary notebooks. "If it wasn't for that corn invading your fields, no one would've discovered what's going on until it was too late."

"It may be already," replied Hargren with concern evident in his voice.

Without warning the overhead lights blazed on in the lab. Berg and Hargren spun around to see armed security guards on either side of the entrance with assault rifles pointed in their direction.

"Lab secure," one of the guards said into his radio.

The door opened and Curt entered the room, followed by Fiker. "Search the rest of the building," Curt ordered.

The two guards moved off to check the other rooms. Fiker cleared his throat. "Dr. Berg, I presume? And you must be Mr. Hargren. What brings you to my lab at this hour?"

"You're not going to get away with this," said Hargren indignantly, holding up one of the notebooks."

Fiker laughed. "Is that so? I'm sorry but I must disagree with you. You see, you are far too late. While you've been worried about your little corn patches I've been finalizing all the details to set my plan in motion. I see you've been reading about it."

"Yes," said Berg, "but what I don't understand is why you would want to poison the world with the Amanitin D toxin."

The two guards came back to the lab and reported that the building was all clear.

"Good," said Fiker. "Tie up our guests so they don't get any ideas about leaving."

The guards went to work and in short order had Hargren and Berg bound tightly back-to-back to a couple of metal chairs. "That's better," said Fiker. "I do hate surprises. Well, unless I'm the one giving them that is."

"Why are you doing this?" Berg repeated.

Fiker glared in annoyance. "A little patience would do you good, Dr. Berg. I don't need to explain anything to you."

Acting on impulse Hargren spoke up. "Dr. Fiker, you're a hero to a lot of people for putting an end to world hunger. Why go to such lengths to help people and then do something like this to harm them? I don't understand."

"I did solve world hunger to help people," Fiker countered angrily. "Don't make me out to be some kind of monster. This is all for the greater good."

Picking up on Hargren's theme Berg pressed him. "What more can you do? Thanks to you everyone has enough food."

"Yes, keep him talking," thought Hargren as Fiker pulled up a chair and placed it in front of them. *"He has to hear himself justify his actions. He can't let it go having us thinking poorly of him."*

Fiker looked at his watch. "I have a few minutes, and as scientists you'll understand and be able to appreciate the work I've done. Besides, Mr. Curt will deal with you soon enough in some creative way."

Fiker sat on the chair backwards and crossed his arms over the seat back. Hargren thought he looked like a dictator but wasn't sure exactly why. He figured it was either the goatee or the prominent square pockets on his olive shirt.

Fiker began speaking. "No doubt you're familiar with the work I've done through Hallita to create crops capable of producing consistent yields where traditional seed had failed. We worked for many years to perfect our genetic modifications until world hunger was solved."

McConnell and the students listened with rapt attention through the wireless transmitter as Fiker spoke.

"We thought that the world would be a better place once everyone had enough to eat. So many wars and conflicts were caused by famine and desperation. If all the people had plenty of food, they wouldn't need to fight over it. We couldn't have been more wrong. The world lauded us for our efforts but there was no end to the violence. Corrupt and petty politicians just found other reasons to satisfy their greed. I despaired for several years despite our success. Everything I'd done was for naught as people were still suffering just as much. Back during the Vietnam War I had a lot of good friends in the protest movements, many of whom I'd kept in touch with through the years. I brought some of them together and we brainstormed what we could do to meet our original goal of a more peaceful world. That was when one of our labs made the breakthrough on Amanitin D. At the time we were testing anything and everything to further our science. That lab had been tasked with working on isolating natural toxins."

Fiker guffawed, "I didn't know what we'd do with it at the time but I saw potential in having exclusive knowledge of the makeup of such a powerful poison. We started running trials to see what it would do and how it worked. Eventually an idea hit me. Nearly the entire world was eating crops grown from my seeds. Hallita had a monopoly. Sure, we worked the political system and weaseled our way around various laws, but the simple truth was that we dominated the seed business with no competition or regulation. Our genetic technology was proprietary and not subject to anyone's review. I realized that we could make whatever changes we wanted and no one would know. I won't bore you with the details as it took us years to perfect the science. We figured out how to encode Amanitin D into the genes of our major staple crops so that the plants would grow normally and the toxin would be delivered through food products into humans. It pains me to think of all the remote villages throughout the world that sacrificed their lives unknowingly serving as test subjects, but what we've done wouldn't be possible otherwise."

"I don't understand," Berg interrupted. "The notes we looked at showed that the toxin has been growing in crops for a number of years. Why haven't we heard of people getting sick or dying? We found Amanitin D in your test corn and it kills the insects and animals quickly."

"That's the beauty of it," Fiker said eagerly. "You've only seen test corn C, which has an older version of the toxin that is effective right away. I have uses for such a plant, but that's not what we're growing worldwide. We made another version of the toxin that builds up in the body very slowly. The structure is lipophilic, meaning it attaches to fat cells. After approximately six years the average person will reach what we call the tipping point. The Amanitin molecules detach from storage in the fatty tissues and enter the bloodstream. By that point the concentration is several orders of magnitude above a fatal dose. We've tested direct exposure at that level and the test subjects averaged no more than an hour before succumbing to the effects. You can rest easy at the moment. The toxin has only been present in the food supply for five years now."

"How does that bring world peace?" Hargren asked dubiously. "Everyone will be dead in a year."

"Not so," said Fiker. "Naturally we developed methods to counteract the effects. We have an antidote that keeps the buildup at safe levels, provided it's administered every six months. Hallita has established distribution centers worldwide to administer the shots. We will require all nations to refrain from violence in order to qualify for distribution. I expect the armies of many countries will be put to good use ferrying isolated villagers to and from the centers."

"But how will that work?" asked Berg. "The government will just seize all of your assets and take the antidote from you. They won't be held hostage by a single person or company."

"If we hadn't planned it so well perhaps what you say would be true," Fiker granted, "but we've had years to think through all the details and plan for the contingencies. The Hallita Farmland Security division has been hard at work designing and putting in place the most sophisticated control and monitoring system ever created. Our antidote is protected by the highest security all the way from manufacturing to distribution. Any tampering by unauthorized parties will result in immediate destruction of the shipment, distribution center or entire network depending on the severity of the incident. Our policy will be zero tolerance and it will be strictly enforced."

"You would destroy the whole program?" asked Hargren in disbelief.

Fiker stared at him thoughtfully. "If necessary, yes. This world will never be at peace left to its own devices. Our system ensures that every country has an incentive to keep its people under control. The consequences would be disastrous if they don't. I'm confident that it would only take one nation serving as an example to dissuade the others from bad behavior. Hopefully, an example will not be required.

And, in case you're wondering, taking out me or the other leaders of the program would not be a good idea. We have multiple failsafe measures that will destroy the entire system in the event of an emergency. Also, a selected few of us will be able to initiate destruction at any time with the press of a button. Believe me when I say the world will have no choice but to comply with our conditions. Hallita has gone to great lengths and expenditures to make peace a reality and we're taking on a great responsibility. Naturally we will be paid accordingly for our efforts and will continue to be the sole supplier of agricultural seed."

Chapter 21

Fiker glanced at his watch. "Oh my, look at the time. I've gotten carried away. It's been a pleasure talking with both of you. As you may imagine, I've had few opportunities to share my excitement with others. I must be on my way to go accept my prize. Mr. Curt, will you see to our guests please? Take them with you tomorrow to San José and make sure they have a chance to watch my acceptance speech. I think they'll find it quite interesting. After that you can dispose of them as you see fit."

"Will do," Curt said as he pulled open the door. Before Hargren or Berg could say a word Fiker was gone.

McConnell observed as Fiker climbed in the Land Cruiser and drove away. "That leaves the three security guards still in the building with Paul and Gary," he said to Kevin and Katrina. "Based on the conversation we heard, they should be safe until tomorrow morning. I'm going to come up with a plan to get them out before then. You two lie low here and monitor the situation. If anything happens give me a call on this radio. The element of surprise is on our side but I'd prefer not to have to go in there."

Once McConnell had slipped off into the jungle, Katrina and Kevin sat alone with their thoughts for the first time in several days. "Do you think Mr. McConnell will be able to get us all out of here?" asked Katrina.

"Probably," Kevin replied, "this kind of stuff is what he's trained to do, which is a good thing. I know I'm not ready to handle this situation. Just thinking about the toxins they put in our food makes me feel like I'm going to throw up. That's what really worries me right now. All those deadly molecules are just sitting in our bodies, slowly building up until they kill us."

"I can't believe they've actually done it," said Katrina. "Dr. Fiker was my hero when I was little. I wanted to be just like him and feed all the starving children in the world. I was so excited about my job after graduation but now I don't know what to do."

"I'm having trouble thinking as far as tomorrow right now," said Kevin. "What if we don't get out of here, or what if they find us? Graduation feels like some kind of abstract idea from another life."

An awkward silence followed as each of them grappled with the gravity of the situation. Katrina was the first to speak again. "You know, besides Dr. Fiker and his people, there are only five of us who are aware of what's going on. Maybe it sounds silly, but the fate of the world could depend on what we do tonight."

"No, you're right," Kevin agreed. "I hope Mr. McConnell has a plan when he returns. If we can get the word out maybe Fiker's plans can be stopped."

Katrina was starting to shiver from the cool night air. Kevin rummaged in the equipment bags and found a blanket which he wrapped around her. "Thanks," she said as he took a seat next to her on the ground. They sat side by side, listening to the feed from the transmitter on the lab building. Ever since Fiker had left, the three guards had been talking incessantly about guns which seemed to be their favorite topic of conversation. If Berg and Hargren were talking it must have only been in whispers.

Katrina was startled by the sound of her name being called. She looked up to see McConnell approaching through the dark jungle. Whispering softly, he informed them that he had a plan. "I have a few things to set in place and then we'll carry out our rescue just as the sun is beginning to rise. Until then you better get some rest. I'll wake you up when it's time."

□ □ □ □ □

Geraldo woke from a deep sleep. *"No, it can't be time for morning workout yet,"* he thought in panic.

"Geraldo?" he heard Spencer calling from across the room.

"What? It's the middle of the night. Can't the pushups wait?"

"I can't sleep," Spencer explained. "What happens when we die? I have to know."

"Why are you asking me?"

"Because you are the man of faith, so you must know."

Geraldo thought for several moments before responding, "Do you have to know right now?"

"Yes, I can't wait. It worries me."

Realizing Spencer was not going to give up on the conversation soon, Geraldo put aside all thoughts of drifting back to sleep. "I don't know," he yawned. "I mean, I know what lots of different people believe, but I don't know what I believe."

Spencer was quiet for a minute. "On the bus today I almost had a fall. I might have died. I am now thinking and it scares me. I need you to say it is ok."

Geraldo was at a loss for words. Through all his studies he had never seriously considered that being a religious leader would mean dealing with conversations like this. Tears came to his eyes as he spoke. "Spencer, I'm such a fake. What was I thinking? I can't lead people if I don't believe in anything. I can't help you; I just don't know the answer. I'm sorry."

"Oh," was Spencer's disappointed reply. "Sorry to wake you."

Geraldo felt awful as he lay in bed listening to Spencer's muffled sobbing. "I'll tell you what. When we get back home let's go see some real religious leaders and you can ask them."

"You mean that?" asked Spencer.

"Yes."

"Thanks Geraldo. Good night."

Geraldo was amazed to hear the sounds of snoring within a few minutes, but was wide awake and unable to stop the flood of thoughts and questions in his mind about how they had all come so close to dying.

▢ ▢ ▢ ▢ ▢

Fiker leaned back and relaxed in the comfortable leather massaging seat on his private jet. It had been an eventful evening with Berg and Hargren showing up at the lab, but that situation was under control and he smiled at the thought of them watching his speech. He looked at his watch as the plane's wheels left the tarmac. It was one in the morning and he was right on schedule. After a few minutes, the plane had reached cruising altitude and the flight attendant came over to see if he needed anything. "My usual," he said, annoyed at the intrusion to his thoughts.

Fifteen minutes later, the attendant returned with a mug of Fiker's favorite coffee. "It's about time," Fiker grumbled. "And, I thought of something else I need. You know how I abhor those cheap little hotel soaps. I neglected to pack my organic hibiscus bath bar. I need you to call ahead to the hotel and have them procure one before we arrive."

Fiker took a slow sip of his coffee as the attendant left to make the call. He relished the complex flavor as he thought about the additional fame and privilege his prize would bring him. He already enjoyed the benefits of wealth and status that his money and position afforded him, but the thought of the nations praising him made him almost giddy with anticipation. After draining the last drops of coffee, he brushed his teeth in the lavatory and then dimmed the cabin lights before retiring to his cabin for the night.

□ □ □ □ □

Geraldo woke to the sound of his alarm beeping. He shut it off and sat up in his bunk. It took him a minute to realize that Spencer had not pulled him out of bed for the customary morning workout but was still sleeping soundly. A mischievous grin spread across his face as he carefully got out of bed and tiptoed across the room. He flipped on the light switch and yanked the covers off of Spencer while yelling in his best drill instructor impersonation. "Get your useless butt out of bed and give me a hundred pushups!" he roared. "We can't have any slackers on this trip! Move it!"

Spencer woke immediately and bolted out of bed, dropping to the floor to do the pushups. Geraldo tried to continue shouting commands but burst out laughing. Spencer stopped and took a second to comprehend the situation. He sat on the floor with a confused look on his face. "I believe I was back in boarding school in Austria. My parents sent me there. Every morning our barracks master made us wake up and do exercise. My senior year I was master. I am keeping it up in college. You did catch me being lazy today. I am sorry."

"You'll have to skip the workout this morning," said Geraldo as he headed for the shower. "We need to get to breakfast."

McConnell roused Kevin and Katrina as the earliest hints of sunrise were showing in the sky. "I have to go make a few last minute preparations. You two wait at the edge of the clearing but stay hidden. When I'm ready I'll notify you over the radio." He explained the plan and then went over it twice to make sure they all understood and there would be no mistakes. "Also, here are some knives. These should make short work of any ropes Paul and Gary are tied with, but you have to be quick."

McConnell gave them a brief instruction on safely handling the blades and showed them how to cut the ropes quickly without hurting the men. He packed a few items from the duffel bags in his back pack and grabbed a gun case. With a quick nod he ran off across the clearing to start his plan.

Stenvick addressed the students as they were finishing breakfast. "I'm sure you are all going to enjoy our trip today. We'll be canoeing a couple hours to the north and stopping at several points to fit in some hikes to scenic overlooks. The river is wide and calm and there are no bridges on the trails, so I expect we'll have a more relaxing experience than yesterday. Make sure you pack your food and drink for the day and we'll board the van in ten minutes."

Having finished speaking he went into the kitchen. Per his instructions, his thermos bottles and mugs were washed and dried and set out for him each morning next to a coffee percolator that the staff set up to brew his special beans. He drained the forty cup tank into the bottles and packed them in his bag along with the cream and sugar.

Talking and laughing excitedly amongst themselves, the students swarmed the food table and worked together to fill their bags with provisions.

◻ ◻ ◻ ◻ ◻

"Oomph," Isaiah grunted as Kyle woke him by smacking him with one of the hotel room pillows.

"Time to get up," Kyle said. "We have to beat them to the canoe rental place."

"Why do they have to do everything so early?" asked Isaiah with a yawn, "I hate getting up before nine."

"If we're successful today then you'll be able to sleep in," Kyle promised, "but for now you have to get ready to go."

A short while later they had checked out of the room, picked up donuts and coffee and were on the road with heavy metal blasting through the speakers in the Mercedes.

Chapter 22

Kevin and Katrina were hiding behind some ferns at the edge of the clearing when their radio crackled.

"It's go time," said McConnell.

They darted out of the jungle and crouched by the side of the lab building around the corner from the front door. As McConnell had instructed, they covered their ears as soon as they heard the sound of an engine starting. A minute later they heard muffled shouts from inside the lab as McConnell drove by the other side in an ancient red Land Rover that he'd found in a maintenance garage the night before. Just after he passed the lab there was a tremendous boom, followed by a shockwave that rattled everything within several miles. As he had promised, the large propane tank exploded in a huge ball of fire that set the nearby storage building ablaze in an instant.

Curt and the two security guards burst out the front door of the lab and ran towards the fire. Kevin and Katrina slipped around the corner and into the building, starting on their task of cutting the ropes without delay. "We're breaking you out," Kevin said as he worked furiously to free Berg. Within seconds they had removed the ropes and hurried Berg and Hargren through the lab and out the back door. McConnell was waiting with the Rover and motioned for them to get in.

"They're coming," shouted Kevin as he looked back towards the fire to see Curt and the guards headed for them in their Land Cruiser.

Dirt sprayed from the tires as McConnell hit the gas and headed for a winding road that led deeper into the jungle and away from the compound. "Keep down," he shouted as he spotted the Land Cruiser in the rearview mirror. He could see one of the guards bracing himself against the roll cage with one hand while bringing up his rifle with the other. They heard the sounds of gunfire followed by shattering glass as a few bullets hit the rear window.

"Paul, we've got to switch places," yelled McConnell. "We can't outrun them and they'll shoot us to bits if I don't do something about it. This rusted heap is a far cry from my Rover."

After a small feat of acrobatics, Hargren was behind the wheel and McConnell was clambering over the seats to the rear as the Rover bounced and skidded on the rough trail. McConnell opened the gun case and pulled out a military issue .223 rifle. He inserted a magazine filled with armor piercing rounds and flicked off the safety.

"Hold on," Hargren yelled just before he hit a sunken spot in the road filled with mud. McConnell was thrown forward against the rear seats as the Rover plunged into the muck and splashed a blinding wave of brown water up over the windshield. Hargren switched on the wipers and regained forward vision just in time to avoid hitting a tree as the road took a turn.

McConnell regained his balance and knelt by the tailgate. He smashed out the remaining shards of glass with the butt of the rifle and then turned it around to aim at the pursuing vehicle. The guard who was standing against the roll cage realized his predicament too late and was hit with a wall of mud as Curt sped into the ditch. McConnell attempted a few shots at the Land Cruiser, but it was nearly impossible to keep a steady aim as they bounced over the rough road. The mud-covered guard popped up from behind the windshield and let loose a spray of bullets, some of which hit the Rover narrowly missing the occupants.

McConnell sent back a three shot volley that took out a headlight and part of the windshield, and then ducked as more bullets peppered the Rover and punctured one of the rear tires. He popped up and quickly took aim before taking a few more shots. The standing guard jerked as the bullets found their mark, and then he slumped down into the passenger seat.

"I think they hit a tire," yelled Hargren.

"Just keep going," McConnell shouted.

Curt grinned as he gained ground on the Rover. "Take out their tires," he yelled to the second guard who was attempting to balance himself against the roll cage while standing on the rear seat. The guard ducked as a volley from McConnell punched through the windshield frame and dashboard, and then he got off a few shots in return. Kevin felt one of the rounds zip by his head as he crouched in the rear foot well with Berg and Katrina on either side.

Hargren hit the brakes and skidded around a tight turn as the trail followed a switchback on its way up the side of a mountain. As they started up the slope, another torrent of fire came from the Land Cruiser when it passed in the other direction on the road below. Windows shattered as a line of bullets marched along the side of the Rover, with the last few hitting the engine compartment. Hargren instantly knew something was wrong when he saw white smoke coming out from the side of the hood. "We're in trouble," he yelled.

McConnell looked up front for a second. "Drive as long as you can, we have to keep moving."

□ □ □ □ □

Ben and Derek were sitting in the rear bench of the van that Stenvick had rented from the university. "This is a lot more comfortable than that bus," observed Derek, "but it has no character."

"I know," agreed Ben. "There's no sense of adventure without the cloud of exhaust. A van like this would never work for our company."

"We could get an older one," Derek suggested, "but I really like the bus idea better. Plus, this would never hold enough equipment. We're packed in like sardines with just the nine of us and our bags."

Melody and Michelle occupied the next row forward. "That landslide was terrifying," said Michelle, "but I don't think I could have taken another trip in that awful bus. It's such a relief to be in this van. We all made it through safe and sound so I suppose I'm kind of glad it happened. I mean losing the bus, not the near-death experience. But,

157

that would have made a pretty good scene for a movie. When I go into film I'm sure I'll never get to do my own stunts like that."

Melody was working on braiding Michelle's hair. "It's good to see you're in a better mood. It almost seems that you're starting to enjoy this trip."

Michelle sighed. "I guess I owe you an apology. I came down here with a pretty bad attitude. This trip was the last thing I wanted to do and I didn't want to get to know any of you, but you've all been so nice to me anyway."

"That's ok," Melody replied. "We've certainly had a rough start, but we still have almost two weeks left. I'm looking forward to the rest of it."

"Ditto that," said Stephanie as she turned around in the seat in front of them. "I wouldn't choose to go through the last couple days again, but our group would never have come together so much if things had gone smoothly. We'll have some amazing stories to tell for years to come."

□ □ □ □ □

The Rover had slowly chugged up the switchback, trailing white smoke as Hargren kept the pedal to the floor and watched the temperature gauge steadily creeping up. Curt kept back far enough to avoid being an easy target but had no trouble keeping pace. The guard scored a few more hits on the Rover that punched several holes in the dashboard and passenger seat. Berg and the students tried to flatten themselves even further into the foot wells, trying to shrink down as small as possible.

"We're coming to the crest," yelled Hargren when he spotted the top of the mountain.

McConnell thought quickly over the map of the trail he'd studied. "Paul, the road bends sharply to the left up ahead. Hit the brakes after the curve and then floor it in reverse."

"Ok," Hargren shouted back.

Curt put on a burst of speed and raced to the top of the hill, confident his quarry wouldn't make it much further judging by the thick cloud of smoke obscuring his sight. He shouted up to the guard. "We'll come around the bend earlier than they expect. Get ready to lay down some fire."

The guard ejected his magazine and pulled a new one from his belt as they approached the bend. Curt began to take the turn but then yelled in alarm as the Rover came hurtling straight at him behind a wall of fire from McConnell. He cut the wheel to the right and nearly flipped the Land Cruiser as he skidded off the trail, narrowly missing a collision and spinning down an embankment before coming to rest against a tree. The guard had been hit and was catapulted out of the vehicle in the sudden move. It only took a glance for Curt to know he would be of no further help.

□ □ □ □ □

"Tell me more about your trip across the country on the scooter," Jennifer asked Geraldo. "That must have been really hard."

Geraldo smiled, "that was probably the craziest thing I've ever done. I was just hanging out with some friends one night and we got to talking about stupid ways that people become famous. We started coming up with ideas, and quickly devolved into joking about less and less practical plans. Someone mentioned going across the country on a scooter, and then I had the bright idea that a Razor scooter would be even more absurd since it's so small."

"And you just decided to go for it?" Jennifer inquired.

"Not at first. We had a good laugh but I pretty much forgot about it for several months. Then, one day we were discussing summer plans in one of my classes. Everyone else had something interesting to do like an internship, vacation or job. I didn't want to admit that I had nothing planned, so I just blurted out that I'd be riding a Razor scooter across the U.S. for charity. As you can imagine, word spread pretty quickly and before I knew it I was the talk of the campus."

"Wow," said Jennifer, "I guess you had to follow through then."

Geraldo nodded, "I pretended I was actually going to do it for so long that I had no choice. It would have been really embarrassing to back out and a lot of people would have been angry since they'd made bets. So, I bought a scooter and began making plans. It was amazing how much media attention I got before I'd even started. People thought it was an outrageous idea but I received all kinds of offers for help and support. I actually became pretty excited about the whole thing, until the day came to start the trip. There was a big crowd to see me off, including some news people, and I made a good show of scooting off the starting line with a smile. I didn't even make it a mile before my legs were killing me and I was wondering what I'd gotten myself in to."

"But you finished the trip, right?" asked Jennifer doubtfully, "or did you cheat?"

"No, I did it for real," Geraldo replied. "It was difficult, but I stuck with it. I think stubbornness alone carried me through some of the hardest parts. I never would have made it if some of my friends hadn't volunteered to drive my support vehicle. They took care of food and water, replacing parts and setting up camp every night."

"I can only imagine what that would have been like," concluded Jennifer.

Geraldo groaned, "Believe me; you wouldn't want to know from experience."

Chapter 23

Curt cranked the engine of the stalled Land Cruiser and jammed the gas pedal down as soon as it started.

"Keep going," yelled McConnell when he saw the pursuing vehicle clawing its way up the slope back towards the road. He raised his rifle to fire as Hargren got them moving forward again, but the last barrage had emptied the rest of the magazine and the opportunity was lost as he reached in his ammo tin for another. Something felt all wrong when he tried to load the new rounds. He looked down to see that two bullet holes had distorted the metal casing so it wouldn't fit the receiver. He picked up the tin and felt the blood freeze in his veins when he saw the two holes passing neatly through all of his spares and rendering them useless.

McConnell snapped back to attention as Curt fired several shots from his .40 caliber handgun. One of them hit the other rear tire which sent a shudder through the Rover as the air exploded out and dropped the metal wheel to the ground. McConnell pulled his .45 from its holster and sent six shots in Curt's direction, which would have hit him had he not ducked his head behind the dash just before the hollow point rounds shredded the stuffing out of his seat back.

McConnell was lining up to fire again when the bare rear wheels hit a large bump and bounced him against the roof. His hand slammed against the edge of the tailgate as he fell back to the floor and the gun flew from his grasp onto the road. Beginning to panic, he tried to pry some of the .223 rounds from the damaged magazines to fire one at a time from the rifle, but the rounds were jammed in place by the distorted metal and he gave up as there was no time to waste.

Hargren had stopped watching the temperature gauge once it hit the mechanical limit in the red zone and he could feel the engine losing power as the noises it made grew more and more dreadful. As the last traces of coolant were depleted and the smoke began to clear, he shouted that there was a bridge ahead. McConnell spun around to look and was hit with a sudden inspiration at the sight. "Take the bridge!"

McConnell saw that Curt was no more than a hundred feet behind the Rover and closing fast as he leaned out over the tailgate. He cringed as two holes perforated the metal in quick succession right next to his head. As they passed onto the suspension bridge, he grabbed the hook from the winch mounted on the rear bumper and flipped the release lever. He knew he had one chance to get this right as he took a length of cable in one hand and hefted the hook in the other.

Curt watched in amusement as McConnell threw the hook. "Ha," he thought to himself as it sailed harmlessly off the side of the bridge, "I bet he never made the little league team." He raised his pistol and took careful aim as McConnell pulled himself back into the vehicle.

"Hold on!" McConnell yelled. "Paul, floor it!"

The engine complained loudly as Hargren found another few millimeters of travel in the pedal, and then there was a violent lurch that nearly stopped them in their tracks.

McConnell whipped around to see that the winch cable had played out and brought the hook up to snag on the railing of the bridge. Wood and ropes splintered and snapped as the momentum of the Rover pulled the cable and a key support from one side of the bridge with it.

"What?" said Curt as he saw the hook snag just feet in front of him. Before he could react the Land Cruiser passed onto the weakened section of bridge as the Rover continued pulling it apart. The deck twisted suddenly to one side under the weight of the vehicle and sent it hurtling off the bridge and into the river a hundred feet below.

Hargren brought the Rover to a stop on the other side of the bridge as the engine sputtered and stalled. "How did you know that would work?"

"I didn't," responded McConnell, "but that bridge didn't look very strong so I figured it was worth a shot. Is everyone ok?"

Berg, Katrina and Kevin exited the Rover and confirmed that they had not been injured. "That was terrifying," said Katrina, still shaking from the experience.

Berg looked at the bridge. "We have to get back to the compound and get out a message. It looks like we can still cross if we climb across the damaged section on the good side."

"I don't think we went more than a mile or two," said Hargren as he stepped onto the bridge.

McConnell grabbed his rifle and gear. "Here, give me a hand with this. I don't want to leave anything with the vehicle."

After a last look over the bullet-riddled Rover, the group started the walk back to the lab.

□ □ □ □ □

Spencer had taken the passenger seat in the front of the van with Stenvick. It wasn't long before their conversation turned to questions about what happened after death. Theology had not been a subject of much importance at the military-inspired boarding school Spencer had attended, and he was awed by the depth of knowledge the professor had on the subject.

"You see, Spencer," Stenvick was explaining, "Psychology can only enlighten us so much when it comes to faith. None of us can prove through observation what happens to us after we die. It takes faith to believe that there is something more. I think it's fascinating to study how faith affects people's thoughts and actions. Personally, I've found that my faith enlightens my work in psychology, and my professional research has served to deepen my faith and gives me new appreciation for it every day."

"What do you believe?" asked Spencer.

Stenvick chuckled. "One of the hard parts about being a professor is that you get in the mindset of never giving straight answers.

I'll begin by asking you some questions. To start with, have you ever read the Bible?"

"No," replied Spencer, "but we have one at home."

"Are you familiar with any of the major religions?"

Spencer thought for a moment. "No."

"Well," said Stenvick, "that doesn't give us much to start with."

"I am sorry," Spencer replied dejectedly.

"No," said Stenvick. "Don't be sorry. It's nothing to be ashamed of. The important thing is that you're looking for answers." Stenvick opened one of the pockets on his trail pack and pulled out a small book which he handed to Spencer. "This is the New Testament of the Bible, which is all about the time Jesus spent on earth. We can talk more about it once you've started reading, but this book has changed my life in ways I never would have thought possible. When I was young, I thought the Bible was just some boring old book that stuffy church people read, but now I believe that it contains the words of God, and it has the most exciting message you could imagine."

Spencer slid the volume in his pocket. "Thank you. I will read."

"I'd recommend you start with John," said Stenvick.

Spencer looked confused. "Who is John? Can't I read by myself?"

"Oh, sorry," laughed Stenvick. "I mean the book of John. It's the fourth book, after Mathew, Mark and Luke. It's a good place to start."

□ □ □ □ □

It hadn't taken long for McConnell to lead the group back to the lab following the trail they'd driven minutes before. He'd been relieved to find his pistol unharmed on the side of the road and checked to confirm that there were several shots left before holstering it. When they reached the building, he had everyone stay behind while he checked to make sure no one was inside or waiting in the vicinity. "All clear," he pronounced once he was satisfied that it was deserted.

Hargren found a phone next to the computers but announced that there was no dial tone after testing it. "Maybe they turned it off since they were leaving," he suggested.

164

"Or when they found out we were here," said Berg.

"I'm going to go check the fence," said McConnell. "I'll figure out a way to break through it and use the satellite phone in my Rover. We shouldn't have to worry about setting off any alarms now with all the guards out of action." He propped open the door and warily checked outside before jogging off into the jungle.

"In the meantime," said Berg, turning to Kevin and Katrina, "let's get to work looking through these files for information on the antidote Fiker mentioned."

"I don't remember seeing anything on the summary pages," said Katrina as she picked up one of the notebooks.

"We should start with the most recent ones," Hargren suggested. "Hopefully there will at least be some mention of what they did."

Everyone looked up in surprise as the door of the lab was suddenly thrown open. Soaking wet, covered with mud and debris, bleeding and with one arm hanging limp at his side, Curt stood in the entrance with his pistol raised and demanded they put their hands up. "Where's that other guy?" he yelled.

They all stood staring at him with blank expressions. "Um, he didn't make it back," Kevin finally stammered. "He was gone by the time we got to the end of the bridge."

"You're lying!" Curt shouted, aiming his pistol at Kevin. "I saw him crossing the bridge with the rest of you. He has to be here."

"No!" Katrina burst out. "He's not with us."

Curt fired off a shot that whizzed over Kevin's head and hit the back wall of the lab, causing the four of them to flinch. "Tell me where he is or your boyfriend gets the next one," he growled, pointing the barrel at Kevin's chest.

"Wait," Berg said, "don't..."

He was cut short as three shots rang out in quick succession. Katrina screamed and Kevin's hands instinctively clutched at his chest. Berg and Hargren stood frozen in place as Kevin looked up in confusion. Curt stood still for several seconds with an expression of bewilderment on his face before the gun dropped from his hand and he collapsed lifeless to the ground.

Megan Monet, the INIAS tour guide, stepped into view in the doorway holding a compact .357 magnum revolver. She was dressed in jeans and a college sweatshirt. "Are there any other guards around?" she asked while quickly looking over the room.

"What are you doing here?" Kevin asked, finally realizing that he hadn't been shot.

"I ran here as fast as I could when I heard the explosion," Megan explained. "I was in the middle of searching the office. All the vehicles were gone so I think I just set a personal record for a five mile sprint. Good thing since it appears I was just in time."

Megan reloaded the revolver and slipped it into its holster as she walked into the room. At the sound of running footsteps approaching outside she made for a desk and barely managed to get behind it with a diving somersault as McConnell burst in and fired in her direction. She came up in a crouch on the other end of the desk with her gun drawn and snapped off two shots, which he ducked to avoid. He quickly returned fire but Megan had already taken cover behind the desk again.

"Stop!" shouted Katrina.

Chapter 24

Silence fell over the lab as the gunfire ceased. "Don't shoot," Katrina implored.

"Who is she?" McConnell demanded.

"Agent Megan Monet," Megan answered from behind the desk. "I'm with the FDA."

Katrina pointed at Curt's body on the floor. "She shot him. I think we can trust her."

McConnell kept his gun trained on the desk as he moved closer to the body to take a look. "Nice grouping, he observed.

"Thanks," replied Megan. "That's how they train us."

"Wait a minute here," Kevin interrupted. "Are you telling me you're not the world's dumbest tour guide?"

Megan laughed. "That's my cover. I'm here to report on the work Hallita is doing. It's the only way the FDA can get an inside look at their operations. Can we put down the guns and talk?"

"Even the accent is gone," Kevin noted out loud.

"Alright," said McConnell. "I guess she's okay."

Megan stood slowly, holstering her weapon as she came around the desk. McConnell finally put his gun away, satisfied that she was not a threat. "Bill McConnell, CIA," he said in introduction. "Rank and title classified."

Megan looked at him skeptically. "Are you with them?" she asked, nodding to the rest of the group.

"Yes. My friend Paul here got me involved. I was just on the way to break through the fence when I heard the shots and ran back. We drove in from the jungle side last night."

"What does the FDA know about Hallita's operations?" asked Berg. "Are you aware of Fiker's plans?"

Megan shook her head. "I've gotten bits and pieces from listening in on conversations, but the security on the work here has been very tight. Playing dumb has allowed me to be a sort of fly on the wall. Most of the scientists pretty much ignore me and figure I'll never understand what they're talking about."

"You convinced me," said Kevin.

Megan smiled and continued, "I overheard a conversation yesterday between Dr. Fiker, Dr. Lake and the late Mr. Curt. I believe you had a meeting with Dr. Lake the other day."

"Yes," Hargren confirmed.

"Anyway, they were pretty upset that some hired thugs failed to take you out, especially when Dr. Lake mentioned the research Dr. Berg has done on Amanitin D. That seems to be the key to a plan Dr. Fiker is going to introduce at the Nobel ceremony."

"It is," said Berg. "Fiker told us about it last night."

Megan listened intently for a few minutes as Berg and Hargren gave an overview of Fiker's scheme. "That makes sense of everything I've observed around here," she said once they finished. "I knew they were preparing for something big. Also, they mentioned a group of students that the thugs are going after. Dr. Fiker was angry that it was taking so long."

"Oh no," Katrina whispered, "That's Dr. Stenvick and the rest of the students."

"We're on a college cross-cultural," Berg explained. "Kevin, Katrina and I got involved in this situation through Paul and became separated from the rest of our group. I need to warn them but none of our phones are working."

"The phone lines and cell tower were turned off late last night," Megan said. "You won't get another signal around here for miles."

"I have a satellite phone," said McConnell, "but I still need to get through the electric fence to reach it. I used a circuit perimeter isolator to get through but it burned out."

168

"I see," Megan said thoughtfully. "Fortunately, I stopped in the security office just a little while ago and deactivated the fence and all the alarms throughout the complex."

McConnell grinned. "That's great. I can use the wire cutters in my bag. I'll go make a call and get some backup in here."

"Don't forget about hacking into the computer," Kevin reminded him.

"Yes. Right. I'll be back soon."

"I'm thirsty," Hargren mentioned absent-mindedly as he looked around the room, spotting a sink by the potting bench and walking towards it.

"Don't drink that," warned Megan. "The water out here is nasty. The vending machine in the hallway has bottled soda and water."

"Oh, ok," replied Hargren. He walked out of the room but appeared in the doorway seconds later. "Does anyone have any change? I don't have any on me."

"Are you serious?" asked Berg with an amused expression. He picked up a metal office chair and carried it to the doorway. "Pardon me."

Hargren stepped aside. "Are you going to check if they keep some change on top of the machine?"

"No," said Berg with a grin. "Stand back." When Hargren had moved away sufficiently, Berg hoisted the chair and swung it against the front of the refrigerated cabinet, shattering the glass and creating a large hole. He set the chair on the floor and grabbed a bottle of water. "Take anything you want. It's on me."

Hargren picked out a cola and stared at the jagged glass. "I don't know why I didn't think of that. You've impressed me once again."

"What are you two doing?" asked Megan as she burst into the hallway. "The front of the machine is unlocked. You could have just opened it."

Berg and Hargren exchanged sheepish glances as their faces turned red from embarrassment. "Oh," was all they could say.

Megan grabbed the side of the door and pulled, opening it easily on its hinges. She took an orange juice and gave the two men a look like a mother scolding her children, then returned to the lab.

Katrina had been surveying the equipment and plants growing on the benches. "Dr. Berg," she called as he came back in the room, "it looks like they have all the same test equipment that we used at the university. Also, the labels on many of these plants indicate that they're samples of current agricultural crops. Maybe we could run some tests to identify how they worked Amanitin D into the genetics."

"I'm not sure if that would work," said Hargren doubtfully. "All of those crops are patented so you won't get a result from the chromosomal sequencer when they match the database, plus with all the communication lines down the machine won't work."

Katrina's disappointment was obvious.

"Good idea anyway," said Kevin trying to encourage her.

Megan spoke up. "Actually, all the testing machines at this facility are unlocked to run independently with no restrictions. Hallita has complete control of the monitoring system but they don't play by the rules. You can test whatever you want and it will give you the results."

"How did you find that out?" asked Berg.

Megan blushed. "One of the scientists had an obvious crush on me. I used that to my advantage and got him to talk. I gave him the idea that I was really impressed by all his knowledge and he just kept pouring out the details. Of course I pretended not to comprehend any of it. It was very unfortunate when he was transferred to another facility."

"It's Bill, don't shoot," McConnell announced before cautiously opening the door and stepping into the lab. He handed a device to Kevin. "Plug that into the computer and you can access whatever you want. I got in touch with our regional office and explained the situation briefly. A team will be here shortly to secure the area and establish a communications base. Believe me Dr. Berg, if there's anything you need to circumvent Fiker's plan just name it and we'll get it."

"We're in," Kevin announced once he was successfully logged into the computer.

"Good," said Hargren with relief, "the lab equipment won't do us much good without the computer to view the results. Bill, can you arrange for some more test equipment and computers to be brought in? If we're going to find out anything useful before Fiker gives his speech we'll need to work very fast and run a lot of tests simultaneously."

"No problem," said McConnell. "Write me a list of what you need and I'll call it in."

"I have a few things to add as well," chimed in Berg. "It's a stretch, but if we can get enough scientists around the world collaborating on working out the antidote we can take away Fiker's bargaining chip. I want computers, video conference equipment and the fastest satellite internet link you've got."

"Sure, anything you want," McConnell confirmed. Once he had the list he darted out the door to go back to the Rover, thinking to himself that this was probably not the last trip he'd be taking to relay their needs before the chopper arrived with the communications gear.

□ □ □ □ □

"They're here," Kyle observed as he watched the entrance to the parking lot through a pair of binoculars. He'd parked the Mercedes out of the way behind some other vehicles and mostly hidden from view by a tree, but with a small gap through which he could see when the group arrived.

"Think I should put a bug on their van?" asked Isaiah as he reviewed the park map and went through Kyle's plan in his mind, trying to think of any detail they'd overlooked.

"Nah," said Kyle after a moment's thought. "We'll get them today for sure. If we fail, which we won't, then we can plant a bug later."

Isaiah clicked through a few screens on his laptop. "I've reserved all the canoes, kayaks and rafts for a few fictitious groups, so no one will be following us down the river for at least a couple hours. That should give us enough time to clean up and get out of here before anyone else comes through."

"Good thinking," said Kyle. "I knew you would come up with some useful ideas once you got over the explosives thing." He looked through the binoculars again. "Alright, they're out of the van and heading for the rental office. If they stick to their itinerary we'll follow in half an hour and pass them while they're doing the hike to the overlook. In the meantime let's go over the plan and check that we've packed everything we need."

☐ ☐ ☐ ☐ ☐

After Stenvick had checked in at the office and everyone had a chance to use the restrooms following the long ride in the van, the group assembled by the river. A somewhat testy conversation in Spanish ensued between one of the river guides and Stenvick, ending with the guide throwing up his hands in frustration and gesturing angrily to the racks of canoes and equipment before storming off.

"Did you catch what that was all about?" Jennifer whispered to Michelle.

"Yes," she explained with a hint of worry in her tone. "The guide wanted us to pay him to lead us down the river. Dr. Stenvick said we didn't need a guide since he's been here before and knows where he's going. The guide said it's against their policy to let groups go alone. Dr. Stenvick said they should have made that clear when he scheduled the trip and that he wouldn't pay a dime more than he had already. They argued that point a bit and then the guide said he wasn't going to help us get setup either and we were on our own."

"Alright," Stenvick called, "let's get this show on the road. We need three of the large canoes from that rack and a paddle and life vest for everyone."

The students went to work gathering the gear and had everything ready at the dock a few minutes later. Stenvick split up the group among the three canoes and asked if they were all familiar with the basics of paddling and steering. Everyone said they knew what they were doing, so they boarded the boats and started down the river.

☐ ☐ ☐ ☐ ☐

172

Berg and the others in the lab were sitting around a table going over their plan for finding an antidote to Hallita's poisonous crops when they heard the low thrum of a helicopter approaching. McConnell went to the door and confirmed that it was CIA. The chopper buzzed in low over the jungle and landed in the clearing in a swirl of dust. As soon as it touched the ground the doors slid open and a team of agents in full combat gear jumped out and formed a perimeter. As the pilot cut the engine an official looking man got out of the passenger seat and walked to meet McConnell at the door.

"Bill," he shouted over the whir of the blades as they shook hands, "what's the situation?"

McConnell led him inside and shut the door against the noise. "To the best of our knowledge this facility is deserted," he began, "but first let me introduce you to everyone and then we'll explain what's going on in more detail." McConnell acquainted the visitor with everyone in the room and then introduced him as Dale Halloway, the CIA's regional director for Nicaragua, Costa Rica and Panama, based at the headquarters in San José.

"That's Incredible," Halloway concluded ten minutes later after being given a quick briefing on the events of the preceding days. He was a moderately tall man in his mid-fifties with neatly combed grey hair, glasses and a well-polished pair of black cowboy boots complementing his suit. He thought for a few moments, rubbing his chin between his thumb and index finger. "As you know, Bill, I don't like to make hasty decisions or take action without proper consideration, but I don't think we can afford to sit on this. We need to get Langley involved right away."

"I couldn't agree more," said McConnell. "We have a chopper on the way with communications gear and another following with some equipment the scientists need. I'd say we'll be ready for video conferencing within the hour. Can you call Langley and schedule a meeting?"

"Sure thing," Halloway agreed. "I'll go make the call right now." Pulling a satellite phone from a leather pouch on his belt he quickly stepped outside to find a clear signal.

☐ ☐ ☐ ☐ ☐

Kyle and Isaiah entered the canoe rental office dressed to look like a couple of seasoned adventure junkies who had never known a steady job. In broken high school Spanish Kyle attempted to check in with the man at the desk. Isaiah stood back with his hands in his pockets and a sly grin on his face as he listened to the exchange for a few minutes. Once Kyle reached the point of talking slowly and loudly in English with the hope of being understood, Isaiah stepped up to the desk. In fluent Spanish he explained that they had reservations and took care of signing them in and paying the rental fee with the much relieved employee.

"Ok, since when do you speak Spanish?" Kyle whispered as they followed a guide down to the boat racks by the dock. "All this time we've been here and you let me struggle through every conversation sounding like an idiot."

"You never asked," responded Isaiah with a shrug of his shoulders. "If you were having problems you should have said something."

As they reached the boats the guide turned and asked a question with his hand extended palm up. Isaiah responded and the conversation quickly turned heated, ending with the guide staring wide eyed at Kyle, backing away and then turning to run.

"What was that all about?" Kyle wanted to know.

"He wanted us to pay him to guide us down the river. I told him no, and then he went off on how all of us Americans are cheap and it's hard for him to make a living, and how we were just like that group that just left. I said that he better leave us alone if he valued his life because you have a violent temper and knifed the last person that made you angry, and that you haven't taken your meds today."

Kyle looked amused, "Nice!" He turned to see the guide peering out the window at them and made a deranged face in his direction. The man jumped back from the window as if he'd been bitten and hid from their sight. Kyle laughed as they gathered the paddles and life vests. Soon they were floating down the river after the students.

Chapter 25

"Why did I think canoeing with Dr. Stenvick would be any easier than hiking?" Jennifer asked Stephanie as they paddled vigorously to keep up with the professor. "My arms are going to fall off if we do this for much longer."

Stephanie sat in the bow of the canoe in front of Jennifer but was raised several inches higher due to Spencer's weight in the stern. "I can barely reach the water with my paddle," she said as she paused to wipe away the sweat that was stinging her eyes.

"Row," Spencer commanded sharply from behind her. "No time for being weak."

Unsure if he was joking or serious, Stephanie plunged her paddle back in the river. "Yes, sir!"

Derek, Ben and Geraldo were trailing the group in the last canoe. They were having difficulty coordinating their efforts and kept arguing about how to stay on a straight course. "Derek, you paddle on the right," Ben directed from his seat in the stern, "and Geraldo, you paddle on the left. I'll count out the strokes. When I say switch you paddle on the opposite side. Got it?"

"Got it," they replied in unison.

"Ok, I'll count by threes," Ben explained. "Paddles in the water on one, finish the stroke through two, and back to the start through three. Ready? One, two, three, one, two, three, one, two, three, switch."

"Hey!" said Derek in annoyance as a spray of water hit him in the back from Geraldo's paddle as it swept across to the other side of the canoe.

"Sorry," said Geraldo as he gently put the paddle back the other way.

Ben yelled at them from the stern. "You're paddling on the same side again." As they both switched to the opposite side he put his head in his hands and groaned.

Meanwhile, Stenvick sat in the bow of the lead canoe completing two strokes for each of Melody's and Michelle's. "What a beautiful day to be out on the river," he observed casually. "There's nothing like paddling through the water to clear your head. Did you two know that I live just up the hill behind Harrisville? It's only a short walk from my house down to the creek that runs through campus. Every morning I carry my kayak and put in by the covered bridge, and then I paddle for about half an hour until I reach my takeout point. I devised a set of wheels and a harness that I use to tow the kayak to make the five mile jog back home. It's a great way to prepare for a big breakfast."

Behind him the girls looked at each other with raised eyebrows. "Is he serious?" mouthed Melody silently.

Michelle shrugged.

□ □ □ □ □

McConnell and Halloway directed the teams that arrived in the helicopters with the communications gear and lab equipment. Working at a furious pace they erected several antennas and setup phone, video conference and internet lines. Under Berg's direction, all unnecessary items were carried out of the lab to make room for a conference area and the additional analysis machines. Hargren was hard at work with Kevin and Katrina running cables and preparing all the equipment for their use.

Megan approached the two CIA men. "I just got off the phone with my supervisor at the FDA. They're going to put all available inspectors and field agents on call in case we can be of assistance."

"Thanks," said Halloway. "I'll make sure your agency is included in our conference call."

McConnell looked doubtful. "What can you foodies do at this point, slap Hallita with a fine?"

"Don't underestimate us," Megan replied. "We may not have all the guns and gadgets that you do, but there are ways we can help."

"We've got Langley on the line," shouted one of the communications techs.

Everyone scrambled to gather around the monitor and silence quickly fell over the room. The video screen showed about a dozen people situated around a u-shaped table. Introductions were made quickly and then the head of the CIA requested a briefing on the situation. "Sir," said Halloway, "I think it would be best if Dr. Berg and Mr. Hargren give you the rundown."

"Fine," barked the CIA director, "speak up so we can hear you."

Berg and Hargren took turns relating how they had traced the suspicious corn to INIAS, investigated the samples from the site, survived the assassination attempt, enlisted McConnell's help, broken into the facility and learned of Fiker's plan. They went on to explain their idea for a crash program to find the antidote using the assistance of trusted scientists all over the world. The CIA director thought for a moment once they had finished, then addressed McConnell directly. "Bill, you've never steered me wrong before. Is this for real? Should we take immediate action?"

"Yes, sir," McConnell replied confidently. "We need every resource working on this right away. If Fiker is allowed to speak and put his scheme in motion the consequences could be dire."

"Ok," said the director. "I'll speak with the President. In the meantime I want you to get started on the antidote. If there's anything we can do to assist, you know who to call. Good luck."

The screen went to a CIA logo as the conference was ended. "You heard the man," said McConnell. "Let's get to work."

□ □ □ □ □

"Here we are," Stenvick shouted, then instructed Michelle to steer their canoe to the left bank of the river. As the bow hit the soft muck at the landing he jumped out and dragged it several feet from the water. Melody and Michelle stepped out to dry ground and helped him pull it the rest of the way up the bank. A minute later Spencer's canoe came in to the same spot and was also pulled from the water. Peering upstream they could make out the last canoe zigzagging its way towards them.

"Over here," Stenvick yelled.

Derek waved to signal that he understood. As the canoe came further towards them everyone watched in amusement as it started heading for the opposite bank, then amidst frantic paddling and shouting hit a rock broadside in the middle of the river. The canoe slid up onto the rock partway, rotating it and dumping out the three occupants before filling with water and capsizing. Ben, Derek and Geraldo coughed and sputtered as they bobbed in their life vests and held onto the overturned vessel.

"Help!" Derek shouted to the onlookers on the bank.

Stenvick chuckled and called back to him. "Why don't you fellows just walk it out of there?"

The shade of red on the boy's faces was clearly visible as they put their legs down and found that the water was only just over waist deep. Thoroughly embarrassed, they lifted the canoe and walked it to the bank to join the rest of the group.

"You might want your paddles for the rest of the trip," Stenvick suggested as he pointed downstream a bit where they were slowly floating away.

The three boys hastily ran into the water and chased after the paddles. When they returned they stood dripping wet as Stenvick explained the basics of how to handle a canoe.

When he'd finished the lesson he addressed the whole group. "The river goes on for about ten miles in a long bend but we can cut that off with a quick two mile portage. Clip your paddles to the sides and carry the boats upside down. With three people the weight will be easy to carry. My group will demonstrate and then the rest of you do the same."

After giving brief instructions to Michelle and Melody, the three of them raised their canoe up in the air and rested it on their shoulders. Before Stephanie and Jennifer had even thought about it, Spencer grabbed theirs in the middle and hoisted it over his head. The girls wondered if they were even needed as they took their places to help.

"Alright, we can do this," Ben said confidently. "One, two, three." To everyone's relief the boys had no trouble lifting the canoe into position. Once the three teams were lined up, Stenvick struck out down a narrow and overgrown dirt path into the jungle. Darkness quickly enveloped them as they traded the open sky and sunlight for the thick tree canopy and dense undergrowth.

□ □ □ □ □

After providing a crash course on how to use the equipment, Hargren directed the CIA staff and they all worked feverishly. The various crop samples growing on the benches were analyzed and the identification info was entered into the computers. The lab buzzed with activity as people hurried in every direction. Berg logged in remotely to his research files and downloaded a contacts list of scientists he associated with around the globe. "Bill," he called over to McConnell, "I need someone who can setup a website on a secure server that everyone can access to upload and share data as we work."

McConnell dialed a number and had a brief conversation. "You have a conference in five minutes with one of our programming teams. Tell them what you want and they'll make it happen. By the way, have you contacted that professor friend of yours to warn him?"

Berg smacked his forehead. "I completely forgot about Rich. It's been so hectic here."

"We have a cell tower up and running now," McConnell informed him. "You should be able to use your phone normally."

Berg hastily dialed Stenvick. "Out of network," he said dejectedly as the call went to voicemail, then he left a message at the tone. "Rich, I hope you get this. You and the students are in danger. There are hired assassins with instructions to take out your group. Apparently they've had a few unsuccessful attempts but they're still trying. Be careful and give me a call when you can."

"Where is their group today?" asked McConnell. "We could send a team out for them."

"I have no idea," Berg admitted. "Rich and I discussed the plan several weeks ago but I don't remember the details. They could be almost anywhere in the country."

Berg was interrupted by someone calling him over for the conference with the programmers. He explained the research method and file types he would be using and discussed how he needed the many helpers to be able to work simultaneously.

"Simple," said the programming team leader. "Give us half an hour and we'll have the site ready for you. We'll send a link and access credentials to everyone on your list."

"Thanks so much," said Berg as they ended the call.

□ □ □ □ □

Kyle and Isaiah pulled their canoe up onto the bank where Stenvick and the students had landed shortly before. The paths where the canoes had been dragged and the numerous footprints were clearly visible in the soft mud. Isaiah checked the photograph they'd taken of the map in Stenvick's dorm room. "They should be walking through the jungle on that trail right now," he said, looking up to spot the entrance.

"I don't like the look of that jungle," said Kyle as he peered into the foliage. "I wouldn't doubt it's full of all kinds of poisonous plants and strange animals. You know, I think I'm starting to feel sorry for those kids. This is one crazy trip they're on."

"Don't go getting soft on me," Isaiah replied.

"Nah," said Kyle, "The way I see it, we'll be putting them out of their misery."

□ □ □ □ □

Melody followed behind Stenvick, holding up the middle of their canoe and keeping a wary eye on the professor. He was swinging a machete wildly in all directions to clear the overgrowth from their path as he hummed the title theme from Indiana Jones over and over again. She'd nearly screamed the first time she walked right into a large spider web that had avoided detection in the dim lighting, after which Stenvick handed her a short branch to clear her way. It didn't take long for the branch to be coated in a thick mess of webs and large spiders that she hastily shook off into the vegetation.

"How are you doing back there, Michelle?" she asked as another web stretched over her branch.

"I'm just fine. It's a lot nicer in here."

Melody stole a quick glance backward and scowled when she saw that Michelle was walking with her head inside the canoe and the sides of the narrow rear section spaced evenly across her shoulders.

"As long as Dr. Stenvick can see where we're going you could walk inside too you know," Michelle suggested.

"Why didn't I think of this before?" Melody thought to herself as she ducked her head under the side and readjusted her hold.

Behind them, Jennifer and Stephanie had given up any pretense of helping and simply followed behind Spencer since he held the canoe too high for them to reach. They were careful to give him plenty of room following several outbursts where he'd thought he'd seen poison ivy on the path and whipped the canoe around violently as he trampled several plants to a pulp with his heavy boots. "I must crush it all," he said as he finished stomping on the latest victim. "You will see. I will defeat it."

The girls were relieved when Stenvick called back to inform him not to worry because poison ivy did not grow anywhere in the region.

□ □ □ □ □

"Dr. Berg," said Halloway as he approached the conference table, "I was just on the phone with President Savatsky. He's in Norway for the ceremony. He was briefed on the situation over dinner and said to let you know that he'll do whatever he can to help."

"That's great," said Berg, astonished at how quickly information had traveled up the chain of command. A wave of hopefulness washed over him and gave him renewed energy.

"Did I hear you say dinner?" McConnell asked, having overhead part of the conversation. "Isn't it a bit early for that?"

Halloway looked at his watch. "The President was eating dinner, in Norway."

"Oh, right," said McConnell. "Well you've got me thinking about it now anyway. I don't think we have any food around here. I'm going to go make a call and have some things brought in."

Hargren called across the room for Berg to join him in the testing area. "Gary, one of the CIA's computer guys was able to copy the programming code from the unlocked chromosomal sequencer and install it in the machines they brought in. We'll be able to read the results from all the machines."

"Oh good," Berg replied with relief. "I was worried we'd be stuck only being able to use the one we found here. My website should be up and running in time to post the results. Let me know when you have the first ones ready. I need to start contacting some colleagues."

As Hargren directed the testing, Berg went to the phones and started calling everyone on his list to explain briefly what was going on and ask for their immediate assistance. He'd only made it through a few conversations when the programming team leader called to give him instructions on using the website. Scientists would be able to log in to transfer files, participate in video and chat discussions and contribute to the organization of the testing plan, all in real time. As the administrator, Berg would be able to direct and coordinate the entire effort from his computer.

Grateful for a long list of professional associates that he could rely on, Berg continued making calls. He felt bad contacting some, knowing it was the middle of the night in their time zones, but not a single one failed to take him seriously and drop everything to aid in the effort. As the minutes passed, the website began to populate with live profile pictures as people logged in and started discussing the problem. Berg assigned tasks based on each person's capability checklist and within minutes he was sure they must have set a record for the fastest implementation of a worldwide research project of this scale.

◻ ◻ ◻ ◻ ◻

When Stenvick led the students out of the jungle and to the bank of the river, they'd been relieved to be finished with the portage and getting back in the canoes again. However, hopes quickly faded when he explained that they simply had to paddle across to the other bank where they would be getting out again for a six mile round trip hike to the top of a waterfall. They pulled the canoes up onto the dirt and stowed the paddles and life jackets before reluctantly donning the packs that they'd just removed to cross the river.

"Forward march," Stenvick bellowed as he struck off into the jungle again. Everyone was relieved to find that the path was clear of overgrowth and well worn. Apparently it enjoyed a higher level of popularity than the portage route, which seemingly hadn't been traveled by anyone since Stenvick's last trip.

"It just occurred to me," Geraldo said to Ben and Derek as he walked in front of them, "how are you two going to run a wilderness tour business if you can't even paddle a canoe straight?"

Kyle and Isaiah exited the jungle and spotted the three canoes on the opposite bank of the river. "Perfect, they're on the hike to the falls," said Kyle. "Now it's time to head downstream and make our preparations."

"Are you sure this will work?" asked Isaiah. "I mean, we're pretty much counting on them not being familiar with the river. Anyone that knew about that portage route has obviously been here before."

"Don't worry," replied Kyle, "I've accounted for that. You said the same thing about the trails at the volcano but they still followed the sign and went the wrong way. This will be even less obvious to them."

Berg finished recruiting his research team and got up from the chair to stretch, confident that scientists worldwide were collecting samples of crops at that very moment and taking them back to their labs for analysis. He walked over to the testing area. "Paul, how are things coming along here?"

Hargren looked up from his computer. "Good, we're almost finished isolating Hallita's Amanitin D molecule and its corresponding genetic code. I'll get the files posted to the site as soon as they're ready."

"What are the other scientists going to be working on?" asked Kevin.

Berg paced back and forth as he explained. "As soon as we give them the information on the modified Amanitin D, they can confirm that the same molecule is present in Hallita crops all over the world. Based on what Fiker said I believe that will be the case, but we have to know for sure. Once that's confirmed I expect there will be a lot of discussion and ideas to try to develop an effective countermeasure. We'll shift resources as needed to pursue the more promising ideas but we'll follow many paths at once. I realize this is an audacious effort given so little time, but our task is easier than the work it took to develop this poison. We know exactly what it is, we just need to find a way to alter it or prevent it from doing further harm until a more elegant solution can be found."

"I guess I don't understand why this is such a rush," said Katrina. "Why do we need to succeed before Dr. Fiker gives his speech? If scientists worldwide have the data they need to beat this won't it be ok if it takes a month or two?"

"I had the same thought at first," Berg said, "and it's not inconceivable that that would still be possible, but the risks are great. If Fiker was telling the truth, none of us have all that long left to live unless we get the antidote. Fiker's demands will be clear and I don't think many countries will be willing to risk going against him on the hope that we'll succeed in time."

"Also," Berg continued, "keep in mind that Hallita has moles everywhere. If they report that research work is being done, that will be the end of antidote distribution for that country. I've informed all of our helpers that strict secrecy is paramount if this is going to work, but they can't keep that up for more than a few days before people start asking them what they're doing. If we don't succeed soon, how many of these scientists are going to be able to continue helping us? Consider this, if Fiker demands that our country gives me up or faces cutoff from the antidote, do you think the public will rally behind me? I wouldn't bet on it. They'll be too afraid for their lives. I fear the same would be true for many scientists around the world. Fiker will be sure to eliminate anyone that could pose a threat to what he's doing."

Kevin spoke up. "Can't the CIA just take out Fiker before the ceremony? Then he won't give his speech and this whole scheme will never become public. You'll have at least six months or so to find the cure."

"That also crossed my mind," replied Berg, "but the risks of taking that path could be even greater. If Fiker is killed, his cohorts will either find another way to get out the message or initiate the destruction failsafe of the whole system, which would destroy all the antidote supply as well as any records of how it's produced. In that case we'd be free to do our research, but the possibility of us failing to come up with a solution is very real. Also, look at how much distrust there is between nations. Half the world would reject our assertion that they need a cure to a problem they're not aware of. They would think it's some sort of plot. I can't say I would blame them given the many misuses of science for political purposes that we've seen over the last half a century, but their mistrust would be their demise. I've thought about this a good deal and I don't see any good outcome if we don't succeed by the time Fiker gives that speech."

"The files are up," said Hargren, putting an end to the conversation for the moment.

"Excellent," replied Berg. "I'll go inform everyone." He went back to his computer and announced that the molecular structure of the Amanitin D molecule was ready for comparison, and then watched as the many eager faces in the video profiles looked intently at what they were downloading onto their own screens. "As I explained before," he announced, "we'll consider any and all ideas for an antidote, no matter how unconventional they may be. Post your suggestions and we'll assign tasks accordingly."

□ □ □ □ □

After paddling for several miles down the river, Kyle and Isaiah pulled their canoe out at a small dock with a sign indicating it was the takeout point for the rental business. They carried the boat partway up the trail heading to a parking lot where buses would pick up the customers and equipment and hid it well out of sight.

"Step one completed," Kyle said as he shouldered his pack and started walking back to the dock. The two men dropped their bags and waded into the water on either side of the wooden platform. "On the count of three," Kyle instructed. On three, they picked the small dock up out of the water and slowly walked it up the trail, hiding it next to the canoe.

"Step two completed," said Isaiah with a grin. "I hope this sign is easier than the one at the volcano." He placed both hands on the sign pole and rocked it back and forth while Kyle pulled it up. They quickly removed it from the wet soil and left it hidden by the dock.

"Ok, step three," Kyle announced. They each fought their way into the dense vegetation with pruning shears and carried an assortment of plants back to the start of the trail, where they pushed them into the soil to create the appearance of an unbroken jungle.

"That's impeccable," Kyle declared as he looked at their work from the riverbank. Then, they shouldered their packs and started walking further downstream, weaving through the trees as they hugged the bank.

Chapter 26

Stenvick pointed out several species of birds that were visible among the trees at the waterfall overlook. The trail had ended at a small clearing near the top of the falls with a wooden railing along the edge of a steep drop off. Far below they could see the spray of water and mist rising into the air from the basin at the foot of the falls.

"This is beautiful," said Jennifer with delight. "We should get a group picture with the falls in the background. Does anyone have a camera with a timer?"

"I do," said Michelle as she pulled one from her pocket. The students piled several packs on the ground to make a raised platform which she balanced the camera on. "Scrunch in close together," she instructed as she viewed the display screen. "Melody and Stephanie, make sure there's a spot for me. I'll set it for ten seconds and then it will take three shots. Ready, go." She pressed the button and hurried over to pose.

"Those came out well," Stephanie pronounced as she looked over Michelle's shoulder to see the pictures. "Can you email them to me when we get home?"

"Of course," Michelle replied, "I'll make sure everyone gets copies."

"Hey, take one of us," Ben yelled from behind them.

The girls turned to see Ben and Derek standing in mock karate poses on top of the fence posts. "You're going to get hurt," Melody warned, "you better not fall off."

Michelle rolled her eyes and muttered something about immature boys as she snapped a few shots of them in different silly poses.

Stenvick was leaning against the railing sipping coffee from one of his thermoses and checking his phone. "Still no signal," he observed to himself. He'd been out of service the entire day and was wondering what Berg and the others were up to. Feeling sorry that they were missing such awe inspiring scenery, he pulled up the camera application and took some photos of the waterfall and the view of the valley from the overlook. With his thermos still in one hand, he balanced the phone between his fingers as he changed a few settings with his thumb. As he reached for an awkward spot on the screen the phone suddenly shifted in his fingers and he lost his grip. Before he could react, it dropped from his hand and he could only watch in dismay as it plummeted out of sight into the river below.

□ □ □ □ □

Kyle and Isaiah had reached a sign hanging suspended on a wire that spanned the breadth of the river. Large print in several languages warned anyone approaching not to pass because of rapids and a waterfall ahead. "Now for step four," said Kyle as he took a rope from his bag and splashed into the water. Isaiah followed him to the middle of the channel with a pair of pliers. Kyle tossed the rope over the wire and pulled it down so Isaiah could reach the sign. Isaiah quickly removed the bolts that attached the metal sign to its bracket and balanced it on his shoulder while Kyle let the wire back up.

"It's a good thing the water here isn't too deep," Isaiah panted as they trudged back to the bank through the waist deep current. "That would have been much harder if we had to swim."

"I know," replied Kyle, "and it would be difficult to keep the sign dry too. We can't have it dripping water on them as they pass underneath."

When they reached the jungle Isaiah set the sign against a tree and opened his bag. He pulled out a rolled-up piece of thick white plastic sheeting and spread it out against the face of the sign.

"That's a perfect fit," Kyle observed. "We won't have to trim the edges, and even the holes for the bolts are lined up exactly."

Isaiah shook his head in wonder as he viewed their work. "We can thank whoever posted the exact measurements to the Internet Movie Sign and Placard Database. If you ask me they need to get a life, but you can't argue that there are benefits to having such obsessive people in the world."

Kyle laughed. "Obsessive doesn't begin to describe this. One passing shot in a made-for-TV movie hardly seems worth all the effort for someone to get out here and record the details like they did."

Isaiah attached the plastic overlay they'd had printed the night before at an office supply store with several pieces of double sided adhesive tape. He smoothed and pressed with his fingers before stepping back to evaluate. The original wording of the sign was not visible at all through the opaque plastic. "It will do," said Kyle. "Let's get it back up there." Isaiah waded out with the modified sign and Kyle pulled down the wire again so he could attach it to the bracket. A few minutes later they'd finished and returned to the bank.

"Now we take up our position to watch and wait," Kyle said eagerly as he started walking further downstream. After they had gone a few hundred feet, they were pleased to see several downed trees obscuring the view ahead and blocking the waterway except for a narrow channel through the middle of the river. The speed of the current increased noticeably as it passed through the restriction, which would not give the canoers cause for alarm and would suit the assassin's purposes well. They walked a little further down the bank and found a suitable location.

"This is good," said Isaiah as he put down his pack and took a seat on a rock. "We've got a perfect view in both directions. I can't wait for the show to start."

Reports flowed in to the lab confirming exact matches of the Amanitin D molecule in crops of all sorts from the numerous locations being tested. "This isn't a hundred percent conclusive," Berg qualified with evident relief, "but I think it's safe to say that Hallita is only using this one poison. We should proceed on that basis." The other scientists nodded and agreed. Berg entered a post in the administrative notifications window that would send email and text alerts to any members not at their computers to stop work on the molecular analysis and check for new assignments.

The scientists offered ideas for antidote tests and Berg gave out the assignments electronically. Proposals ranged from standard antibiotics and drugs used to treat poisoning from other amatoxins to more interesting solutions such as weight loss pills and radiation. Also of great variety were the methods used to conduct the tests. The scientists with facilities capable of artificially synthesizing the molecule would work on direct chemical reaction trials. Others had highly sophisticated computer modeling software to analyze solutions. The rest would do what they could with plant extracts and their own blood and tissue samples.

Berg and Hargren consulted and informed McConnell that they would need some additional supplies including a team of medical personnel, blood pathologists and testing equipment. McConnell stepped out of the lab and relayed the instruction at the field post that had been set up at the edge of the clearing. Halloway was busy giving constant status updates to various officials in the CIA and White House, and Megan was discussing plans with the FDA administrators. McConnell was amazed at the level of cooperation between agencies, having expected the usual turf wars and resistance to sharing information. Seeing that the chopper with the food supplies had not arrived yet, he went back into the lab to wait.

□ □ □ □ □

"Quiet, someone's coming," Kyle whispered as he motioned to Isaiah to duck down and lie still on their vantage point above the river.

Isaiah squinted to make out the shape floating downstream towards their position. "This is going to be good," he said with unguarded excitement.

Kyle checked his watch and looked again at the approaching craft. "This seems early for them to be here. We passed their canoes minutes after they left for the hike. You know... I think that's a kayak, and I only see one boat. I thought you said there would be no one else coming through for a few hours after us."

Isaiah looked guilty. "I reserved all of the other *available* boats, but there was a reservation after us for a two-person kayak that I didn't mention. I thought they'd make a good trial run for our plan if they showed up on time, since they'd end up between us and our targets."

"These are just innocent civilians," Kyle whispered angrily. "We can't just indiscriminately send people to their deaths. What were you thinking?"

Isaiah shrugged and raised his eyebrows in a gesture indicating he didn't know. "I don't see what your problem is. We don't know them. Besides, it will look more like an accident if those students are not the only group to go over."

Kyle thought for a few moments and reluctantly agreed that Isaiah had a good argument. As the kayak drew closer, they stopped talking and watched intently to see what would happen. A man and woman who appeared to be in their twenties were paddling the tandem kayak. They did not seem to be concerned about the increased speed of the current until they rounded a bend and quickly entered a gorge. Near vertical rock walls rose along the banks, narrowing through a section of rapids until ending at a deep crevice where the water spilled out into thin air to fall several hundred feet before crashing violently on the rocks below.

The woman was sitting in the front of the kayak and started screaming when she saw the rapids ahead of them. "We have to turn around!" they could hear her yelling. Unfortunately for the kayakers, it was too late. They tried to paddle backwards or turn the kayak but the force of the current was too strong and swiftly carried them into the gorge. They were spun violently in circles, bouncing from one rock to another and rolling several times on their way through the rapids until hitting the final stretch of smooth, fast flowing water leading to the brink of the falls. The kayak straightened as it covered the last few yards and then sailed gracefully into the air as the water dropped away underneath.

The sounds of screaming faded after a few seconds as the kayakers fell out of earshot of their spectators. "Flawless!" Kyle applauded, giving Isaiah a high five. "It worked. Now we'll just have to be patient for the next performance."

"See," said Isaiah, "I told you a test run would be a good idea. Actually, we should take some video of the students. I don't want any funny business when it's time for us to get paid. We should have some proof to show Mr. Curt."

"That's not a bad idea," replied Kyle. "There's something about that guy that I don't trust, and I need the money."

□ □ □ □ □

"I think we've got the hang of this," Derek said from his seat in the front of the canoe. He, Geraldo and Ben had finally worked out their paddling arrangement and could maintain a straight line or turn in either direction as needed.

"Dr. Stenvick, how far will we be going?" asked Melody as she paddled behind the professor in the lead boat.

"We should be at the takeout soon," he replied. "There will be a dock and a sign. I'd like to take a longer trip but it's not possible due to the waterfall. Once we return the canoes we'll take another hike in a different section of the park."

"Oh look, that's new," Stenvick announced when he saw the sign hanging above the river, notifying them in several languages of the takeout ahead. "I've never had any problems finding the dock, it's well marked. But, maybe some folks missed it and they had to put this up." The three canoes slipped silently under the warning sign as Stenvick kept an eye on the bank, wondering if there had been a change to the dock that made it harder to locate.

As they approached the downed trees, he figured something must have happened in the year since he'd been there last, such as a storm or flood that would explain the new sign and the differences in this section of the river. "Head for the middle of the stream," he yelled back to the other canoes. "It looks like there's a clear path through the trees there." Michelle steered the canoe into the middle of the V as the water narrowed to flow through the small passage, and she could feel the boat accelerate as the current picked up speed.

When they cleared the leaves and branches obscuring their view, Stenvick looked for the familiar dock but didn't see anything recognizable along the banks. He turned to scan the area directly behind the trees in case they were hiding the takeout from view, but there was nothing there aside from the dense jungle. He looked to confirm that the other two canoes had both navigated the passage, and then turned back to continue paddling, unsure why a sense of unease was starting to gnaw at him.

"I think it's getting easier to paddle," Stephanie said to her companions in the second canoe. "Don't you feel like we're moving faster?"

"I think you're right," Jennifer agreed. "It's still hard to keep up with Dr. Stenvick's canoe, but it does seem like we don't have to paddle so hard to move. Also, the trees are going by quicker than they did before."

"Maybe we're getting better at it," suggested Stephanie. "There is a technique to proper paddling. I'd say we must have gotten it."

Stenvick stopped paddling as his canoe rounded a bend in the river. "Michelle, Melody, hold your paddles a minute. I don't recognize where we are, and I don't remember a bend like this before the takeout."

"The sign said it was coming up," said Melody. "I've been looking and I haven't seen it yet so it must be close."

"I hope so," Stenvick replied with concern apparent in his voice. "I've never been down the river this far. Maybe they moved the location of the dock, but I'm feeling kind of anxious since I don't know how far it is to the falls."

□ □ □ □ □

Isaiah and Kyle watched with bated breath as the lead canoe came to the end of the turn in the river and started picking up speed when it entered the gorge. The location of their trap could not have been more perfect, as by the time the canoers could see what was ahead it was too late to paddle to the bank or attempt to stop. The bend in the river looked wide and peaceful from the start, but changed almost instantly as the banks closed in at the end, causing the current to double in speed beyond the already faster rate it had taken after the trip through the trees.

Chapter 27

Stenvick froze in his seat and stared ahead in shock at the tumultuous rapids looming before him. Realizing something had gone terribly wrong, he quickly stood to get a better view, careful however not to upset the canoe. His eyes scanned the steep rock walls lining each side and culminating in the narrow gap of the falls and his mind raced into action. They couldn't turn back against the strength of the current and there was no way to get out up the steep walls of the ravine. Once they passed through the notch it would be a long fall to certain death.

The walls of the ravine were almost vertical until they neared the falls, where the angle grew much shallower as the terrain pulled away to either side and opened to a broad valley. Several stubborn trees clung to life around the top of the notch with their roots digging into the thin soil and cracks in the rocks. *"We have to get to those trees,"* thought Stenvick, *"but how?"* He looked around in the canoe, taking inventory of everything they had with them; Hiking packs, paddles and life vests. Suddenly an inspiration hit him.

"Keep to the middle of the rapids," Stenvick shouted over his shoulder, "and make sure the canoe stays straight. When we hit the smooth section at the end give me your paddles." Melody and Michelle had no idea what he was thinking, but they didn't have time to second-guess his instructions. The canoe was now hurtling forward into the whitewater. The roar of the foaming torrent was deafening as they took the first plunge into the chute. "Turn left!" Stenvick yelled as they headed straight for a rock. Michelle jammed her paddle into the water and pulled hard, sweeping the bow away from the obstacle and sending them into another dip that bounced them in their seats as they were drenched with spray.

Stenvick yelled out another few turns as they careened down the course, narrowly avoiding impacts that would likely throw them from the canoe and dash all hopes of reaching safety. "Quick, give me your paddles," he shouted as they cleared the last of the rocks. The girls handed him their paddles and watched in alarm as they raced straight for the notch. Stenvick hurried to arrange the three paddles together in his hands with two blades pointing one way and the third opposite. With seconds to go, he leaned out over the bow and held the paddles perpendicular to their path in his outstretched arms. "Hold on!"

Just as the tip of the canoe reached the terminal notch in the gorge, he jammed the cluster of paddles into the water and under the bow, summoning all his strength to hold them in place until they hit the rocks on either side of the boat. As he felt them make contact, he quickly let go and clung to the bow for dear life. The front of the canoe rode up onto the paddles and headed for the sky until coming to an abrupt stop as the wide middle section wedged between the rocks. Stenvick looked down to see nothing but mist below him before turning around and scrambling to the middle of the canoe.

Balancing as best he could on the awkward angle of the boat bottom, Stenvick pulled open his pack and took out the climbing rope with the grappling hook on the end. A quick glance showed him that the second canoe was in the rapids and would be on them soon. He swung the hook several times and threw it up the bank where it looped around a tree. "Quick, use the rope to climb up to the trees!" he shouted over the deafening roar of the falls. Melody and Michelle had already shouldered their packs over their life vests and clambered up the steep and slippery bank with the help of the rope. They gained handholds and footholds among the trees where the rocks took a shallower angle.

Stenvick put on his pack and climbed a few feet up the rocks. Holding the rope with one hand, he waved and shouted to Stephanie's boat to slow down their pace as much as possible. The two girls and

Spencer back-paddled for all they were worth, but they still crashed into Stenvick's canoe at an alarming pace. At the sound of a loud crack, Stenvick looked to see two halves of a broken paddle fly out over the falls. The weight of the second canoe pressing into the stern of the first pushed it down and into the flow of water, wedging it against the bottom of the channel. Stenvick watched as the sides of his boat began to buckle under the stress and push further into the notch.

Stenvick dropped down to the canoe and handed the rope to Stephanie. She wasted no time in climbing it as Michelle and Melody cheered her on from above. Jennifer and Spencer followed soon after. Stenvick was relieved to see Derek, Geraldo and Ben clear the rapids and hurtle towards him. He shouted and waved for them to slow down. The boys did their best to slow their momentum before hanging on as they slammed into the back of the second canoe, pushing it forward and driving it up at an angle as it rode the first canoe like a ramp.

Another crack split the air as a second paddle broke under the impact and the lead canoe lurched forward a few more inches. Stenvick could see that the cross rails were bending as the sides were crushed inward and knew that it wouldn't hold much longer. The three boys had to climb into the second canoe to reach Stenvick and the rope. Their weight pushed the back of the canoe down into the water, allowing the current to push on it and add more stress to the first canoe plugging the notch.

The sound of the third and last paddle failing sent a chill through Stenvick and he felt his canoe grind into the notch even further as the sides gave in. Ben was the last from the third canoe to take the rope and climb, leaving only the professor. They had all gone up the rope one at a time to avoid putting too much weight on the small tree and its tenuous grip on the earth. Stenvick held the end of the rope and waited as Ben completed his ascent. As he placed a foot against the rock and started to pull himself up he could feel the canoe giving way beneath him. With a sickening crunch, the sides collapsed and the three vessels shot out over the falls.

Stenvick shakily climbed the rope and joined the students at the top of the slope. Everyone cheered as they reached down and pulled him to safety. He unhooked the grapple, coiled the rope and stowed it back in his bag. "Let's get further up the bank and away from danger," he instructed while taking one last look back at the raging waterfall. A short while later, they all sat high above the gorge waiting for their adrenaline levels to fall back to normal before risking any further movement.

□ □ □ □ □

Isaiah pressed stop on the small video camera he'd been using to film the events on the river. He let out a long sigh and turned to see Kyle teary eyed and shaking.

"That should have worked," Kyle started mumbling. "The landslide should have worked. The bridge should have worked. I can't take this. I've never failed a mission before, but no matter what we do they make it through completely unscathed. No one is that lucky."

Isaiah awkwardly patted his hand on Kyle's shoulder, trying to think of some way to make him feel better. "I know!" he said with as much enthusiasm as he could muster, "let's take the night off. We'll go grab some pizza at Sylvia's. I'll even pay."

Kyle took a deep breath and looked at the distant group of students sitting on the top of the opposite bank. He wiped his eyes with his sleeve and his face took on a steely quality. "Isaiah," he said darkly, "I've made up my mind. Let's put the sign and takeout dock back and put a tracker on their van on our way out, and then we'll go have that pizza. I don't care what Mr. Curt wants, tomorrow we'll follow them on the road to their destination. When they arrive we'll be right behind them, and then we'll finish this. Bring your guns and explosives. This is personal."

□ □ □ □ □

Stenvick finished off a thermos of coffee, then rose from the log he was sitting on to address the students. "Kids, I don't know what happened back there. I've been down this river many times before, but today I must have missed something. I'm sorry that I led us all into this situation and I'm glad you're all safe."

198

"Dr. Stenvick," said Melody, "I was looking for the takeout too. We didn't pass any place that you'd be able to easily get a canoe out of the water."

"Hmm," Stenvick pondered, "I think I'll have some words with the folks back at the rental office. We could have been killed down there. This is nothing short of criminal negligence. This is unacceptable!"

"I am glad we were not," said Spencer. "I do not have answers yet. I do not want to die now. I have not done with reading. I have questions. My beliefs are insufficient."

Stenvick frowned. "Well, fortunately we've all been given more time to think about that. Speaking of thinking, I don't know what possessed me to go up this bank of the gorge. The other bank would have worked just as well, and now we're on the wrong side of the river from where we need to be." He pulled out a map of the area and located their position by the falls. "The quickest way would be to ford the river at the takeout spot, but I don't know how deep it is and we couldn't find it anyway so that doesn't appeal much to me."

Broadening his search on the map, Stenvick spotted a solution. "Ah, here we go. Four miles downstream after the falls, there's a hiking trail that crosses the river over a bridge. We'll have to find a route down the valley through the jungle, but that will be no problem if we just keep the water to our left. Then we can follow the trail for about eight miles back to the rental place."

"Dr. Stenvick," Stephanie asked warily as she eyed the position of the sun, "I don't think we have more than a couple hours or so until dark. Can we make it that far before we lose the light?"

Stenvick looked at his watch and considered her question. "You bring up a good point. I was hoping to fit in another hike once we returned the canoes, but I don't think this plan will leave enough time for that." Unaware of the shocked expressions around him he continued. "I suppose we'll have to make do without the hike. These delays are making it difficult to stay on schedule. Twenty-six hours is simply not enough time to fit in everything we need to do in a day. Let's get moving."

"Don't you mean twenty-four hours?" Derek asked curiously.

Stenvick looked at him with an odd expression and then seemed to recall something. "Oh yes, I remember the twenty-four hour day. It was impossibly short so I left that behind years ago. I almost forgot that people still follow that schedule."

Pulling his machete from a sleeve on the side of his pack, he started humming again and took off into the jungle. Derek and Ben looked at each other in confusion, but decided to let the matter drop.

□ □ □ □ □

As the medical team unloaded and setup their equipment, Berg briefed them on the blood work and testing he'd need them to do. Taking advantage of the diverse group of people who had gathered at the site, two nurses went around drawing blood samples and writing down the vital statistics of each person. The pathologists were given the information on the Amanitin molecule and tasked to find out how it was presenting itself in the blood or fatty tissues of their test group.

McConnell was busy preparing a large gas grill that he'd had one of the choppers fly in. Per his instructions, they had also brought several coolers and boxes packed with enough food to supply the small camp for several days. Once the grill came up to temperature, he hummed happily and started laying on shrimp kabobs and steaks, pleased to be in his element with something to do while the scientists worked. Megan walked over and eyed the sizzling meats. "I'm famished. I hope you're making enough to share."

"Certainly," McConnell replied. "I had lots of food delivered and I love cooking for large groups. Are you here to audit my sanitary code compliance?"

Megan laughed. "Not at all, that's a whole different department of the agency. I just wanted to make a special request on a steak."

"Sure," replied McConnell, "how do you like it done?"

"I want it cooked extra well. I can't stand to see any trace of pink inside. Cook it well, then more well."

McConnell gave a pained expression. "You're asking me to burn a steak? That will come out as tough as shoe leather. I don't know if I can do it, it would be like asking a Doctor to do harm to their patient. Why would you even want it that way?"

"Promise you won't laugh," Megan implored.

"I promise."

"Ok, I'll explain. When I was little, my father loved to grill steak. I would've enjoyed it done medium well, but he had to cook it rare every time. It was barely seared on the surface and completely raw inside. Actually, I'm pretty sure he forgot to even put it on the grill sometimes. It oozed blood all over the place and the texture was horrible. To this day, steak gives me nightmares and the only way I can handle eating it is if it's practically charred through."

"Megan, I'm sorry to hear that," McConnell responded. "If it means that much to you I'll burn your steak until it almost catches on fire."

Megan surprised him with a quick hug that felt like it would crack his ribs if she squeezed any harder. "Thanks for understanding. Most people just look at me like I'm crazy when I ask to have my steak cooked so well."

□ □ □ □ □

Kyle and Isaiah climbed into the Mercedes and confirmed that they were receiving the signal from the tracking bug they'd installed on the university van. "I better check in with Curt," Kyle said resignedly when he pulled out his phone and saw that he finally had a signal after being out of service on the river. "He's not going to be happy that we failed again."

"Why don't you just tell him we got them?" said Isaiah. "We'll gun them down tomorrow morning, and then go pick up our payment before he knows what happened. By the time they get the news we'll be on our way out of the country."

Agreeing with Isaiah's plan, Kyle's mood brightened considerably as he placed the call. Isaiah waited in anticipation of hearing the conversation. Curt would be annoyed that it took them so long, but the news of their supposed success would be a welcome change. Kyle ended the call before the voicemail picked up. "No answer. That's odd."

Isaiah shrugged. "Maybe he's out of service at the moment, or using the restroom or something. Try again in a few minutes."

Three minutes later Kyle dialed again with the same result. After half an hour with no response, they decided to give up for the time being and make the drive back to the city. They figured that Curt would surely contact them when he could, once he saw the missed calls.

Berg, Hargren, Katrina and Kevin gathered around the pathologists when they announced that the blood results were ready. Every sample they tested contained Amanitin D molecules attached to the lipids, although the concentration varied widely from person to person. Their results were consistent with the data being posted to the website by other scientists. As they concluded the meeting, Halloway sauntered over and informed Berg that he was needed for a conference to discuss their progress.

The video monitors showed several committees at the CIA, FDA and White House, as well as the President from his hotel room in Norway.

"Dr. Berg," said the gruff CIA director getting immediately to the point, "what's your status? Do we have an antidote?"

Berg swallowed and chose his words carefully. "We're making good progress on that. We've confirmed the presence of Hallita's toxin in crops around the world. And, we've confirmed that the toxin has built up in varying amounts in our bodies and is being stored just as Dr. Fiker said. Testing is ongoing on multiple fronts to find a method to neutralize it."

"So the answer is no," barked the director. "I knew we shouldn't leave this in civilian hands."

"Hold on," cut in President Savatsky. "Dr. Berg and the team he's put together are the most competent experts in this matter that we could hope to assemble. I'm confident of that and I trust that they're our best chance of solving this. Dr. Berg, based on your experiments so far, do you think you'll find the answer in time?"

Relieved by Savatsky's more amenable manner, Berg explained further. "Mr. President, I can't give you a guarantee, but I can promise you that we're working as hard as possible to reach our goal. My team has found many ways to break down the molecule. We can make it detach from the fats and we can break it down into harmless constituents, but doing so in a manner safe to our bodies is the hard part. None of the methods that have worked in the lab would be survivable, or we'd be trading one toxin for another that's just as fatal if not more so. However, we still have many promising ideas to try."

When Berg had finished, Savatsky held up his hand to prevent any discussion. "Thank you, Dr. Berg. I know you're busy so we won't take up any more of your time. Keep working and we'll check in on your progress later. I'm making plans with the CIA and FDA for how we'll handle this if you succeed, and also for the possibility that you don't. For now, I'm hopeful and you have my complete support."

Berg let out the breath he'd been holding once the screen went black. Halloway gave him a pat on the back. "Relax, you handled that well."

"I sure hope so," Berg replied.

McConnell wandered around the lab after the conference, looking at the various test plants. He read the label on a pallet of mushrooms. "*Amanita phalloides* (Death Cap)." "*So these little buggers are what this whole thing is all about,*" he thought as he eyed the harmless looking fungi. "*I wonder what they taste like.*" A humorous thought suddenly hit him. Picking up the tray and making sure the label was facing out, he carried it over to Berg. "Gary, would you mind if I use these in a chicken and mushroom dish? It doesn't look like anyone else needs them."

Berg was deep in thought but looked up to see McConnell holding the tray of Death Caps. "Bill, no!" he burst out in alarm. "Those are fatally poisonous. What are you thinking?"

McConnell laughed. "I'm just kidding. I thought we could use a little humor to liven up the mood around here. Imagine the headline; 'Mycologist dies from eating mushroom while attempting to save the world from it.' Wouldn't that be ironic?"

Berg stared at him with a stunned expression on his face.

"Come on, Gary, it's a joke," McConnell said uncertainly as his laughter died off. "Sorry, I'll just put these back and leave you to your work."

Berg snapped out of his thoughts. "Bill, that's it! We have to test!" He quickly called everyone together to explain. "Bill just reminded me of something," he said once they had all gathered. "When I was very young my grandparents would take me with them to go searching for wild mushrooms to eat. They had many friends who would join them, including this one old man who would collect Death Caps and put them in his basket. My grandfather told me to never touch those mushrooms and that the old man was mad to eat such poisonous things, and that I should stay away from him."

Berg considered for a moment. "That must have been at least thirty years ago. I nearly forgot. Anyway, one day when my grandparents were busy I approached the old man and asked him why he ate poisonous mushrooms. He said he liked the taste, and then he bent down and whispered to me. 'Can you keep a secret?' he asked me. I said yes. Then he told me about how he could eat as many Death Caps as he wanted as long as he drank a can of cola at the same time. He took a can from his bag and opened it, then took a big sip before popping a mushroom in his mouth and eating it. I was amazed and frightened and ran back to my grandparents, but I saw him a few more times at the mushroom hunts. He would smile and give me a knowing look to remind me to keep his secret safe."

"Do you think he was telling the truth?" asked Hargren.

"I can't say for sure," Berg replied. "It was a long time ago and he certainly could have been pulling my leg, but my grandparents said he only collected Death Caps and he pulled the mushroom that he ate right from his basket. As unlikely as it seems, I'd like to test his claim to see if there was any truth to it."

Kevin spoke excitedly. "There's lots of cola in that vending machine you two broke. We can test it right now."

The last traces of the sun were disappearing below the horizon as Stenvick chopped his way through the dense jungle. He followed the slope of the land downward as it dropped after the waterfall to eventually level out with the river. By his estimation they had made it approximately halfway to the intersection with the trail that would lead

204

them to the bridge. "It will be dark soon," he announced. "If you brought a flashlight or headlamp, this would be a good time to get it out."

The group stopped and several students put their packs down to retrieve small flashlights. Stenvick removed most of the contents of the main compartment of his bag until he reached something at the very bottom. "I knew I'd need this eventually," he said as he pulled a battered green metal case from the bag and set it on the ground. He unlatched the lid and flipped it open to reveal an old Coleman camping lantern safely nestled in protective padding. Reaching into the bag again he also produced several bottles of fuel.

"I got this for Christmas when I was a boy," Stenvick explained as he filled the tank from one of the bottles. "I take it with me on every hike, as well as enough fuel to last two days for occasions such as this." He lit the wick and the flame burst to life, sending a warm glow over their surroundings. "Also, the fuel is really handy for starting camp fires with wet wood. You just have to make sure to keep a safe distance when you light it!"

The professor paused and looked thoughtfully at the students surrounding him. The soft glow of the lantern cast flickering shadows over their tired faces and he could see that the stress of the day's events had caught up to them. "Let's take a break for a few minutes," he said, setting the lantern on the ground and sitting cross-legged against his pack. "You know, we've run into a number of close calls on this trip. It seems like misfortune has been following us everywhere we go."

"Amen to that," cut in Geraldo.

Heads nodded amidst murmurs of agreement from the circle of students.

"Many people would say we've been very lucky," continued Stenvick. "Despite everything that's happened we're all still together and none of us have been injured. It's not hard to imagine that our situation could be much different right now. I'd just like to take a moment to reflect on that and thank God for His protection over us in the midst of disaster. Even though we can't see them, I'm certain His angels have been working overtime watching out for us these last few days."

Geraldo spoke from across the circle. "Do you really believe that? I mean about the angels and God and all that? You wouldn't be saying the same things if one of us had been hurt, or killed."

"Yes, Geraldo, I do. I don't expect God to keep me or any of you safe from all danger, but I've prayed for the safety of our group every day. I've done what I can to watch out for us, but I know that we wouldn't have made it through some of those situations on our strength alone. I've been around a lot of years and I've felt God's hand of protection many times. I don't know what tomorrow may bring, but I put my trust in Him and I'll praise Him for as many more days as He decides to give me. I don't want to see any of you hurt, and I'm thankful that you haven't been."

"But what if one of us fell off a cliff and died tomorrow?" Geraldo pressed him. "How could you be thankful then?"

Melody spoke up before Stenvick had a chance to respond. "Everyone dies, Geraldo. People have accidents every day. That doesn't mean God abandoned them. No one can live forever. If I die tomorrow I know what's next for me. I'm not worried about it. I'd be with Jesus and I know that Dr. Stenvick and everyone else could rejoice about that even while they're sad that I'm gone. But, Geraldo, if you died tomorrow it would be a different story. Where would you be going? You can't just 'pick a religion' when you reach the gates of heaven."

"Well," said Stenvick, "there's some food for thought. Melody is right, Geraldo. I can praise God no matter what happens. Injury and death are just part of life. I don't want anything bad to happen to any of us, but bad things are unavoidable and that's just reality. It's up to us to decide how we're going to react."

"Dr. Stenvick is right," Derek chimed in, "and he's not the only one that's been praying for our group."

Geraldo looked to Derek and then around the circle at the nods of agreement. "What, are you all in on this or something?"

"I am not in on it," said Spencer, "but I want to find out what it is."

The conversation continued for a few more minutes until Stenvick stood and announced that they needed to get moving. He packed everything back in his bag and started off again, chopping methodically at the vegetation and holding the lantern high to light the way.

Chapter 28

Berg checked in with the other scientists and was disappointed to find that none of their experiments had shown any promise yet. He kept the cola idea to himself until they'd had a chance to try it first at the INIAS lab, not wanting to look foolish or desperate to his colleagues. Hargren and the students were working to setup multiple tests to see if the cola had any effect on the toxin, but even with all the technology at their disposal they would still have to be patient until the results could be analyzed.

"It must do something," Kevin observed as he watched one of the test tubes of concentrated Amanitin D that they'd found in the lab. They'd prepared several small samples and added cola in different ratios. Each tube bubbled and fizzed for several minutes before the liquid stilled.

"How could it?" asked Katrina. "It's just a soda. That old guy must have been off his rocker or just playing a trick on Dr. Berg. Even with the best medicine available, people are still lucky to survive eating a Death Cap."

"We'll just have to wait and see," responded Kevin with a hopeful tone. "I like cola, and I'd certainly drink more if I knew it might save my life."

Kyle tried dialing Curt again as he sat across from Isaiah waiting for their pizza at Sylvia's. Despite several attempts, they'd still been unable to reach him and were starting to worry. Isaiah dipped a rye stick in a creamy cheese and herb sauce and twirled it slowly to stop any drips. "I can think of three possibilities. He lost the phone, he's dead or he's cut off communication and has ordered a hit on us so we won't be a liability. You have to admit we haven't been very successful so they might look for other options."

"That possibility has certainly been on my mind," Kyle agreed. "Until we hear otherwise, I think it's safest for us to assume the worst. Hey, did you ever check our car for bugs? Curt lent it to us from INIAS, so I wouldn't be at all surprised if he's been monitoring our movements and conversation."

"I'll do that right after dinner," Isaiah mumbled through a mouthful of breadstick. "I should've thought of that earlier."

Kyle thought for a moment. "Curt doesn't know where the students are going tomorrow. We never talked about the location while we were in the vehicle, so even if there is a bug we can pull it off now and take care of them tomorrow, and then we'll blow up the Mercedes and leave the country."

"I like that idea," said Isaiah, "although I could really use the money."

"We can't think about that now," Kyle responded. "At least we have another job lined up after this. Sometimes the smart thing to do is to cut your losses and disappear if you want to stay alive in this business."

They halted the conversation as the waitress arrived with the pizza and placed it on the table. After taking in the mouthwatering smell of the steam rising off the surface, they attacked it voraciously. They'd ordered the special of the day which was an extra-large pizza loaded with double portions of bratwurst, kielbasa, sausage and potato on a golden egg crust with a hearty garlic cream sauce and mounds of mozzarella and goat cheese melted over the top.

"Wow, this is good," Kyle said before taking another large bite.

Isaiah nodded his head and grunted in agreement.

□ □ □ □ □

The weary group of students trudged behind Stenvick into the grounds of the canoe rental place, exhausted after the twelve mile hike from the waterfall and anxious for the chance to finally sit and relax during the trip home in the van. A light was on in the office and one of the employees stepped out to meet them as they approached. Stenvick walked up to the man and an argument soon followed, which Michelle translated for the students.

"Dr. Stenvick is saying there was no sign for the dock. The man is saying it's clearly marked, and is asking where our canoes are. Stenvick says they went over the falls. The man says we'll have to pay to replace them. Stenvick says it's not our fault, we couldn't find the dock, and they should have a warning sign before the falls. The man says they do. Stenvick says they don't. The man says if we had paid for a guide we wouldn't have had this problem. Stenvick says we shouldn't need a guide to find a dock that he's used many times before."

The argument continued back and forth until the man from the office took a swing at Stenvick, which the professor caught in his palm inches in front of his nose. A look of shock came over the burly man's face as his blow was stopped so easily by the diminutive tourist. Despite being half the size of his attacker, Stenvick maintained his grip, pressing his thumb into a pressure point and bending back the man's wrist. The man grimaced in pain as he was forced to a kneeling position on the ground. Stenvick shouted something in Spanish and the man nodded his head, at which point Stenvick let go.

"Dr. Stenvick threatened to sue since we were nearly killed due to their negligence," Michelle explained. "The guy says he's sorry, and asks that we please don't call the police. He'll go inspect the signs tomorrow morning. He apologizes for the inconvenience and says to forget about the canoes."

□ □ □ □ □

Everyone gathered around the computer in the INIAS lab as Hargren pulled up the results of their tests with the cola. "This is very interesting," he began. "It seems that the cola reacts with the Amanitin D molecule and alters the structure, possibly by breaking some of the bonds. However, it only has this effect in the direct test tube reactions

211

with the concentrated toxin and the pureed plant matter. I see no indication of any changes in the blood samples. The lipid bonds must be too strong."

"Fascinating," observed Berg. "So if I understand correctly, the Amanitin D molecule is resistant to this reaction once it's stored in the fats, but before that it's vulnerable?"

"Yes," Hargren confirmed.

"Then the old guy may have been telling the truth," said Kevin. "Drinking the cola at the same time would mix it with the mushrooms and alter the toxin before it can be absorbed."

"Maybe so," agreed Berg, "but Amanitin D is not the only toxin found in the Death Caps. We don't know what effect the cola would have on the others, if any."

Katrina spoke up. "But Amanitin D is the only toxin Hallita is using in the food. The others don't matter for our purposes. If the cola alters the structure of the molecule then maybe it's no longer toxic and is safe to eat. Even if we can't get rid of the poison in our bodies, we might be able to stabilize the situation if we can prevent any more from building up."

Berg looked troubled. "That's a possibility, but there's no way for us to prove it quickly. We'd need to run animal tests to monitor the levels in the blood, and then confirm any results with human trials. That could take months."

"How quickly does Death Cap poisoning show symptoms?" Katrina asked.

"Well," said Berg, "you'd start seeing symptoms in a few hours if you ate a couple mushrooms, but that would be due to the other forms of Amanitin toxins. Amanitin D is naturally present in very small amounts. The long term buildup to the tipping point is what gives it its potency, but it would be impossible to eat enough Death Caps to get a sufficient dose before the other toxins would kill you. Fiker worked this out so that when the tipping point is reached, the molecules break from the fats and enter the blood stream all at once. It would be like taking one of those test tubes of concentrate directly. They contain the equivalent of tens of thousands of Death Caps. According to Fiker, human test subjects died within an hour of exposure."

"Dr. Berg," Halloway called from the other side of the room, "It's time for your 11:00 PM conference."

"Ok," said Berg as he walked over to have a seat at the monitors. The screens went live and showed the same board rooms as before.

"How's it going, Dr. Berg?" President Savatsky inquired.

"Sir, we don't have a cure, but we might have a solution that will buy us sufficient time to find one." Berg felt his nerves go on edge as all eyes around the conference tables focused on him expectantly.

"Please explain," Savatsky prodded.

"Well, we followed a, um, lead, and our tests have confirmed that the toxin is altered when mixed with cola."

"You mean the soft drink?" bellowed the CIA director.

"Yes, sir," Berg replied. "We have some evidence to show that it neutralizes the toxicity of the molecule, possibly rendering it safe to eat, but without more time to run trials I can't guarantee that."

"How long will the trials take?" demanded the CIA man.

"Probably several months," admitted Berg.

"What's your gut feeling?" Savatsky asked. "Do you think it will work?"

Berg thought for a few moments. "My opinion is that it's more likely to than not."

"Mr. President," barked the CIA director, "Dr. Fiker has checked in to his hotel and our team is in place waiting for orders. If Berg here says it will work let's move in and take Fiker down."

"No," Berg countered sternly, cutting off the director and surprising everyone on the call. "I'm hopeful of this solution's effectiveness, but that's no guarantee and at the moment Fiker is the only one with an antidote. If you attempt to take him out now, he or his cohorts might destroy the whole program and we'll be in serious trouble. Even if we find the cure, how can we convince the world that they need to take it?"

"Hold on folks," said Savatsky as the red faced CIA director was about to explode in anger. "Dr. Berg, your solution might work but there's no way to know for sure until well after Fiker gives his speech, correct?"

"Correct," confirmed Berg.

"And what about the rest of your team, have they found any other possibilities?"

Berg shook his head and explained that they had not.

"This is a difficult decision," stated Savatsky, "but the lives and wellbeing of the American people are my responsibility. I can't approve any action against Fiker that could endanger our access to the antidote without concrete proof that we don't need it."

Silence fell over everyone on the conference as the implications of the President's words sunk in. Katrina came up behind Berg drinking from a bottle of cola and stood by his shoulder. "Dr. Berg," she said hesitantly, "we need successful human trials before we can say for sure that the cola makes the toxin safe, right?"

"Yes," Berg responded sadly.

Katrina continued. "And a vial of Amanitin D would cause certain death within an hour?"

Berg nodded his head. "Yes. Why are you bringing this up?"

Katrina faced the monitor. "Mr. President, you'll have your proof in an hour."

Before anyone could react, Katrina produced a vial of the toxin she'd been hiding behind her back, raised it to her lips and downed it in one large gulp, then chugged the rest of the bottle of cola.

"No!" Kevin screamed when he saw what she did. He rushed to her, followed closely by Hargren and the others in the lab.

"What was that?" Savatsky asked. "What did she drink?"

"Amanitin D," stammered Berg in a voice barely above a whisper. He spun around to face Katrina. "Katrina, what have you done?"

Katrina's face had gone pale and her voice was shaking with fear as she responded. "We have to know for sure. This is the only way."

"Why, Katrina?" Kevin cried. "You could die... and I can't bear the thought of losing you."

"You what?" Katrina asked in confusion.

"Dr. Berg," Savatsky interrupted from the video screen, "will this young lady prove if your solution is effective?"

Berg turned to the screen, having forgotten all about the video conference. "Yes, sir. We'll know within the hour."

Hargren and Kevin hurried Katrina over to a chair and started checking her temperature and pulse.

"We'll wait one hour," said Savatsky. "Good luck, Dr. Berg. Our prayers are with that young woman."

"Her name is Katrina," Berg snapped, his face revealing a jumble of emotions.

Berg ended the call and rushed over to join the others by Katrina. Megan and McConnell burst into the lab with the medical team following close behind. Katrina's face had grown very pale and beads of sweat were forming all over her skin. Without warning, she gasped and clutched her hands to her stomach, then doubled over screaming. Kevin caught her as she fell from the chair and lowered her gently to the floor, where she began convulsing violently.

▢ ▢ ▢ ▢ ▢

Spencer sat in the front of the van again for the ride back to the university. "Dr. Stenvick," he began, "I got to read some of that Bible. I have questions."

"That's great," replied the professor, "but when did you get to do that? We've been busy all day."

"I did it when we walked in the jungle. I use my headlight to see and tell Geraldo to watch out for roots to trip on. Why did people kill Jesus? He was a nice guy."

Stenvick sighed. "That's a good question, Spencer. You see, Jesus spoke the truth everywhere He went, and that made a lot of people angry. The religious leaders of the day had become corrupt and were putting themselves and their own rules before God. Jesus called them on it and it made them furious. They thought getting rid of Him would take care of the problems He was causing them. They didn't want to deal with their guilt and admit they were wrong, so they killed Him."

"I think that is sad," said Spencer. "I thought telling truth is the right thing."

"It is," Stenvick agreed, "but it's not always the popular thing to do, especially when people don't want to hear it because they're doing something wrong."

Spencer spoke again after a moment. "Is it true that Jesus died and then came back?"

"Yes," said Stenvick. "I've studied the historical evidence, and there's no doubt about it."

"And we can live forever if we believe Him?" Spencer queried.

"Yes," Stenvick replied. "God's standard of holiness is absolute perfection. It's obvious we could never live a good enough life to earn our way to heaven. It's such a relief to know that Jesus took care of that for us. It's like a huge weight has been lifted right off my shoulders."

Spencer laughed. "That is why you pack so much in your bag!"

Stenvick chuckled heartily. "That's a different matter, but good observation. My faith is the reason for my joy in life. It's why I'm so excited to get up every day and go explore the wonderful world God created."

"I like that," Spencer said excitedly. "I wanted to know why you can be so happy. Geraldo says it is because of all that coffee you drink, but I knew it must be a different reason."

Stenvick smiled as he took a sip from his thermos. "I like my coffee well enough, but it's just a drink. No amount of caffeine could give me the joy I've found in Jesus."

"Good," said Spencer with relief. "I like tea better."

The conversation continued until Stenvick pulled to the curb in front of the dorm. As the interior lights blinked on, the students awoke and reluctantly roused their sore and tired bodies to unload.

"What time is it?" asked Jennifer.

"Almost 11:30," responded Stenvick. "All of you should get to bed right away. We have to be up bright and early tomorrow to head to the turtle reserve."

The students groaned as they marched into the dorm. Within minutes most of them were sprawled on their bunks fast asleep.

It had been only a few minutes, but it felt like an eternity to those surrounding Katrina and trying their best to find some way to help her. Her convulsions slowed and gradually lost intensity until she lay shuddering and drenched in sweat. "Her pulse is 220," warned one of the nurses.

"Is there anything we can do?" Kevin pleaded.

Suddenly Katrina's eyes opened wide and she took a quick gasp of air before a torrent of foamy bubbles erupted from her mouth like soda spraying from a bottle that had been shaken. When it ended she coughed and fought for breath, then collapsed, panting heavily.

"Are you ok?" Kevin asked cautiously after a minute had passed. In response, Katrina let out a loud burp and then asked in a weak voice for him to help her sit up. Hargren and Kevin gently raised her to a sitting position. Her clothing was soaking wet and her skin was cold and clammy to the touch. The nurse checked her temperature, pulse and blood pressure again. As the minutes passed, her vital signs began to fall back closer to normal levels.

"Help me back on the chair," Katrina whispered softly. She sat as though in a daze, but the color started to slowly come back to her face and her breathing grew stronger and steadier. After a little while, the nurse said her vitals were back to normal. Katrina asked for a drink and eagerly sipped at the cup of water one of the medical technicians handed her, and then as if awakening from sleep she looked around at the crowd of people surrounding her with confusion evident on her face. "What happened?"

"You drank a vial of the toxin," said Berg.

"I know that," Katrina interrupted. "I mean, what happened after that? I started to feel sick and I think I fell, and now you're all staring at me."

"Trust me, you don't want to know," Hargren answered. "How are you feeling?"

Katrina paused to consider his question. "I feel like I've been beat up and drowned, but ok other than that I suppose. And I'm hungry."

"You had quite a reaction to the toxin," explained Berg as he checked his watch, "but if you keep improving over the next thirty minutes I'd say we've found our solution."

Dr. Fiker sat alone for breakfast at a small table in the café of his hotel in Oslo. His private jet had landed a couple hours earlier and the limousine he'd ordered had been waiting to pick him up. Having slept on the plane, he didn't even touch the bed when he entered his suite. He'd quickly showered and put on a fresh suit before leaving again. He closed the leather binder containing the speech he was finalizing as the waiter approached.

"Sir, have you decided what you would like?" the waiter asked in perfect English with a crisp Norwegian accent.

"Yes," Fiker replied slowly as he picked up the menu. "I would like four organic eggs scrambled with freshly churned butter and dill picked this morning. Toast six pieces of sourdough bread to a golden brown color and drizzle butter and honey over them. Also, I want a glass of freshly squeezed orange juice and a plate of thinly sliced strawberries dusted with sugar."

"Those are not among our menu selections," the waiter replied, uncertain of whether Fiker was joking or not. Seeing the intense look on Fiker's face he conceded, "But for you we can put that together, and can I get you any coffee or tea?"

"Ah yes," Fiker exclaimed. "I nearly forgot." He picked up a leather briefcase from the floor next to his chair and laid it on the table, opening the lid to reveal several bags of coffee beans with labels in Spanish, as well as some related supplies. He set a digital food scale on the table and placed a paper cup on it, calibrated the empty weight to zero, and then carefully measured out the beans and handed the cup to the waiter. "Grind these beans to international standard size four, and then brew them in twelve and a half ounces of bottled spring water at ninety five degrees Celsius. Make sure to use a new gold plated filter from an unopened box."

"Of course, sir," the waiter replied. "And how do you take your coffee?"

"Serve it in a large stoneware mug," Fiker instructed, "preferably brown or green. Mix six ounces of coffee with twelve grams of sugar and twenty nine milliliters of hazelnut flavored organic non-dairy creamer. Cover the surface completely with miniature marshmallows, and then top it with freshly whipped cream dusted with cinnamon and nutmeg. Bring out a soup spoon with it."

"As you wish," said the waiter. "Will that be all?"

"Yes," Fiker replied as he put away his coffee supplies and set the briefcase back under the table.

As the waiter left, Fiker opened the binder and continued checking over his speech. Concern plagued the back of his mind since he'd not been able to contact Curt at the facility, but he rationalized that the man would be quite busy handling the move. Dr. Lake had informed him that the distribution facility in San José was ready to go and they were just awaiting his signal to bring the systems online. Fiker was excited. Years of painstaking work had gone into preparing for this day, and now there were mere hours to go until he would usher in an age of peace such as the world had never known. He chuckled at the thought that perhaps he'd be back in this same place next year to receive the prize a second time.

□ □ □ □ □

As the hour following Katrina's ingestion of the Amanitin D vial drew to a close, it was clear that she was going to be fine. Aside from a bad case of hiccups, she'd shown no further reactions to the toxin and was feeling much herself again after having something to eat. One of the nurses took a sample of her blood and gave it to the pathologist, who ran a full battery of tests and found no differences compared to her previous sample.

Berg and Hargren went around to everyone who had been tested and asked about their dietary habits and level of cola consumption. They'd just finished entering the data in a spreadsheet along with the blood toxin levels when Halloway announced that the President was on the line. Berg rose from his seat but gave one more instruction before leaving. "Paul, see if there are any trends in the data. If you find anything interesting bring it over right away. Katrina, come with me." Seconds later they stood in front of the screen and greeted Savatsky and the familiar set of committees.

"Katrina, how are you?" the President inquired with genuine concern showing in his expression.

"It worked!" she declared. "They just checked a few minutes ago and I'm ok."

Savatsky wiped the sweat from his brow as relief washed over his complexion. "I'm glad to hear that. I've been worried sick for the past hour wondering what would happen to you. You're a brave young woman, and though I would never have given you permission to do what you did, on behalf of all of us I'd like to say thank you. Our country, and the world for that matter, is in your debt."

Not one for sentiment, the CIA director cut straight to the point. "Dr. Berg, is this a solution or a lucky stunt? Do we still need the antidote?"

The head of the FDA also spoke up. "I agree. The girl appears to be fine at the moment, but do we have any proof that drinking cola will have any long term effect on the toxin buildup?"

"Yes!" Hargren shouted from across the room. Seconds later he appeared next to Berg with a printout. "I just charted the results of our blood tests and the dietary survey of the people here with us," Hargren explained. "There's a direct relationship between cola consumption and toxin level. Those of us who drink it rarely or never have the highest toxin concentrations, while those who drink it often have the lowest. One of the computer programmers here insisted that he's been drinking only cola since he was in college. Apparently he doesn't like water. The amazing thing is that his blood toxin levels are in the range of statistical insignificance!"

"What's the size of your sample population?" asked the FDA director.

"Thirty three of us," Hargren replied.

"Is the data consistent? Are there any outliers or aberrant values?" the director asked.

Hargren shook his head. "No, it's a clean trend. Everyone fit the curve."

"That's incredible," stated the director. "Mr. President, I think we're good to go. As the head of the FDA I never imagined that I'd be recommending soft drinks as an essential part of the daily diet, but it looks like we'll need to do that until a long term solution is found. Maybe we can increase our promotion of diet, exercise and proper dental care at the same time."

"This is good news," Savatsky concluded. "Dr. Berg, you and your team have exceeded expectations. Everyone, we'll proceed with plan A so start your preparations. Dr. Berg, get some rest if you can. The Nobel ceremony will be broadcast live from Oslo starting at noon their time, which will be five in the morning where you are. I'll need you to be refreshed and ready during the acceptance speech and standing by at the phone. I have a plan and I'll need to coordinate with the Nobel committee. Good night for now, we have to get to work."

Berg sat staring at the blank screens in disbelief. "I can't believe it, Paul," he said to Hargren. "We've had some of the brightest scientists in the world working on this problem, but the solution came from a crazy old mushroom hunter."

Hargren chuckled. "What was that proverb you always used to share in Mycology? There are no moldy mushroom hunters, or, hunters shouldn't hold mushrooms, I can't remember."

Berg recited the phrase, "there are old mushroom hunters and there are bold mushroom hunters, but there are no old bold mushroom hunters. I guess we've found an exception."

Berg put out a notice on the website that they'd found a temporary solution to the problem. He thanked everyone for their efforts and promised that details would follow soon. Now that there was no longer pressing work to do, the tiredness that had been building up over the last few days suddenly weighed on him. With a big yawn, he trudged over to one of the cots that had been brought in and laid down to catch a few hours of sleep. Hargren took a cot near him a minute later and was quickly dozing off.

Kevin and Katrina sat on the grass behind the lab building looking up at the stars. The sky was clear and with the lights in the CIA camp dimmed, the view was impressive. "Did you mean what you said earlier?" Katrina asked after they'd sat in silence for a few minutes.

"What do you mean?" Kevin asked hesitantly.

"Right after I drank the toxin, you said you couldn't bear the thought of losing me. Did you mean that?"

Kevin was silent for a moment, trying to find the right words. "Yes," he finally stated, then quickly realized that she would want more of an explanation.

"We've known each other for quite a while now," Kevin continued. "I've always felt so comfortable talking to you, kidding around with you; you've been a great friend. I've been too shy to say anything for a while because I didn't want to make things awkward between us, but when I saw you take that poison it felt like my heart was being ripped out of my chest. You were standing there holding the empty vial and there was nothing I could do. The truth is, Katrina, I couldn't bear the thought of losing you then, and I can't imagine life without you. I guess what I'm trying to say is that I love you."

Katrina sat next to him very still and quiet as silence fell between them. Kevin's feelings had been obvious to her ever since they first met when they were assigned as lab partners in Organic Chemistry. "I…" she stammered, tears welling up in her eyes. "I know. I've known for a long time, and I've been waiting for you to put it into words." Taking his hand in hers she continued. "You can't imagine how hard it was for me to drink that toxin. I didn't want to die and I was scared out of my wits, but I had to do it. I couldn't live with myself if I backed out after the idea came to me. I didn't want to hurt you, and I knew I would if things went the other way, but I had to take the chance. I hope you can understand."

Katrina sniffled and wiped her tears on her sleeve as the emotions she'd been holding back flooded to the surface. Kevin wrapped an arm around her shoulder and pulled her next to him. "I understand," he said gently, "and that's why you're so special to me."

Katrina cried for a few minutes as she leaned into him and they sat in silence. "I can't imagine life without you either," she finally said, "and I love you too."

Chapter 29

Berg woke from a fitful sleep to find Halloway gently shaking him on the shoulder.

"Dr. Berg, the Nobel ceremony is underway. Dr. Fiker will be speaking live in fifteen minutes so get ready to watch."

Berg rubbed his eyes and yawned, then pushed himself off the cot and plodded to the restroom. When he returned, the room was buzzing as people gathered around the video screens. They sipped coffee while eating sausage and egg breakfast sandwiches that McConnell had prepared. Halloway explained that the video feed being broadcast to the major news networks was on the left hand screen, and the secure satellite transmission from the CIA was on the right.

The guests in the auditorium rose to their feet and applauded as the Nobel Committee chairman completed his remarks and welcomed Dr. Fiker to the podium. Fiker smiled broadly as he gazed out over the audience, and then motioned for everyone to take their seats. The applause and conversation died away until the energy of anticipation was palpable in the room as the guests eagerly waited for the speech to begin.

"I am greatly honored, yet humbled to be standing here before you today," Fiker began with a measured and dignified air. "I have asked myself; what have I done to deserve such recognition? How have my actions bolstered the cause of peace? Is the world a better place because of anything I have accomplished? Some say that famine is no more thanks to the agricultural advances I have introduced through Hallita. It is true that food resources are plentiful like never before, yet people still go hungry."

"I cannot help but feel that I am not deserving of this prize of peace. I look at the world today and I see wars between nations, conflicts between peoples and corruption in governments. None of these things have changed as a result of my work. When I launched Hallita it was with an ideal in mind of a world where every man, woman and child had plenty to eat. No one would go hungry and no one would have to fight over scarce resources. I am saddened that despite all I have accomplished, that ideal has not become the reality I had hoped for."

"This question has plagued me for many years; what more can I do? Ladies and gentlemen, I have found the answer to that question and will share it with you today. I have-"

The news feed suddenly went black, and then to static for a few seconds before the desk anchor appeared on the air and announced that they seemed to be having technical difficulties and would resume the broadcast as soon as possible. Berg and the rest of the group in the lab focused their attention on the screen with the CIA feed which was still coming through.

"-A world with no more wars," Fiker was saying. "I have found a way to ensure that nations will settle their disputes through peaceful diplomacy, and governments will work solely for the good of their people." Fiker paused for effect as whispered murmurs passed through the auditorium. "Allow me to explain. It took many years, but our world gradually transitioned to an agricultural model where Hallita now controls the production and distribution of nearly all seed that is planted. Farmers have come to depend on our products, and regulators ceased their oversight long ago."

"I had an epiphany. There is an old proverb that says the way to a man's heart is through his stomach. If that is true, then you can control a man's actions by controlling what he eats, and that is what I have done. You have all been eating my crops for many years. I control those crops, and what is in them. Unbeknownst to you all, you have been ingesting a toxin that I created." Fiker paused and raised his hands for silence as the crowd began to stir and grumble. "Please, hear me out before you pass judgment."

"As I said, you have been eating a toxin. It grows in the crops, finds its way into your food and builds up in your bodies over time. It…" Fiker stopped as he noticed everyone in the audience turning their heads away from him and to the sides of the stage. Turning around to see what had caught their attention, he saw the large CIA logo on the projection screens. Soon the logo disappeared and was replaced by a live video image.

"Berg!" Fiker cried out in shock when he saw the professor smiling at him from the screen.

"Dr. Fiker," a voice boomed over the audio system in the room, though it was not from Berg.

Fiker looked in every direction until spotting a figure walking down the aisle and waving his hand. Squinting to make out the face, he realized it was President Savatsky. "What's going on?" Fiker asked indignantly. "Don't come any closer or I'll destroy the whole system and the antidote will be gone."

Savatsky paused as Fiker drew a small box from his pocket and held it up for everyone to see. "I wouldn't do that if I were you," Savatsky warned. "The situation is not as you think." Slowly turning and facing each way, he addressed the stunned audience. "Ladies and gentlemen, allow me to introduce Dr. Gary Berg of Harrisville University. Dr. Berg, would you please explain what is going on?"

Berg gave a brief summary highlighting the events that had led up to his arrival at the INIAS lab, then explained his research with the Amanitin D molecule and the work his team had accomplished over the last few hours to find a solution to Fiker's toxin.

When Berg related how Katrina had risked her life to prove the effectiveness of the cola, Fiker burst out that that couldn't be possible. His face red with rage, he hardly noticed as government agents surrounded him, confiscated the transmitter and cuffed him. They seated him in a chair near the podium and guarded him at gunpoint as Savatsky took the stage.

□ □ □ □ □

225

The television in the UCR cafeteria was tuned to the Nobel broadcast as Stenvick and the students were eating their breakfast. Two news anchors were discussing the problem with the live signal from Norway and rehashing what everyone already knew in order to fill the time. One of them paused as they listened to an instruction through their earpiece, and then announced that they would be returning momentarily to Oslo for a special address from the President.

"Look, that's President Savatsky," Geraldo stated, drawing everyone's attention to the television. The screen switched to a view of Savatsky at the podium with an angry Dr. Fiker seated under guard nearby.

"This can't be good," Ben observed.

Spencer shuffled over to the television and reached up to adjust the volume so they could hear what was being said. A Secret Service agent standing by Savatsky leaned over to whisper something in his ear, at which point the President nodded and faced the camera.

"Greetings," Savatsky began, his rich baritone voice ringing through the auditorium. He stood with a characteristically straight and distinguished posture. His keen eyes, mottled salt and pepper beard and kind face gave a visceral portrayal of his deep wisdom and character. Few men could match the air of sophistication and intellect that he possessed even in the most casual settings. "I ask that our television viewers please accept my apologies for cutting the transmission. Also I would like to express my thanks to the organizers of this event for their cooperation in this delicate matter. It is with profound sadness and a heavy heart that I address you today. Those of us in this room and all of you viewers elsewhere have come together to witness and celebrate the bestowing of a great honor, the Nobel Peace Prize. This ceremony is a time to recognize the achievements of an individual who has made a positive contribution, and who has shown us a glimpse of the best parts of humanity in a world that so often brings out the worst."

"This man seated before you, Dr. Nathan Fiker, appeared to be such an individual. However, events have unfolded over the last few days that have shown him to be otherwise, culminating in his own admission before the audience in this room of a diabolical plan to impose a reign of terror on us all. I must be clear that the situation is now under control and there is no cause for panic. Yet, there are certain things that require explanation and action on the part of us all."

"I am fully aware that as the President of the United States, I do not retain the trust or good will of all people. That is why it was necessary to wait for this moment to address you, when the leaders of the world were gathered here to witness today's proceedings together. They can all attest to the truth of what I say, and we will all need to cooperate to work through the challenges before us. You see, Dr. Fiker has been working through Hallita for many years to tamper with the food crops we all depend on. His motivations were noble, but his methods unconscionable. In order to better explain, I would like to introduce one of the people responsible for bringing this scheme to light, Dr. Gary Berg."

Chapter 30

The group in the UCR cafeteria stared in disbelief when they saw Berg on the video feed from the INIAS lab, surrounded by Kevin, Katrina, Hargren and many other people. Berg began to speak after a short pause. He provided a brief overview of how he had come to Costa Rica on Hargren's bequest and of the events that had transpired since. Leaving out some of the more alarming details, he proceeded to explain how the food they all ate would eventually cause a fatal sickness if left unchecked. Steps would have to be taken to introduce new crops, but in the meantime drinking cola with each meal would delay the effects until they could research a more permanent fix.

When Berg was finished, President Savatsky explained that Hallita had built facilities worldwide intended to act as distribution centers for an antidote to the toxic substance in the food. As Berg and a small army of scientists raced to find a solution to the problem, he had been coordinating with the CIA, FDA and intelligence agencies the world over. Hallita's facilities were seized the moment the television transmission of Fiker's speech was cut, and were now being searched for any information that could prove useful in undoing the disaster Fiker had brought about. Also, he had spoken with the management at several cola manufacturers and they were taking immediate action to ramp up production worldwide.

President Savatsky was silent for a few moments, then with emotion evident in his voice he continued. "Dr. Fiker wanted a world free of war, and free of conflict. Who among us does not? Those are goals we should all strive for, but peace cannot be forced upon us, manufactured by the actions of one man. Peace cannot be maintained where there is no freedom. That is an essential truth of our humanity that men like Dr. Fiker fail to grasp. They believe that control and fear will bring about submission and compliance, but the human spirit was not created to submit in fear to the unjust rule of men. It will always rebel and resent those who attempt to suppress it."

"We have much work to do. I would ask that all nations set aside their wars and struggles to focus on fixing the greater problem at hand, our food. I do not ask this as a demand, or with any threat. There will be a time and a place to resolve disputes and I don't pretend to suppose that conflicts will cease. Despite our differences, we are all human beings. We share the same earth, drink the same water and breathe the same air. Let's work together to plant new crops that will provide safe food to sustain us all."

A lone figure in the audience stood and began clapping his hands as President Savatsky finished his speech. Others joined him until the entire room erupted in a standing ovation that lasted for several minutes. Fiker was escorted off the stage as the President made his way down to the crowd to shake hands and greet those who wished to speak with him.

The applause was still going strong when the picture switched back to the news anchors, who struggled to provide commentary that did justice to the events they had just seen. Derek looked at the baguette and cereal he was eating with suspicion. "I'm going to have some breakfast cola," he announced as he got up from his chair and headed for the drink dispensers. Despite the early hour, everyone else in the room agreed and a line quickly formed.

The door to the cafeteria opened and a man in a suit entered. "Excuse me," he yelled out to get their attention, "Is there a Dr. Richard Stenvick here?"

Stenvick rose from his seat, "That's me."

The man approached holding a cell phone in his outstretched hand and introduced himself as CIA. "Telephone call for you, sir," he explained. "Dr. Berg is on the line."

Stenvick took the phone and put it to his ear. "Gary?"

"Rich!" Berg exclaimed, "I'm sure glad to hear from you. Are you all ok?"

"Yes," Stenvick replied, "I just saw you on the television. What's going on?"

"I promise I'll explain everything later. Right now we have to finish up some things here at INIAS. Did you get my message?"

Stenvick explained that he had not, and that he'd lost his phone. "Why?" he asked, "what was it about?"

"I guess it's not important now," replied Berg hesitantly, "but be careful. The CIA has assigned a security detail to your group. Hopefully it will just be a precaution but please don't give them any difficulty."

"Ok," Stenvick agreed with confusion evident in his voice. "We'll be leaving soon for the turtle reserve. Do you plan on joining us?"

"No," Berg responded. "Go ahead without us. We'll meet up when you return."

◻ ◻ ◻ ◻ ◻

Kyle and Isaiah sat in the Mercedes and watched through binoculars as the students piled into the van several blocks away. Three men in suits and dark sunglasses followed the students out of the building and got into a black SUV parked behind them.

"Who are they?" asked Isaiah.

"My guess is some sort of agency guys, maybe CIA," said Kyle. He tried calling Curt again, but there was still no answer. "I don't like this. First we can't get in touch with Curt, and now these kids have what looks like a security detail."

"No problem," said Isaiah confidently. "They're headed out to a remote part of the coast. Whatever weapons those spooks might have, they'll be no match for my rocket launcher and no one will be around to see it."

Kyle grinned. "You're right. We'll sneak in after them once they've made camp for the night and finish this once and for all."

Chapter 31

"We did it!" Hargren exclaimed triumphantly to the others gathered in the lab.

"We certainly did," agreed Berg, beaming with the thrill of success. "I just wish I remembered the name of that old mushroom hunter. We couldn't have done this without him."

Megan, McConnell and Halloway approached and interrupted the conversation. "We've just been on a conference call," McConnell said. "The situation appears stable for now. Once the dust settles there will be a lot to do. Our teams are packing up anything of significance from the Hallita sites, and all the key players have been taken into custody."

"What will be done with INIAS?" Kevin inquired.

"I'll be staying here for a while," responded Megan. "The FDA will be sending down a team to look through all the research that's in progress here, and to make sure nothing else grows out of control. I'll be acting as a sort of tour guide."

Katrina burst out with a small laugh despite herself as she saw the look on Kevin's face.

"What? I didn't say anything," Kevin pleaded in a tone of mock innocence.

"No," said Megan, "I'm not going back to playing Miss Airhead. For your information, I was halfway through getting my Doctorate in biochemistry at Wisconsin-Madison when the FDA convinced me to join them as a field operative."

Kevin was stunned. "That's where I'm going for my Masters! Who was your research advisor? I've been following Dr. Oh's work and I really hope I can get a spot in his lab in a few years."

It was Megan's turn to be surprised. "I worked with Carl Oh. He tried to convince me to stay on but the FDA position was too exciting to turn down."

Katrina smiled with amusement as Kevin proceeded to pepper the agent with all sorts of questions about her research work and how she ended up at INIAS. Their conversation was eventually ended when McConnell came over to inform them that he'd be taking the students, Berg and Hargren back to his home to rest up for a while before having a celebratory dinner.

Ten minutes later, after gathering what little gear they'd brought in and taking some colas from the vending machine for the trip, McConnell led them back through the jungle and through the hole in the fence to where his Rover was parked. He carefully navigated the river and reached the dirt road they'd entered from. Mist swirled around the vehicle in the early morning light as they bounced along the trail, chatting excitedly about their adventure as well as McConnell's plans for the dinner.

Stenvick and the students arrived at the coastal reserve in time for lunch. The three CIA agents kept a wary eye on the parking lot as the group climbed out of the van and sat down at several picnic tables. Everyone had been talking about the news that morning for the entire ride from San José.

"Now that we've arrived," Stenvick announced before they began to eat, "please remember that we're here to focus on the natural wonders around us. I know you're all excited about what our fellow travelers have been up to, as am I, but we can't let that distract us. We'll hit the trail in fifteen minutes to go see the turtle nesting area on the beach."

234

"I love turtles," Michelle said to the girls at her table, "especially the babies. They're so cute."

"You should visit our greenhouse sometime," Stephanie suggested. "We have a bunch of fish pond displays and there are lots of little turtles lounging around. They're pretty tame and lazy since we let the customers feed them."

"Thanks, I'd like that," Michelle replied.

Jennifer was watching the CIA agents. "How do you think those guys will hold up trying to follow Dr. Stenvick? They're wearing suits and dress shoes. They must not have gotten the memo about what we're doing."

Melody giggled. "Maybe this will be their initiation beach day! Unfortunately for them we're staying out here overnight and I don't think they brought any luggage."

The girls laughed as they finished their meal and got up to prepare for the hike.

□ □ □ □ □

Later that afternoon, Kevin woke in one of the guest rooms at McConnell's place to a sweet smoky smell wafting through the air. He took a hot shower and put on the new clothing that had been left on the dresser for him. Leaving the room, he walked down the hallway to the kitchen to find Berg and Hargren sitting at the counter, talking with their host as he managed numerous pots and pans cooking on the gas burners.

"Did you sleep well?" McConnell inquired.

"Yes, thanks. What is that wonderful smell?"

McConnell grinned and pointed to a large rectangular appliance along the wall. It was polished stainless steel like the rest of the kitchen and had several temperature gauges on the hinged front door. Kevin could see a smoldering bed of coals through the glass panel of a bottom section, and noticed a round vent pipe heading up through the ceiling.

"I neglected to show you this when you were here last time," McConnell stated. "It's my smoker. I've got fifty pounds of ribs in there coated with my special barbecue sauce."

Kevin turned at the sound of a door opening in the hallway and smiled when Katrina appeared in the kitchen a moment later. She was dressed in jeans and a blue hooded CIA sweatshirt much too large for her. Kevin couldn't resist the thought of giving her a hug.

"Did you sleep well?" McConnell asked again.

"Yes," Katrina responded with a yawn. "Whatever you're making smells delightful."

"How are you feeling?" Kevin asked as she approached.

"I'm fine, just a little tired," she said as she wrapped her arms around him and leaned into the hug he eagerly gave her.

They were both startled by a sharp rap on the front door followed by Halloway bursting in carrying several shopping bags. "Hi everyone, I brought the soda," he announced cheerfully.

Over the course of the next hour, they all pitched in to finish the meal preparations. Megan arrived along with a few of the other agency people who had been at the lab with them. None of them had required convincing to attend the feast put on by McConnell.

□ □ □ □ □

At the turtle reserve, Stenvick set a rapid pace as they hiked along the beach towards the nesting site. The soft sand shifted and gave way under their hiking boots as they plodded along. As the girls had expected, the CIA men struggled to keep pace behind them and had to remove their dress shoes.

"Those guys have no idea what they've gotten themselves into," Ben remarked as he looked back to the men following at a distance.

"I know," said Derek. "The CIA should ask Dr. Stenvick to help with their physical training."

"Here they are," Stenvick announced, halting suddenly. A few turtles were lounging on the beach in front of them. "We'll take a half hour to observe, but don't cross over the fences. This area is protected."

McConnell arranged enough seats for everyone at his dining room table. He instructed them to grab a plate and serve themselves buffet style from the dishes in the kitchen. He'd removed the racks of ribs and cut them into manageable portions, then slathered them with more of the barbecue sauce.

"This is a wonderful meal," Megan complimented him when she'd filled her plate. "Thanks for inviting us all here."

"No problem," McConnell replied. "It's not every day that you get to be a part of something like this, and I wanted to celebrate our success properly."

"What will happen to Dr. Fiker?" Katrina asked as they took their seats around the table.

Halloway explained that he was being taken back to the United States and would be held in custody until his fate could be determined. McConnell's phone rang. He took the call and listened for a few seconds. "Yes, we're at my place," he responded. "You can bring it by here, and make it quick if you want some food while it's still hot."

After ending the call, he put the phone back in his pocket and turned to Hargren. "That was Ralph. His shop is finished with your Bus and he's going to drop it off here so you can all get back to the city tonight."

"I forgot all about that," Hargren replied. "I don't think I'll be hanging on to that vehicle for very long, but I appreciate you getting it fixed up for the trip back. It will give me some time to find a suitable replacement for the Trooper."

They all dug in to the scrumptious meal and shared stories about the events of the past few days. Berg answered a number of questions about the work he had done to isolate the Amanitin D molecule, and explained the science behind Fiker's toxin as best he could. After they'd talked for a while and could barely fit any more food in their stomachs, Ralph came in and joined them at the table. He looked tired but greeted everyone and helped himself to a heaping plate of food from the kitchen.

"Bill sure knows how to cook up a good meal," he said, "and I wasn't going to pass up the chance for those ribs. I have your VW outside, Paul. Let me just finish this food and then we'll unload it off the trailer."

237

□ □ □ □ □

Kyle started the engine of the black Mercedes and buckled his seatbelt. "You ready?" he asked Isaiah.

"Yes," Isaiah responded grimly, "let's do this."

"I just want to go over the list one more time," said Kyle. He listed off several machine guns, sniper rifles, a rocket launcher, grenades, explosives and knives.

Isaiah confirmed that they'd packed each item, including all necessary ammunition.

"And we also have the food and water?"

"Yes."

"What about the fake passports, cards and cash?"

"Yes, we got them all."

"Ok," Kyle concluded, "I think we have everything. Let's go."

Pulling away from the curb, he quickly accelerated into the flow of traffic and they were on their way.

Chapter 32

"Wow, that was good," said Ralph as he wiped his mouth with a napkin after finishing the last of the ribs on his plate. "Let's go unload that Bus."

"Come on folks," McConnell ordered, "follow me outside. You won't want to miss this."

With some confusion as to why unloading an old Volkswagen off a trailer was such an interesting event, the whole group rose from the table and followed McConnell out the front door to the courtyard. Ralph had parked a large flatbed truck and trailer in front of the garage. Heavy canvas tarps and straps covered the vehicle on the trailer.

"That seems a bit excessive," Hargren observed. "Were you trying to protect the worn paint and dents?"

Ralph chuckled. "Not exactly. Bill, you want to give me a hand with the straps?"

McConnell helped him release the ratchets and remove the straps holding down the tarps, and then they paused before uncovering the vehicle. "Paul," McConnell said, "It was really too bad that your Trooper was destroyed in the course of your investigation. I know how much you loved that vehicle and it really dismayed me to hear about its demise. Ralph is the same way. He gets sentimental about vehicles. So, I hope you'll accept this as our thanks for all you've done in bringing Fiker's scheme to light."

The two men grabbed hold of the tarp, counted to three and then pulled it off the Bus in one fluid motion. The look of surprise on everyone's faces was priceless, and Hargren quickly took on a baffled countenance.

"That's not the Bus we brought here. What did you...? How did...? I don't understand."

The vehicle sitting on the trailer in front of them was a Volkswagen Bus, but certainly not the tired old wreck that had barely made the trip from the city. The body was perfect and rust free, with gleaming yellow paint and new glass all around, and it sat much higher off the ground on a tube frame with large off road tires and heavy duty suspension with a 4x4 drive train. It was outfitted with custom brush guards, lighting and a roof rack, and every fastener and piece of trim was polished and shining in chrome or stainless steel.

"I told you Ralph was a genius with custom work," McConnell said proudly.

Ralph stepped forward to offer an explanation. "This was the quickest turnaround I've done, but we already had most of what we needed at the shop, and I was able to order the rest in quickly enough thanks to Bill's connections and expense account. I threw out everything except the metal shell of the body. We sandblasted, welded, banged and polished until it was as good as new. I already had the undercarriage all ready to go except for an engine and transmission. We do enough custom jobs like this that it makes sense to stock several sizes of chassis and complete the final touches when we bolt on the body."

"You might not know this," Ralph stated, "but parts are still easy to come by for these vehicles. I had a complete interior rebuild kit, window glass and hardware shipped over. Of course, all of the components are upgraded designs and I swapped heavier duty equipment for many items. I hope you like the tan leather seats. I thought they were the nicest option. I do have to apologize though, the supercharged V8 and transmission needed considerably more space than the originals, so I had to move the rear seat forward a bit and install a cover over the enlarged engine bay. Oh, and before I forget. The new engine needs a lot of air for proper performance, which was a challenge to provide since it's located in the rear. I installed two scoops on the roof that feed the engine. We blended the air ducts down each side along the interior walls pretty well so they shouldn't be in the way."

Hargren was in awe as he listened and gazed upon the vehicle. "Thanks, this is amazing. Really, I wasn't expecting anything like this. Bill said you'd check the fluids and brakes, and things like that."

Ralph directed a sly grin at McConnell. "Did he? Sure, I check those things before we deliver a vehicle, but I'd never waste my time trying to repair rusty old junk or doing oil changes. The only reason anyone brings a vehicle to my shop is to get back something completely different. Bill's Rover was an interesting and rare exception since we wanted to maintain the appearance to suit his purposes."

Ralph undid some final straps and removed the blocks holding the tires in place, then asked everyone to stand clear before climbing up into the cab and starting the engine. The V8 came to life with a roar and growled angrily through the custom stainless exhaust as he slowly idled the Bus off the trailer. Once it was safely parked, he hopped out and gave the keys to Hargren before bidding them all farewell and driving away in his truck.

"Well," said Berg with a bit of sadness mixed with excitement, "We should head back to the university. Do you think you could give us a lift, Paul?"

Hargren laughed. After saying their goodbye's to McConnell, Megan, Halloway and the others gathered there, they climbed into the Bus. Hargren beeped the horn and they all waved as he pulled around the fountain and out the gate.

Following a full day of hiking on the beach and numerous trails crisscrossing the reserve, Stenvick's group sat around a camp fire roasting hotdogs and marshmallows. The CIA men were stationed at three points a good distance away from them, staying hidden in the darkness of the night and keeping watch for anyone approaching. If they were annoyed at the sounds of Stenvick playing his Guatemalan whistle they were keeping the frustration to themselves.

The students sat in several small groups, talking and sipping bottles of cola as they held their hotdogs on sticks over the fire.

"I wonder if these are toxic hotdogs," Derek thought out loud as he stared at the sizzling surface of the gradually darkening meat. "Dr. Berg said the molecule is in our food."

"I don't know," Ben replied. "I can't imagine it would be present in everything, but it kind of takes the excitement out of eating my favorite meals."

Derek agreed. "I don't know if I'll be able to handle drinking so much cola. I like it, but it just doesn't go well with everything. I want a nice cup of coffee with breakfast, not a cold soda."

Ben laughed, "I think you can still have your coffee, but you need to drink a cola at the same time. Maybe it won't be so bad. Maybe they can figure out what's in it that does the trick and put that into other drinks."

"Yeah," Derek agreed, "or even a powder or pill."

Each of them sipped from their bottle as they contemplated the thought.

"Do you think there's really someone out there that wants to hurt us?" asked Michelle. "Why do we need CIA protection?"

"I'm sure it has something to do with Dr. Berg," said Melody. "If he made Dr. Fiker and the people at Hallita angry, they might have found out we were with him on this trip and go after us for revenge."

"But we didn't do anything," Michelle argued. "Besides, weren't all of Fiker's people arrested? I thought everything was under control."

"I think it's just a precaution," said Jennifer, "and if Dr. G saved the world, the government will probably do anything to make him happy."

"Well I'm glad the CIA guys are with us," Stephanie said emphatically. "We'll need them to defend us if the turtles decide to invade our camp tonight."

All the girls burst out laughing.

Spencer watched the ten hotdogs roasting on the end of his stick with disdain. "These are not sausages. In Austria we did not have these."

"They're not supposed to be sausages," Geraldo explained. "They're hot dogs. There's a difference."

Spencer seemed unconvinced. "They are so small and they look funny. I do not understand why you eat them."

Geraldo shrugged his shoulders. "We're used to them I suppose. It all depends on what you grow up with."

"Like your beliefs?" Spencer asked.

"I guess so," Geraldo replied thoughtfully, then laughed. "I don't think I've ever heard anyone make a connection between faith and hotdogs, but I guess you could look at it a bit like that."

"How?" asked Spencer.

"Well, I'm happy with hotdogs because they're what I'm used to, but you believe the sausages in Austria are better because they're what you're used to."

"No," Spencer retorted, "Austrian sausage is better. There is no arguing. Jesus would agree. He is very wise. You need to talk to Him. You need to read His book."

"You mean the Bible?" Geraldo asked.

"Yes," said Spencer. "It is a good book. Dr. Stenvick gave it to me. I am so happy. It will give you answer if you let it."

Geraldo spoke thoughtfully. "I've read a lot about the Bible, but honestly I haven't really looked at the book itself. Maybe I'll give it a try."

"No maybe," barked Spencer. "You will read every morning after push up time."

Kyle gripped the wheel tightly as he drove on the narrow two lane highway heading towards Limón. "Isaiah, would you stop that. I'm nervous enough driving this road without you playing with that thing."

Isaiah popped the pin back in the grenade he was holding. For several minutes he'd been pulling it in and out like someone obsessed with flicking their lighter. "How about you just pay attention to the road and don't worry about what I'm doing," he responded testily.

Kyle hit the brakes as an old pickup passed and cut him off, nearly colliding with him as it swerved to avoid the traffic in the oncoming lane. "I can't wait until we're out of this country," he

243

grumbled. "How can people drive like this? You can't see anything around the curves and there's a cliff right at the side of the road."

"I think they get used to it," Isaiah suggested as he pulled the pin and put it back again, "just like we got used to heading into battle after a while. Once you do something dangerous often enough, the fear starts to go away."

"That or they're just crazy," said Kyle. "Regardless I don't like this road."

The car behind them started honking in frustration as Kyle slowed down for a sharp curve ahead. "I'm not going to blindly speed into that!" he shouted as if the driver behind could hear him.

"At least he won't try to pass right now," Isaiah said, seeing a line of delivery trucks slowly rounding the bend in the other lane.

Suddenly a tall yellow Volkswagen Bus jacked up on huge off-road tires whipped around the curve in front of them, its headlights and blazing light bar blinding them as the beams swung in their direction. Kyle gasped, hit the gas and turned hard to the right to avoid a collision. He could hear horns blaring behind him as the yellow VW swerved back into its own lane, but the Mercedes was now skidding on the narrow strip of gravel by the edge of the road and didn't have enough traction to steer back onto the asphalt. There was no guardrail along the edge to halt their momentum so they hurtled off the cliff, falling for several seconds before slamming into the steep slope of the mountain and then bouncing off. They were both screaming in terror as their stomachs crashed around violently in their chests. Kyle shouted to hold on and tried desperately to maintain control of the wheel as they careened down the impossibly steep terrain. Isaiah dropped the grenade without even thinking and grabbed onto the dashboard. After a few seconds they flew off the edge of a sheer drop and were sailing smoothly through the air when the grenade exploded.

□ □ □ □ □

Two days later...

Stenvick took a seat across from Berg in the cafeteria. "Well, you've had quite an adventure. Are you ready to do some hiking?"

"I sure am," Berg replied. "After what we've been through I'm really looking forward to the peace and quiet of the woods."

Stenvick held back a laugh but responded with a wry grin. "Yep, you won't find any excitement with our group. Just plants and trees and lots of walking..."

"What?" asked Berg, noticing his friend's odd expression.

"I'll explain later, Gary, but you could say we had a few stressful moments of our own. Today we're visiting a nature preserve where we expect to see all sorts of fungi. You'll have lots of teaching opportunities. We've gotten used to going along without you, but who knows how many interesting things we've missed."

"That sounds wonderful," said Berg. "So, I see you've adjusted your diet. I've never drank so much cola in my life. How's it going for you?"

Stenvick surveyed the glasses of cola lined up on his tray in an alternating pattern with his coffee mugs. "It's torture," he said with a grimace. "Do you know how much harder I'm going to have to exercise to burn off all these empty soda calories?"

Berg raised an eyebrow. "Umm, how is this different from all the cream and sugar you put in your coffee?"

"It just is," Stenvick said while gulping down a glass of cola. "Plus, now I have to carry all this extra weight in my pack."

The professors switched their attention to the television when Spencer turned up the volume and called for everyone to watch. The morning news was showing coverage of a Mercedes that had fallen from a cliff and exploded, killing both occupants.

"Poor guys," said Stenvick. "This has not been a good week for traveling around here."

Epilogue

Four months had passed since the University group returned safely from Costa Rica. The spring semester was winding down at Harrisville and the students were busy studying for finals. President Savatsky was on campus to host a special luncheon in the private dining room for the members of the trip.

"It's a pleasure to finally meet all of you," he said once the entire group had gathered. "As you may imagine, my schedule has been quite full dealing with the aftermath of the Nobel ceremony. Negotiating with all the major soft drink manufacturers to produce more cola has been quite an endeavor. The National Guard has been very helpful distributing it to people in need. I had breakfast with the President of Mexico this morning and I'm expected in Canada for dinner, then I'll fly overnight for London. But, I'm not here to discuss my calendar. I want to know how you've all been since your trip, and if you, Dr. Berg, have reconsidered your answer to my proposal."

Berg placed a half-eaten Amanita-shaped cookie back on his plate and finished chewing the red and white frosted cap. "I was honored that you asked me, and I must admit that heading a department to clean up our Nation's crops would be appealing to me, but my answer remains no. Teaching and research are my passions. This is where I belong. There are plenty of qualified candidates that will do a great job for you. I'm sorry, but it's just not the job for me."

Savatsky sighed. "Very well, I can respect that. If you ever change your mind just give me a call."

Berg smiled and promised that he would.

President Savatsky turned to Kevin and Katrina. "I hear congratulations are in order. Is that correct?"

"Yes!" they said in unison, and then Kevin explained. "We just got engaged last week. We're going to get married."

"That's wonderful!" Savatsky said excitedly. "Have you set a date?"

"Not exactly," replied Katrina, "but the wedding will be sometime this summer before we move to Wisconsin for Kevin's graduate school."

"Excellent," said Savatsky, "and do you have any plans out there as well?"

"I do," she replied. "It turns out the company I was going to work for, Global Proactive, was little more than a front for Hallita to distribute their seeds to areas without large scale farming. The FDA gave me a grant to start a new organization with a similar focus to what Global Proactive was supposedly doing."

Savatsky grinned. "That's great. Good luck to both of you."

He stepped over to Berg again. "Have you heard from Paul recently? I haven't spoken with him in several weeks."

"Yes," Berg replied, "he's doing well. He said the work on the new lab facilities at UCR is coming along nicely thanks to the funding you arranged. He's working out of the lab at INIAS for now to continue his research."

"That's good to hear," Savatsky stated. "I need to get down there soon. He promised to take me on a jungle drive in his Volkswagen."

Berg chuckled. "That will be an experience you won't forget!"

Derek and Ben were having an animated conversation when the President came over to greet them. "We should ask him," said Ben.

"Ask me what?" inquired Savatsky.

Derek turned to him. "You seem like an intelligent academic type. Do you ever feel like there's not enough excitement in your life?"

"Well," the President considered, "I wouldn't say that at the moment, but I suppose there are times I feel that way."

"Here's what we're thinking," Ben explained. "We want to start an adventure tourism company where the participants are faced with dangerous situations like we ran into on our trip."

"All perfectly safe and controlled of course," Derek pointed out, "but they won't know that."

"Why would anyone sign up for such a thing?" Savatsky asked.

"They wouldn't," said Ben, "we're thinking that their family or friends would send them on the trip to give them a break from their daily boredom."

"Interesting," the President said thoughtfully. "Actually, several coworkers come to mind that would be fun to send on that sort of adventure. Let me know if you actually go through with it."

"Miss De la Puenta," Savatsky said in greeting as he approached Michelle. "How are you? I happened to meet with your father a few weeks ago. He told me all about your plans to be a movie actress."

"I'm well," Michelle replied with a smile, "but I'm rethinking the movie idea. I could land some roles because of my family's money and connections, but I don't want to be famous unless I earn it. I'm going to audition anonymously for some smaller films and see where my talent can take me."

"That's quite admirable," said Savatsky. "If we see your name in lights someday, I'll be happy to know you got there on your own merit."

The President found Spencer and Geraldo talking by the table of cheese and sausage. "Congratulations on your wrestling win, Spencer. I hear you've set a school record."

"Yes," Spencer replied. "I will do it next year and make four in the row."

"I believe it," said Savatsky, "and, Geraldo, what are your plans after graduation?"

"I've been thinking about that quite a bit since the trip to Costa Rica," Geraldo said seriously. "While we were down there, the other students and Dr. Stenvick really challenged me. I also owe a lot of thanks to Spencer. He's been a very enthusiastic workout and devotional instructor. He says good habits lead to good character, and now that we're roommates I really haven't had any choice on developing good habits. I sold my truck and I'll use the money to support myself for a couple years doing volunteer missions work. I want to be a pastor, but I've realized that I need to spend some time listening to God and serving people first. Then we'll see what I'm called to do next."

Savatsky patted him on the shoulder. "Ministry is certainly not something to be taken lightly. I hope you find the direction you're looking for."

President Savatsky introduced himself to Melody, Stephanie and Jennifer, and listened intently as they shared several stories about the events of the trip. Stephanie shared how Stenvick had fearlessly come to her aid on the rope bridge, and that she was planning to take a course with him the next semester. Melody talked about some of the discussions Stenvick led during their rare breaks from hiking on the subjects of birds, human nature and the benefits of maintaining good friendships. Despite the grueling physical activity, she was sure she'd learned more in those two weeks than in an entire semester.

Jennifer, addressing Savatsky as "Mr. Pres," shared her favorite moment when Stenvick got back at Ben for the fake bird calls with a practical joke of his own.

"He got all of us in on it and convinced a few park guides to help. When we reached a certain portion of the trail, the guides made a funny bird call from the jungle all around us. Dr. Stenvick looked panicked and yelled for everyone to prepare for an attack of the yellow spotted wobbly stompers. We all huddled in a tight cluster on our knees with our heads down, but made sure to leave Ben out. He started getting very anxious and afraid, pleading for us to let him into the huddle as the noises got closer and he could hear large creatures crashing through the jungle towards him. Then, the three guides appeared in ridiculous bird costumes and attacked him with water balloons. Everyone had a great laugh at his expense."

Chuckling heartily, Savatsky excused himself and reached out to shake hands with Stenvick. "It's nice to meet you face to face. Have you had a good semester?"

"Yes," Stenvick replied. "I've been having a fascinating time teaching Advanced Psychology. We've done an entire segment based on the events of my trip. We've discussed Dr. Fiker's motivations and view of the world, as well as Katrina's willingness to risk her own life for the greater good. Also, I've started training seriously for several triathlons this summer. I was feeling quite out of shape by the time we got home from Costa Rica. I enjoy leading those trips, but those two weeks without exercise always leave me feeling like sludge."

Savatsky laughed and nodded. "We all make sacrifices for the things that are important to us. I can see the way these kids look up to you. Take heart and know that you're making a difference."

A waiter called for everyone's attention and announced that they should take their seats for the meal to be served. Once the dishes had been set before them, Savatsky stood at the head of the table and conversation ceased as all eyes turned toward him.

"I'd like to propose a toast," he said while raising his goblet of cola. "To all of you; May your futures be bright and your food be safe."

Glasses clinked around the table amid cheers and laughter.

"President Savatsky?" asked Derek, "what happened to Dr. Fiker?"

Savatsky looked at him with a smirk. "Let's just say he's busy pulling weeds out of a very large garden."

The End

Author's Note

This story is a work of fiction. No part of this book should be taken as a guide or recommendation for safe practices involving fungi. Much of the science portrayed in the novel is the product of my imagination and was invented as needed to suit the story. As Dr. Berg would surely advise, please consult a trained mycologist before collecting wild mushrooms to eat.

Also, the GMO industry has certainly brought about many worthwhile advances. Many good scientists have devoted years of research to worthy goals. As with all new technologies, only time and testing will prove the benefits and drawbacks of GMO products. There are many valid concerns about the current state of the industry, and I would urge the reader to study the issue and draw his or her own conclusions.

254

Acknowledgements

I owe much appreciation to the many friends and family members who provided inspiration for this story. Thanks to all those who offered their comments and criticism throughout the editing process.

To my wife, your tireless support and assistance made this book possible. Thanks for your critiques and advice, and for always pushing me to do the best job I could even when I felt like it was "good enough." Sharing this project with you has been an amazing experience and I couldn't have asked for a better partner.

To my parents, thank you for providing so many opportunities to experience the world and develop my creativity. Your enthusiastic support of this project has meant a lot to me. I smile each time I remember your laughter over certain portions of the story.

To Morris, thanks for all your help with edits, suggestions and recommendations for how to improve my writing style.

To Nancy, thanks for pointing out some much needed stylistic changes and for all your recommendations on cultural authenticity.

To Gary, though I've never shared your level of passion for the natural sciences and I've suffered many mosquito attacks on our hikes together while you "botanize," I respect the work you do and your commitment to it. I've learned a lot from you over the years and I always enjoy our conversations.

To Paul, did you ever fix that oil cap? The times we've spent together have always been a lot of fun. Thanks for being our vacation tour guide and for introducing me to "beep and wave" and "manly missions."

To Rich, I've enjoyed hearing about your adventures for many years. I hope you've found this story amusing and that it inspires you to continue exploring. I know you've truly been an inspiration to many people.

To Bill, thank you for helping to get us through so many situations and minor emergencies, even if they only involved rusted exhaust and not the fate of the world. We're very thankful for your abilities and willingness to help.

To Kevin and Katrina, I may have taken "a few" liberties with how you met and fell in love, but regardless of how it happened I'm glad you did. We don't get to see you often enough, but when we do it's one of the highlights of our year.

To "Nathan" and Sarah, sorry to make you the bad guys, but it was kind of natural given the dictator shirt and the laughs we've had over your ambitions to take over small countries. Both of you impress me with your talents and abilities. I look forward to seeing what mark you'll make on the world, and I know it will be for good!

To Megan, you've shown a lot of strength in your dedication to your work even through tough situations, and I admire how you pull through and overcome. You have a gift for understanding people, and I'd recommend you as an undercover agent any day.

To Kyle and Isaiah, don't get any ideas... I hope you maintain your friendship for a lifetime and find good outlets for your talents.

To Spencer, your impersonations and witty humor always make me laugh. You also have a good heart and I appreciate the concern you show for others.

To "Geraldo," I've had a lot of fun joking with you over the years about crazy ideas and your ridiculous alter-ego. I'm glad you put so much emphasis on teaching the unique nature of our faith and the importance of living out our lives as followers of Christ. Keep it up.

To Derek, all of our times at Capt. J's have been a blast. I'm always amazed at the crazy things you do before rushing to work. I hope we can enjoy many more commemorative mugs of coffee together.

To Ben, you have a great sense of humor and I always enjoy our time together. It's a good thing you married Sarah, now you don't have to text her constantly. And remember, there's going to be a charge for that.

To Michelle, I appreciate your kindness and the ways you compliment and encourage. You always think of the needs of others.

To Melody, I appreciate your calm and considerate manner. Keep up your crochet and design work, it's impressive.

To Stephanie, thanks for all the good times playing music and drinking coffee. We've certainly had a lot of fun adventures together.

To Jennifer, your cheery outgoing personality and sense of humor will surely brighten many a patient's day.

To Sylvia and Paula, thanks for all the good meals, hospitality, love and encouragement you've provided over the years.

To Ben, I couldn't thank you enough for all the help you've been on our many projects. Your dedication to finishing the job is exemplary and you've been like family to us. I don't know what we would do without you.

To Dale, thanks for all the work you do to keep things organized and running smoothly. I admire your wisdom and thoughtfulness.

To Ralph, keep putting on those hood scoops! You truly have a gift for vehicular projects and I've always been amazed at your productivity.

To my coffee maker, thanks for brewing so many mugs of coffee for me to enjoy as I worked on this book.

Finally, I owe the greatest thanks to God, the Creator and Sustainer of all. Without Him nothing is possible. I'm thankful for the many blessings He has given me, and that He has afforded me the time and talents to take on this project. He is the source of all joy, and through good and bad times my hope is in Him.

About the Author

You Bring the Coffee, I'll Save the World is Michael Emberger's first novel. He and his wife live in New Hampshire with their dog Harper and a flock of pet chickens. Michael has a degree in Engineering and enjoys working on construction projects. His favorite beverage is coffee.

Connect at www.facebook.com/MichaelJamesEmberger

Offers from Our Sponsors

Paul Hargren School of Defensive Driving

Bring this book for 20% off one of the following single day courses:

       Aggressive Driving 101

       Passing on Blind Curves

       Anticipatory Gear Shifting

       Accident Avoidance

Ralph's Custom Garage

Bring in your copy of this book for a free estimate on a custom vehicle conversion, by appointment only.

Mama Sylvia's Costa Rican Pizzeria

Buy one pizza get one free (of equal or lesser value) when you show this book to your server.

K&I Inc.

Show this book to get $50 off any job. Minimum two day contract, restrictions apply.

CPSIA information can be obtained at www.ICGtesting.com
Printed in the USA
LVOW10s1557231015

459498LV00005B/638/P